Emilie Ruete

Memoirs of an Arabian Princess

An Autobiography

Emilie Ruete

Memoirs of an Arabian Princess
An Autobiography

ISBN/EAN: 9783744752855

Printed in Europe, USA, Canada, Australia, Japan

Cover: Foto ©Raphael Reischuk / pixelio.de

More available books at **www.hansebooks.com**

MEMOIRS OF AN ARABIAN PRINCESS.

MEMOIRS OF

AN ARABIAN PRINCESS

An Autobiography

BY

EMILY RUETE
Née Princess of Oman and Zanzibar

NEW YORK
D. APPLETON AND COMPANY
1888

.

This version of "The Memoirs of an Arabian Princess" is rendered from the German, in which language the work originally appeared.

PREFACE.

Nine years ago I made up my mind to write down some sketches of my life for my children, who at that time knew little more about my origin than that I was an Arabian and a native of Zanzibar. Tired out in body and in mind, I did not then expect to live to be able to tell them, when they had grown up, of the many changes in my life, and of the recollections of my youth. I therefore resolved to write my memoirs for them, and this I have done for love and devotion to my children, whose affection has been my only solace for many long and anxious years, and whose tender sympathy has kept me from despair in my heaviest troubles.

Originally, therefore, my memoirs were not intended for the general public, but for my dear children alone, to whom I desired to bequeath the same, in token of a fond mother's love, and I only yielded to the repeatedly expressed wishes of many friends in having them published now.

These pages were concluded years ago—with the exception of the last chapter, which was added recently, after a voyage I was permitted to undertake, with my children, to my old home, Zanzibar, in the course of last year.

May this book, then, go out into the world and gain as many friends as it has always been my good fortune to make for myself!

CONTENTS.

CHAPTER I.

IN Bet il Mtoni, the oldest of our palaces in the island of Zanzibar, I was born, and there I lived until the age of seven.

Bet il Mtoni, distant about five miles from the city of Zanzibar, lies on the sea coast, surrounded by most beautiful scenery, and quite hidden in a grove of palm and mango trees, and other gigantic specimens of tropical vegetation. The house of my birth is called "Mtoni house," after the little river Mtoni, which rises only a few miles inland, runs through the whole palace into numerous fountains, and flows directly behind the palace walls into the splendid and animated inlet which severs the island from the African continent.

Only one large-sized courtyard divides the numerous buildings of Bet il Mtoni, which, on account of their heterogeneous styles, invented as occasion required, with their numberless and puzzling passages, must be called, on the whole, ugly rather than beautiful.

I do not distinctly remember now the arrangement of the vast number of rooms these buildings contained, but I can well recall to my mind the large bathing

accommodation at Bet il Mtoni.   There were a dozen
baths in one row at the extreme end of the courtyard,
and in rainy weather these popular resorts could only
be reached under the shelter of an umbrella.   Apart
from them lay what was called the "Persian" bath,
a Turkish steam bath, whose ingenious and tasteful
architecture was unequalled in Zanzibar.

Each bathing house contained two baths, five yards
long by four yards wide, and just deep enough to let
the water come up to the breast of a grown-up person.

These refreshing baths were a favourite resort with
all people in the house ; most of them stayed in them
for many hours every day, to pray, sleep, work, and
read there, even to take their meals ; and from four
o'clock in the morning till midnight they were never
once empty.

On entering these bath-houses, which are all alike,
two raised resting-places may be observed to the right
and left for prayer and repose, which are covered with
the finest coloured mats.   Every other article of
luxury, such as carpets, was banished from these
rooms.   Every Muslim (Mahometan) requires a
separate and perfectly clean dress for prayers, intended only for this purpose, and which ought to be
quite white.   Of course this rather inconvenient religious precept is only followed by extremely devout
persons.

The places of repose are separated by narrow
arcades from the bath-rooms, which are all in the
open air ; two arched bridges of stone, with steps
gradually rising, lead again to other rooms lying
apart.

Each bath-room was allotted to a special set of occupants; woe to the person who did not keep within her proper bounds! A very rigorous spirit of caste ruled at Bet il Mtoni, which was observed by high and low alike.

Tall orange trees, as high as the largest cherry trees in these parts, throve in dense rows in front of the bath-houses; their branches often sheltered us while young, when we were afraid of punishment from our excessively strict teacher.

Man and beast lived amicably together in the large courtyard, without being in the least inconvenienced by each other's presence—peacocks, gazelles, guinea-fowls, flamingoes, geese, ducks, and ostriches roamed about in perfect liberty, and were petted and fed by old and young. We children vastly enjoyed hunting out the many eggs that lay about here and there, especially the large ostrich eggs, and to hand them over to the head cook, who would reward us with presents of sweetmeats.

Twice a day, early in the morning and in the evening, all children above five years of age had riding lessons in this court from one of the eunuchs, during which the members of our little zoological garden roamed about as freely as ever. When we had made sufficient progress in this art, we were each mounted by our father. The boys got permission to choose a horse from the royal stud, while we girls received large white donkeys from Mesket, which are often much more expensive than horses. Of course we were provided with a complete harness for these handsome beasts at the same time.

Our chief amusement in these family houses consisted in taking long rides, as we had neither theatri-
cals nor concerts to entertain us.   We frequently had
races in the country, which as frequently ended in an
accident.   Once I nearly lost my life in such a race.
Afraid of being overtaken by my brother Hamdân, I
had paid no attention to a very large crooked cocoa
tree right in my way, and my forehead had almost
come in contact with its stem before I had even
noticed it.   Quick as thought I threw myself
back, and in this way mercifully escaped a horrid
death.

The numerous flights of stairs were one of the peculiarities of Bet il Mtoni, which were unusually steep,
and had huge steps, apparently made for a race of
giants.   Straight up they went, without a turning or
a landing place ; one's only assistance a very primitive
kind of railing, which, being in constant use, needed
as constant repair.   I remember even now how all
the people living in our wing of the house were
frightened one morning when both railings of our
stone staircase were found to be missing, and I am
yet surprised that of the many persons passing up
and down no one came to grief.

Statistics being a thing quite unknown in Zanzibar,
nobody of course could tell how many people actually
lived in our house.   I think I do not exaggerate, however, in estimating the total number of inhabitants at
Bet il Mtoni at one thousand.   To understand this it
must be remembered that great numbers of servants
are employed in the East by all people of quality and
by those who want to appear rich.   At least an equal

number of persons were lodged in my father's city palace, Bet il Sahel, or "Strandhouse."

In the wing nearest to the sea at Bet il Mtoni were the apartments of my father, Sejid Saîd, Imam of Mesket and Sultan of Zanzibar, and those of his principal wife, who was a distant relation of his. He resided, however, only four days a week in the country with us, and the remainder he spent in his city palace, Bet il Sahel. The title "Imam" is a religious dignity, which is but rarely conferred on a sovereign. Originally we owe this distinction to our great-grandfather "Ahmed"; the title has since that time been hereditary in our family, and every member of it is authorized to append it to his signature.

Being one of his younger children I only remember my father with his venerable, snow-white beard. He was above middle height, his features had a very fascinating and engaging expression, and his whole appearance commanded respect. In spite of his warlike propensities and his delight in conquest, he was a model father and sovereign. Justice he valued as the highest of all things, and in this respect he knew no difference of person, not even between one of his own sons and the lowest slave. He humbled himself before God; nor was he self-conceited and proud like so many high-born people. It happened, and not rarely either, that he would ride over by himself to the wedding of a simple slave, who had gained his regard by many years of loyal service, to offer his congratulations to the young couple in person. He always used to call me, "Old woman," as I was very fond of cold milk soup (Arab, "farni"), which is

the favourite meal of all our old and toothless
people.—

My mother was a Circassian by birth, who in early
youth had been torn away from her home. Her father
had been a farmer, and she had always lived peacefully with her parents and her little brother and
sister. War broke out suddenly, and the country was
overrun by marauding bands ; on their approach the
family fled into an underground place, as my mother
called it—she probably meant a cellar, which is not
known in Zanzibar. Their place of refuge was, however, invaded by a merciless horde, the parents were
slain, and the children carried off by three mounted
Arnauts. One of these, with her elder brother, soon
disappeared out of sight ; the other two, with my
mother and her little sister, three years old, crying
bitterly for her mother, kept together until evening,
when they too parted, and my mother never heard
any more of the lost ones as long as she lived.

She came into my father's possession when quite a
child, probably at the tender age of seven or eight
years, as she cast her first tooth in our house. She
was at once adopted as playmate by two of my sisters,
her own age, with whom she was educated and brought
up. Together with them she learnt to read, which
raised her a good deal above her equals, who, as a
rule, became members of our family at the age of sixteen or eighteen years, or older still, when they had
outgrown whatever taste they might once have had
for schooling. She could scarcely be called pretty,
but she was tall and shapely, had black eyes, and
hair down to her knees. Of a very gentle disposition,

her greatest pleasure consisted in assisting other people, in looking after and nursing any sick person in the house; and I well remember her going about with her books from one patient to another, reading prayers to them.

She was in great favour with my father, who never refused her anything, though she interceded mostly for others, and, when she came to see him, he always rose to meet her half-way—a distinction he conferred but very rarely. She was as kind and pious as she was modest, and in all her dealings frank and open. She had had another daughter besides myself, who had died quite young. Her mental powers were not great, but she was very clever at needlework. She has always been a tender and loving mother to me, but this did not hinder her from punishing me severely when she deemed it necessary.

She had many friends at Bet il Mtoni, which is rarely to be met with in an Arab harem. She had the most unshaken and firmest trust in God. When I was about five years old I remember a fire breaking out in the stables close by, one night while my father was at his city residence. A false alarm spread over the house that we, too, were in imminent danger; upon which the good woman hastened to take me on one arm, and her big Kurán (we pronounce the word thus) on the other, and hurried into the open air. On the rest of her possessions she set no value in this hour of danger.

My father had only one Horme (plural Harîno), or legitimate wife, at my time, as far as I recollect; his other wives, or Sarari (singular Surie), numbering

seventy-five at his death, had all been purchased by
him gradually, and the former, his first wife, Azze
bint Sêf, a princess of Omân by birth, reigned as
absolute mistress over the household. In spite of
her very small size, and of her plain exterior, she
possessed an immense power over my father, who
willingly submitted to all her arrangements. She
treated all the other wives and their children in a
very imperious, haughty, and pretentious manner;
happily for us she had no children of her own, who
could not have failed to be as disagreeable in their
way! All my father's children, thirty-six in number,
when he died, were by his Sarari, and there was
consequently no difference between us.

Bibi (mistress, lady) Azze, who had to be addressed
as "Highness" (Sijjide),* was feared by old and
young, by high and low, and liked by no one. Even
now I remember her well, and how stiffly she used to
pass by without a kind word to any one. How
different was my dear old father! He talked kindly
to everybody, no matter what rank the person addressed might be. My exalted stepmother knew
very well how to keep her station, nor did any
one dare to approach her without her own invitation
or encouragement. I never saw her walk about
without a retinue, except when she went with my
father to the bath-house, which was set apart for
their special use. All who met her in the house
were as deferential to her as a recruit to his officer.

Though her imperiousness was felt very acutely by

---

* Bibi is Suahely ; Sejjide, Arabian. Both words mean "Highness."

all, it had not sufficient power to deprive the residents
at Bet il Mtoni of all charms of life. My brothers
and sisters, of all ages, were supposed to go every day
and wish her good morning; but rarely were her
vanity and pride gratified by more than one visitor
at the appointed time—before her breakfast hour—so
greatly was she disliked by us all.

My older brothers and sisters lived at Bet il
Mtoni; some of them, Schẽcha and Zuéné, for
instance, were old enough to have been my grand-
mothers. The latter had a son, Ali bin Suut, whose
beard had turned grey already when I knew him first;
she was a. widow, and had found a shelter in her
paternal home after the death of her husband.

It is generally believed by Europeans that with us
the sons are greatly preferred to the daughters; but
such was not the case in our family. I know not a
single instance in which the son was more liked by
father or mother, merely because he happened to be
a son. Though the law in some cases favours sons
more than daughters, and grants them larger privi-
leges—as, for instance, in the division of inheritances—
yet the children are everywhere loved and treated
alike. It is, of course, but natural, and only human,
that in the South, as well as all over the world,
one child, whether boy or girl, is secretly more beloved
by his parents than the other, but this is never shown
openly. It was thus with our father also; for the
two of his children he loved best were not sons, but
daughters, Scharife and Chole. When I was nine
years old I was once wounded in the side by an
arrow, by my wild brother Hamdan, who was about

2

my own age; fortunately the hurt was not a severe one. As soon as my father heard of this affair, he said to me: "Salme, go and call Hamdâm." And the boy was so terribly scolded for his misbehaviour, that he remembered it for a long time after. This instance proves how greatly people are often misinformed on foreign matters. It stands to reason that a good deal depends everywhere upon the children themselves, and it would wrong good children to treat them in the same way as bad ones.

The Bendjle was the prettiest spot at Bet il Mtoni. It was an immense round tower in front of the main building, and close to the sea, large enough for a ball, had such a thing been known in our country. It looked very much like a gigantic merry-go-round, with a vaulted ceiling in the same style as the building. The entire framework, the floor, railing, and the tent-like ceiling were constructed of painted wood. My dear father used to walk up and down in this place for hours and hours together, plunged in deep thought, and with head bent down. A bullet which he received in battle, and had settled in the hip, caused him frequent pain, and made him limp a little.

Some dozens of cane chairs were placed all about this lofty balcony, and a large telescope was put up for general use. The view from this raised "Bendjle" was surpassingly beautiful. Several times during the day my father, Azze bint Sêf, and all his grown-up children would take their coffee here. Any one wishing to speak to my father privately would be sure of finding him here alone for several hours in the day.

Il Rahmâni, a man-of-war, was anchored off the Bendjle all the year round, whence they fired the signals in the fasting season; the crews required for the many rowing boats had their quarters there. A tall flagstaff was erected on the shore to signal whenever these boats and crews were wanted.

Both at Bet il Mtoni and at Bet il Sahel the meals were cooked in the Arab as well as in the Persian and Turkish manner. People of all races lived in these two houses—the races of various beauty. The slaves were dressed in Suahely style, but we were permitted to appear in Arab fashion alone. Any newly-arrived Circassian or Abyssinian woman had to exchange her ample robes and fantastic attire within three days for the Arab costume provided for her.

Bonnets and gloves are no less indispensable articles of toilet to any Western lady or woman of respectability than jewellery is to us. Trinkets are considered so necessary, that even beggar-women may be seen plying their trade decked out in them. My father had special treasure chambers in both his houses at Zanzibar, and in his palace at Mesket, in Omân, amply stocked with sovereigns and gold pieces of Spanish and other coinage; besides these, however, they contained large assortments of feminine adornments, from the simplest article to the diamond-set crown, expressly procured to serve as presents. Each time an increase to the family had taken place, either by the purchase of a Sarari, or by the frequent births of princes or princesses, the doors of these chambers were opened, to take out presents for the new arrival according to its rank and

station. On the seventh day after the birth of a child
my father used to pay a visit to the infant and its
mother to present some article of jewellery to the
baby. In the same way a new Surie received at once
the necessary jewels, and had her servants assigned
to her by the chief eunuch.

Though himself very simple in all his ways, my
father was very particular about all people around
him. No one was permitted to appear before him
except in full dress, and this was the rule with his
children as well as with the youngest eunuch. The
little girls used to wear their hair in thin plaits, as
many as twenty sometimes, with the ends collected
together, and a heavy gold ornament, set with precious
stones, suspended from their centre. Sometimes a
gold coin was attached to each plait, which looked
much prettier. These ornaments were taken off at
bedtime, and re-attached in the morning. The girls
had their hair dressed in this pony fashion up to the
period when they had to go about veiled. Once I ran
off to my father without these ornaments in my hairdress, to get some of the French sweetmeats he used
to give us every morning. Instead of obtaining these,
however, I was promptly sent back in charge of a
servant—I had appeared before him not properly
dressed ; but I took good care never again to commit
the same offence.

My sister Zejâne and my stepmother Medine were
my mother's most intimate friends. Zejâne was
the daughter of an Abyssinian ; Medine, a Circassian,
who came from the same part of the country as my
mother, like Sara, another stepmother of mine

Sara's two children were my brother Madjid and my sister Chadudj, of whom the former was the junior by some years. My mother and Sara had solemnly promised each other, that whoever survived the other should replace her with her children. Chadudj and Madjid, however, were nearly full-grown when Sara died, and they did not need my mother's help as long as they lived in their paternal home. It was the custom in our family for boys up to the age of eighteen or twenty to remain with their mothers in our father's house, and to submit to the general house rules. At about this stage of life each prince was pronounced of age, though this depended entirely upon his behaviour. When of age he was numbered amongst the grown-up people—an honour which was always eagerly coveted. A separate residence was then assigned to him, together with horses, servants, and everything else he required, also an adequate monthly allowance.

My brother Madjid had now obtained this honour, more on account of his conduct than of his age. He was very modest, and won all hearts by his kind and gentle manners. Not a week passed but he rode over from the city (he lived at Bet il Sahel with his mother) to see us, and he always liked to play with me, though he was my senior by twelve years.

He came over perfectly delighted one day to tell my mother that he had just been pronounced of age, and that, being his own master now, he had received a house of his own. He insisted at the same time upon our removing to his new place to live with him, and he was joined in this request by Chadudj. My

mother begged him to consider that she could not
well accede to his wishes without first consulting my
father, but promised to inform him of the result as
soon as she had done so. On her part she declared
herself willing to live with him as long as it suited
both himself and his sister.   Madjid at once offered
to save her all trouble by speaking himself to my
father, and next day, indeed, he informed us that the
latter had given his consent. Our removal being thus
settled, it was arranged, after a long consultation, that
we were to take up our new residence with him in the
course of a few days, after he had completed all /
necessary arrangements at his place.

CHAPTER II.

BET IL WATORO.

My mother did not find it easy to reconcile herself to the prospect of her impending removal. She was very much attached to Bet il Mtoni, where she had lived from her childhood; she was not fond of any change, and was very much afflicted by the separation from Zejâne and from my stepmother Medine. She told me, however, afterwards that her own scruples had been outweighed by the consideration of making herself useful to the children of her dear departed friend.

As soon as it became known that she had decided to remove to town, every person she met cried out, "Have you lost all trust in us, Djilfidan, that you are going to leave us for ever?" "Oh, my friends," she replied, "I do not leave you of my own free will, but it is my fate to part from you!"

I am sure a good many people will shake their heads with a feeling of pity on reading the word "fate." Maybe such persons have hitherto shut their eyes and their ears to the will of God, and have spurned to take any notice of it, laying a far greater stress upon what they call chance. It should be borne in mind, how-

ever, that I once was a Mahometan, and grew up as
such. I am, moreover, speaking of Arab life, of an
Arab home, and there are two things above all quite
unknown in a real Arab house, the word " chance "
and materialism. The Mahometan not only believes
in God as his Creator and Preserver, but he is convinced at all times of His presence, and he feels likewise sure that not his own will, but the will of the
Lord is done in little things as well as in great.

It took us some days to complete all our arrangements, and then we waited for Madjid's return, who was
to arrange about our journey. I had had one brother
and two sisters, all nearly of my own age, as companions at Bet il Mtoni, and I was very sorry to leave
them, little Ralub in particular, who had been greatly
attached to me ; on the other hand, I was right glad of
the opportunity of getting away from our excessively
severe teacher.

Our large room looked something like a beehive
during the parting scenes with so many friends and
acquaintances ; everybody brought a parting gift in
proportion to his means and affection. This is a custom very much in use with us, for no Arab will deny
himself the pleasure of presenting a parting gift to his
friend, even if he has nothing to give but the merest trifle.
I remember a case in point which occurred in my early
youth. We had made an excursion from Bet il Mtoni
to one of our estates, and were just about to step into
our boats to return home, when I felt some one tugging
at my dress from behind. Turning round, I saw a
very old negro woman, who handed me a parcel,
wrapped in plantain leaves, with the words, " This

trifle is my parting gift to you, bibijangu (my mistress), it is the first ripe fruit of my garden." Undoing the leaves, I found they enclosed—one cob of newly-gathered Indian corn. I did not know the poor old woman at all, but afterwards she proved to have been an old *protégée* of my mother's.

Madjid arrived at last with the news that the captain of the *Rahmâni* had been ordered to send a cutter for us next evening, and another boat for our luggage and for the servants who were to accompany us to the city.

My father happened to be at Bet il Mtoni at the time, and next day my mother went up with me to bid him good-bye. We found him walking up and down the Bendjle as usual, and he came at once to meet us as soon as he saw us. My parents began talking at once about our journey, and, to stop the many questions with which I continually interrupted them, one of the attending eunuchs was ordered to bring me sweets and sherbet. I was of course very curious to know something about our new home and about life in town. I had only once been there for a very short time, and had not even seen all my brothers and sisters, nor my numerous stepmothers who lived there.

We then went to the apartments of my august stepmother to take leave of her. Azze bint Séf was graciously pleased to dismiss us standing, which with her was a great honour, as she always remained seated when she received people. We were also permitted to kiss her hand before turning our back upon her for ever.

We had still to run up and downstairs a good many

times to shake hands with all our friends, of whom, however, we met but few in their rooms. My mother resolved, therefore, to say good-bye to them after prayers, which all had to attend.

The cutter lay off the Bendjle ready to receive us at 7 p.m.; it was a fine big boat with a crew of fourteen oarsmen, with an awning over the stern, carrying our standard—a plain, blood-red flag. The passenger seats were covered with pretty silk cushions for ten to twelve persons.

Old Djohar, a trusty eunuch, came to report everything ready to my father, who was watching our departure from the Bendjle, and took the helm; he was to convey us to our new destination in company with another eunuch. All our friends in tears accompanied us as far as the house door, and their cries, "Wedâ, wedâ" (farewell, farewell), ring in my ears to this very day.

There was no landing pier on the flat shore, and we had to get into the boat either by being carried in a chair or by walking through the dry sand and over a plank; my mother got into the cutter in this manner, attended on both sides by some eunuchs, while another carried me in his arms and placed me in the stern sheets. The light of the coloured hanging-lanterns in the boat, together with the glittering stars above, cast a magic brightness over the sea, and the oarsmen pulled away, keeping time by the tune of a melancholy Arab song.

We kept close in shore, and I was soon fast asleep in my mother's lap. I was suddenly and rather roughly roused up by a number of persons calling out my name; very much frightened and half asleep yet, I learned that we had arrived at our journey's end. We were just below the lighted-up windows of Bet il Sahel, which were occupied by crowds of people—they were my stepmothers and sisters with their mothers, most of whom I had never seen before, and who were curious to have a look at me. My mother told me they had commenced crying out my name as soon as the boat had come in sight.

On landing, I was received by my young brothers in a very lively manner. They wanted us to go with them at once, but my mother had to decline, as she did not wish to keep Chadudj waiting, who was watching our arrival from her house. I was very sorry that I was not allowed to join my young relations at once, but my mother remained firm, and I was consoled by the promise that we were to spend a day at Bet il Sahel as soon as my father had returned to it.

We therefore passed on to get to Madjid's residence, Bet il Watoro, which was close by, and from which there was also a splendid view over the sea. Chadudj received us at the bottom of the staircase and bid us heartily welcome: she conducted us to our rooms, and her chief eunuch, Emân, brought in some refreshments. Madjid was below in his reception room with his friends, waiting for permission to come up and join us. How delighted he was, good, noble fellow, to welcome us in his new home!

Our own room was of but middling size, and looked out on the mosque close by. It was furnished like all Arab apartments, and there was nothing wanting to our comfort. As the dresses worn by day are not taken off at night, and all Arabs of standing are accustomed to the strictest cleanliness, there is no need for separate bedrooms, and the room allotted to us quite sufficed for our wants.

Rich and distinguished people generally furnish their houses in the following style: Persian carpets or very fine and soft matting cover the floors; the thick, whitewashed walls are divided from floor to ceiling into several partitions by deep recesses; these recesses are again subdivided by shelves of wood, painted green, forming a kind of open cabinet. Upon these shelves are symmetrically ranged the choicest and most expensive objects of glass and china. To an Arab nothing can be too costly to decorate these shelves; a handsome cut glass, a plate beautifully painted, or an elegant and tasteful jug, may cost any price; if they look pretty they are sure to be purchased.

The bare and narrow walls between the recesses are carefully concealed by large mirrors reaching from the low divans to the ceiling; these mirrors are generally expressly ordered from Europe. As a rule, pictures are prohibited to a Mahometan as imitations of Divine creation: of late, however, they are tolerated now and then. Clocks, again, are in great favour everywhere, and some houses contain quite a rich collection of them; they are placed above and in pairs on each side of the mirrors. The walls of the gentlemen's rooms are decorated with costly weapons from Arabia, Persia, and Turkey, and this is done by every Arab according to his means.

A large curtained bed of rosewood, of Indian workmanship, very prettily carved all over, is placed in one corner of the room. Arab beds are very high, and to get into them it is necessary to mount upon a chair or to call in the assistance of a chambermaid. The empty space beneath is often occupied by the children's or sick nurse.

Tables are rarely seen, and only in the houses of people of high station, but there are chairs of all kinds and colours. Wardrobes, chests of drawers, and the like are not in use; we had, however, a chest or trunk with two or three drawers, and a secret drawer to put away money and jewellery.

Windows and doors stand open all the year during the day; they are only shut for a short time during the rainy season. In our country we do not at all understand what "draught" means.

At first I did not like our new residence at all; I missed my young brothers and sisters very much, and Bet il Watoro appeared to me very small compared to gigantic Bet il Mtoni. I was by no means pleased that I was to stay here for ever. I could not sail my boats here, unless I chose to do so in a washtub, as there was no river near, and all water had to be fetched from a well outside the house. My dear mother, whose greatest pleasure was to give away all she possessed, wanted me to send my beautiful sailing boats to my brothers at Bet il Mtoni, but I could not make up my mind to do that at once. For the first time in my life I felt indeed very unhappy and downcast.

My mother, on the other hand, soon reconciled herself to her new duties, and was so busily engaged all

day in directing and arranging things in company
with Chadudj, that she did not even find time to look
after me. Dear Madjid alone took some trouble about
me, and showed me over the house from top to
bottom ; but nothing could please me, I was perfectly indifferent to everything, and I urged my
mother incessantly to return at once to Bet il Mtoni
and to my dear relations there. This could not be
done, of course, and the less so as she really proved a
great help to my brother and sister.

Fortunately I soon discovered Madjid to be a great
friend of all kinds of live beasts, of which he had quite
a collection, amongst others any number of white
rabbits, which spoiled the new house completely,
much to the annoyance of my mother and sister.
He also kept a great many fighting cocks of all
countries ; I have never again seen such a fine collection together, not even in zoological gardens.

I was soon his constant companion on his visit to his
favourites, and he was kind enough to let me share in
all his amusements. Before long I owned a number
of fighting cocks myself, and I felt not quite so lonely
now at Bet il Watoro. We inspected our champions
nearly every day, which were led up and down by
servants. A cockfight is, indeed, by no means an uninteresting affair—it is very entertaining, as it takes
up the entire attention of the spectator, and often it
is intensely amusing.

Afterwards he gave me fencing lessons with swords,
daggers, and lances, and taught me to practise with
gun and pistol when we went into the country. In
fact he made quite an amazon of me, greatly to the

distress of my dear mother, who declined to learn anything about fencing and shooting. All this, of course, did not improve my taste for fancy needle-work, and I preferred much to handle all kinds of weapons to sitting quietly at the bobbin-machine for hours together.

The perfect liberty I enjoyed in all these pastimes—for as yet a new teacher had not been found for me—made me soon feel in better spirits, and my objection to lonely Bet il Watoro soon vanished. Nor did I neglect riding, and, by Madjid's orders, Mesrur the eunuch improved me in horsemanship.

My mother being too busily employed in the house to have much spare time for me, I got soon attached to a clever Abyssinian woman, who grew very fond of me, and who taught me her language; but I have long since forgotten all I learned from her.

A lively intercourse was kept up with Bet il Mtoni, and whenever we went there we were always received most affectionately by all our friends. The communication between the two places was kept up by slaves carrying verbal messages to and fro. Eastern people are not very fond of letter-writing, even when able to write. Every person of note or wealth keeps some slaves who are employed as runners only. They must travel a certain number of miles daily, but they are well treated otherwise, and special care is taken of them. They are trusted with the most confidential messages. Upon their honesty and secrecy depends frequently their master's welfare, and even more! It is by no means a rare occurrence that the most intimate relations between people have been severed and

destroyed for ever by an act of vengeance on the part
of these messengers. In spite of this great drawback,
people cannot be induced to learn to write, and to
make themselves independent for life. The saying,
"Leave the world to take its course," is nowhere more
true than with us.

My sister Chadudj was very fond of society. Hardly
a day passed without any number of visitors being in
the house from six o'clock in the morning till midnight. Those who arrived very early were received
by the servants, and conducted to a room, where they
could rest until eight or nine o'clock, when they were
welcomed by the lady of the house. Later on I shall
have occasion to say more of these ladies' visits in a
separate chapter.

I did not at all succeed in being on the same
friendly terms with Chadudj as I was with Madjid.
She was rather forbidding, and I never got to love her
fondly. There was too great a contrast between good,
noble Madjid and her. Nor was I the only one who
was of this opinion. Everybody who became more
intimately acquainted with them soon found out who
of the two was the more amiable. Above all, she
could be very cold to strangers, and ungracious, and
on this account she had many enemies. She had the
greatest dislike to all novel and foreign things, and
nothing annoyed her more than the call of a European
lady, though it never lasted above half or three-
quarters of an hour.

In other respects she was very circumspect and of
a practical turn, considering her station; she was
never idle, and when she had nothing else to do she

sewed and embroidered dresses for the children of her
married slaves as assiduously as the fine shirts for
her brother. Among these children there were three
very pretty boys, whose father was superintendent of
buildings in our service. These boys were called
Selim, Abdallah, and Tani, and, being only a few years
younger than myself, they soon became my daily companions, as I had no others of my own age in the
place, till I went over more frequently to my brothers
and sisters at Bet il Sahel.

CHAPTER III.

THE long-looked for day at last arrived on which I was to pay a visit to Bet il Sahel with my mother and Chadudj from early morn till night. It was on a Friday, the Mahometan Sabbath, that we left our house as early as half-past five, wrapped in our big black shawls with gold borders (called Schele). We had not far to go, only some one hundred paces, to get to our destination.

The faithful but rather cross old gatekeeper did not receive us in an over friendly manner. More crossly even than was his wont, he told us that he had been on his feeble legs for the last hour admitting lady visitors. Said il Nubi, as the crusty old fellow was called, was a Nubian slave of my father's, whose beard—I cannot express myself otherwise, as the Arabs wear their heads shaved bare—had grown white in long and loyal service. My father thought much of him, as Said had once stayed his master's hand in a moment of great though righteous wrath from committing an act of rashness, which he would have deeply regretted all his life.

The little ones, however, did not know much about

Said at the time, and it gave us great pleasure to play all sorts of tricks upon the crotchety old fellow. Our designs were chiefly directed against his enormous keys, and I believe there was not a spot in all Bet il Sahel where they had not, at one time or another, been hidden. My brother Djemschîd above all showed great skill in making them disappear so completely, that even we could not find out their hiding-place.

We found the people occupying the first floor all astir already; only those who were still engaged in their morning devotions remained as yet invisible. Nobody would have dared to disturb them, even if the house had been on fire. We had chosen this day because my father happened to be there, and the same reason had caused many others to come too.

Nor were all the ladies who arrived friends or acquaintances of ours—many, indeed, were perfect strangers to all of us. Most of them had come from Omân, our native country, and on purpose only to obtain some pecuniary aid from my father, which was rarely denied them. Omân and our kinsfolk there are very poor, and our own prosperity dates from the time of my father's conquest and occupation of Zanzibar.

Women are as a rule forbidden by law to speak to a strange man. There is, however, an exception to this in two cases: they may appear before their sovereign and before a judge. As hardly any of these visitors in question were able to write or send a petition, there was nothing left for them but to undertake the short voyage from Asia to Africa, and to prefer their

request in person. All of them received presents
according to their position and rank freely, and without the numerous questions that a poor applicant in
Europe is usually subjected to. It is taken for
granted in our country that no respectable person
will ask for assistance merely for the sake of begging,
and this view proves correct in most cases.

I was most affectionately received by all my
brothers and sisters, especially by my dearly beloved
and never-to-be-forgotten sister Chole. Hitherto my
mother had been the only one whom I really and
fondly loved, but I now began to adore this "light of
our house" from my very soul. She was my only
ideal soon, as she had been our father's favourite
child before, and she deserved, indeed, to be admired
by all. She was admitted to be a girl of rare beauty
by all who were unprejudiced and without envy. No
one can remain quite insensible to beauty—it was so
with her in our house, as there was, indeed, no one to
equal her in our whole family, and the fame of her
beauty had spread far and wide. Fine eyes are very
common in the East, but hers were so eminently
beautiful, that she got the name, Nidjm il subh, or
" Morning Star." An Arab chief, taking part on a
certain feast day in the popular game of sham fighting in front of our house, was observed with his looks
fixed upon a certain window, quite unconscious of the
blood which gushed from his wounded foot, and of the
pain this wound must have caused him. It was my
sister Chole whom he had seen at the window by
chance ; her beauty had so overwhelmed him that he
accidentally pierced his foot with his iron-pointed

lance, and wounded himself without so much as noticing it, until one of my brothers drew his attention to the fact. For years after poor innocent Chole was teased by my brothers about this affair.

Bet il Sahel, which is a good deal smaller than Bet il Mtoni, lies also close upon the seashore; it is a bright and cheerful-looking place, and a very pleasant house to live in.

There is a splendid view of the sea and the shipping from all its windows, which delighted me much. The doors on the upper floor, which contains many rooms, open upon a long and wide gallery of such grandness as I have never seen equalled. The ceiling is supported by pillars reaching down to the ground, and these pillars are connected by a high parapet, along which chairs are placed. A great many coloured lamps, suspended from the ceiling, throw a magic glow over the whole house after dark.

The gallery looks down upon a courtyard, always full of bustle and noise; I have sometimes been reminded of all this in after years by market scenes on the stage, reproducing something like a picture of it on a small scale.

Two large separate flights of stairs lead from this court to the rooms on the first floor. Crowds of people are continually going up and down these stairs, and the crowding is often so great that it takes some minutes before one can get to the staircase at all.

One corner of the courtyard is taken up by the slaughter-house, according to the Eastern custom of killing one's own meat. In another spot negroes have their heads shaved; tired-out water-carriers

stretch themselves rather lazily on the ground, heedless to all calls for water, until they are uncere-
moniously roused and reminded of their duty by one
of the eunuchs; generally they do not wait for the
approach of those taskmasters, but get up and run
off with their big "Mtungi" (water jars), amid the
jeerings of the bystanders. Not far off a dozen or so
of nursemaids sit basking in the sun with their little
charges, telling them thrilling stories and fairy tales.

The kitchen is put up in the open, near one of the
ground-floor pillars; the numberless cooks quarrel
and fight continually, until one of the head cooks
steps in, dealing blows right and left, and restoring
order for a time. The quantities of meat boiled here
are enormous, the beasts being always cooked whole.
Fish of so large a size was often brought, as had to
be carried by two negroes; smaller ones were only
bought by basketsfull, and poultry by the dozen. Flour,
rice, and sugar were counted by bags, and butter, imported in a liquid state from the Isle of Socotra, by
jars of about a hundredweight each. Spices alone
were taken by the pound (ratti).

The quantities of fruit consumed were still more
enormous. Thirty to forty porters, and sometimes
as many as fifty, came in daily laden with fruit, not to
count the small boats arriving from the seashore
plantations. I should not overestimate the daily
supply of fresh fruit at Bet il Sahel, in putting it
down as equal to the load of a large railway truck.
During the mango season (embe) more than double
this quantity was consumed every day. Great carelessness prevailed in the conveyance of the fruit, and

large quantities were made quite unfit for use owing to the manner in which the baskets were treated and flung on the ground by the slaves.

A wall, about six feet deep, ran along the shore to protect the house against the sea, with a grove of very fine pomegranates behind. Several of the best horses were brought out every morning from the stables, and fastened to this wall with long ropes, to roam about and wade in the soft sand at low tide. My father took great delight in his thoroughbreds from Omân; he inspected them daily, and himself tended them when they were sick. It is well known how tenderly attached an Arab is to his favourite horse. My brother Madjid had a splendid brown mare, and he ardently wished to obtain a foal from her. This wish was at last fulfilled, and when "il Kehle," the mare, was about to foal, he ordered his head groom to call him, be it night or daytime. We were actually roused from our sleep one morning, between two and three o'clock, and informed that the happy event had taken place. The groom who had brought the glad news received a reward of fifty dollars from his happy master. This is by no means a single instance; the attachment to horses in Arabia proper is said to be carried still farther.

After prayers we went to see my father in his apartments. Fond of joking as he always was, he turned to me after a while, saying: "Well now, Salme, how do you like this place? Would you like to return to Bet il Mtoni? And don't they forget here to give you your—milk soup?"

About ten o'clock all my elder brothers came in

from their houses to breakfast with my father. Besides us, his children and grandchildren, who were admitted after the age of seven, no one but his legitimate wife, Azze bint Sêf, and his sister Asche sat down at his table. No Surie was ever permitted to take meals with him, however high she might stand in his favour. Social distinction in the East never shows itself more than at meals; guests are on the most friendly and intimate footing with their hosts—often more so than would be the case in Europe—but at meal-time this equality ceases, and the strictest observance of rank is adhered to by common consent. Even the Sarari have established a division of rank among themselves. The handsome Circassians, well aware of their better breeding, decline to break bread with the coffee-coloured Abyssinians: thus by tacit understanding they dine apart. I have already mentioned that among us children no distinction of colour was made.

It soon struck me that the occupants of Bet il Sahel seemed much happier and more cheerful than those of Bet il Mtoni, and I began to understand the reason of this afterwards. In this latter place Azze bint Sêf ruled supreme; she ruled over husband, step-children, and their mothers—in short, over every one and everything within her reach, while at Bet il Sahel all, my father not excepted, were more free and at liberty to do as they liked; there was no one here to give orders but my dear and gentle father. I think he was himself so conscious of the great difference between the two houses, that for years he had not sent any one to live at Bet il Mtoni, except by desire, although there was plenty of room to spare in the

palace, while Bet il Sahel was always overcrowded.
This state grew so bad at last that he conceived the
happy thought of building wooden pavilions on the
large gallery aforementioned. Finally, however,
another house was built on the shore some miles to
the north of Bet il Sahel, to serve as residence to the
younger generation, which was called Bet il Râs
(Strandhouse).

A painter would have found many models for a
picture in our gallery, for a more variegated company
could not easily be met with. The faces of the people
showed eight to ten different shades of complexion at
least; and it would, indeed, have puzzled even a clever
artist to make out the many-tinted garments worn.
The noise was truly appalling—quarrelling or romping
children in every corner—loud voices and clapping
hands summoning servants, the Eastern equivalent for
ringing a bell—the rattle and clatter of the women's
wooden sandals (Kabakib)—all combined in producing
the most distracting din.

Our chief amusement was listening to the babel of
languages spoken in our midst. Arabic was the only
language really sanctioned in my father's presence.
But as soon as he turned his back, a truly Babylonian
confusion of tongues commenced, and Arabian, Persian, Turkish, Circassian, Swahely, Nubian, and
Abyssinian were spoken and mixed up together, not
to mention the various dialects of these tongues. This
excitement seemed, however, to disturb no one, and
only sick people complained of it sometimes. My
father, too, had got quite accustomed to it, and never
interposed.

All my grown-up sisters presented themselves in festive array on this day, partly because it was our Sunday, and in honour of our father's presence. Our mothers walked about, or stood together in groups, talking, laughing, and jesting with each other so amicably that a stranger, unaware of the fact, would never have guessed them to be the wives of one man. The clashing of arms on the staircase announced the arrival of my numerous brothers and their sons, most of whom intended to stay with us all day.

Things were kept up at Bet il Sahel in a much more sumptuous and extravagant style than at Bet il Mtoni, and I met there a far greater number of handsome and pretty faces than at the latter place, where my mother and her friend Medine had been the only Circassian women. But the majority were here Circassians, who beyond a question are more distinguished in outward appearance than Abyssinians, though even amongst the latter great beauties are to be found. This natural superiority was the cause of a good deal of ill-will and envy, and one beautiful Circassian in particular was treated coldly, and even hated by the Abyssinian women on account of her beauty.

It cannot be a matter of surprise that under these circumstances a kind of ridiculous "hatred of race" had broken out among my brothers and sisters. In spite of many good qualities they have, Abyssinian women are almost always of a spiteful and vindictive disposition, for, their passions once roused, they know no bounds or decency. We, that is, the children of Circassian mothers, were generally called "cats" by those who had Abyssinian blood in their veins, merely because some of us were the unfortunate possessors of blue eyes and a fair complexion, for which they nicknamed us "Highness." My father was never forgiven the fact that he had chosen his two favourite children, Scharife and Chole—both by Circassian mothers, the former even blue-eyed—from the hateful "race of cats."

At Bet il Mtoni we had always led a kind of monastic life under the rigid rule of Azze bint Sêf, whilst Bet il Watoro was still more lonely and dull. I was therefore well pleased to join in the merry doings of Bet il Sahel, and soon made friends with the brothers and sisters, and two of my nieces, of my own age, Schembûa and Farschu, the only children of my brother Chalid. They came to Bet il Sahel from their own house every morning, and went back in the evening and took part in the lessons and games of their uncles and aunts. Chalid's mother, Churschît, was a Circassian, and quite an exceptional woman. She was uncommonly tall, and possessed a great strength of will combined with a high degree of common sense; I have never met any woman like her in all my life. Later on, and during the time that Chalid represented my father in his absence, it was said that it was she who actually governed the country, and that her son was only her tool. Her advice and counsel in all matters concerning our family was considered quite indispensable, and much depended always upon the decision she came to. She took in at a glance as much as if she had owned the hundred eyes of an argus, and on all momentous occasions gave proof of a wisdom and sagacity truly Solomonic. She was not, however, very much liked by the little folks, and we rather avoided coming near her if we could help it.

When about to return to Bet il Watoro in the evening, I was rather dismayed on hearing my father tell my mother that I was still to go on with my lessons, *i.e.*, reading; and upon her telling him that as yet no other teacher had been found, he decided that I was to come to Bet il Sahel, and return home every night, like my nieces, so as to take part in the general lessons there. I was not very much pleased when I heard this; lessons had never attracted me, the less so as my last teacher had inspired me with a thorough dislike to all learning. I got soon reconciled, however, to the new arrangement in consideration for the companionship of my brothers and sisters, on all days except Fridays, and my charming sister Chole promising my mother to watch over me. She kept her promise faithfully, quite taking the place of a mother.

My own dear mother was very much downcast at my father's decree, which took me away from her six days in the week, but there was no help for it; she made me promise, however, to show myself several times a day at a certain place, from which she could see and nod to me in the distance.

CHAPTER IV.

ALL I can say here of my new teacher is, that I shall always remain deeply grateful to God for having given me such a faithful friend in youth. She was very strict, but also very just. I was often quite alone with her, as her other pupils did not much care to enter her darkened sick chamber, and preferred to keep out of her reach instead, taking advantage of her helpless state. I could not, however, bear to hear her ask for me, and leave her alone in her sufferings. She was highly pleased at my obedience, it is true, but my refractory brothers and sisters not only laughed at me for my pains, but often cuffed me.

In course of time I liked Bet il Sahel very much, for there was plenty of room for roaming about, and we played any number of foolish pranks, which were not left without punishment when found out; but I had generally the best of it on such occasions, as Chole was too tender-hearted to punish me as I deserved.

We had some splendid peacocks at the house, one of them was rather savage, and could not bear the sight of children. One day, when we were walking

round the cupola of the Turkish bath, which was
connected by a suspension bridge with Bet il Sahel
and Bet il Tani, this peacock suddenly and furiously
darted at my brother Djemschid. We threw ourselves on the beast, and conquered it at last, not
feeling inclined, however, to set it free without punishment. We resolved upon a very cruel revenge, viz.
depriving the animal of its magnificent plumage;
and miserable enough the pugnacious bird looked
after this. My father was fortunately absent at the
time, and when he returned the affair was hushed
up.

Two Circassian women had arrived from Egypt,
and after a time it appeared to us as if one of them
was rather haughty and indifferent to us. We were
rather galled at this, and put our heads together to
find out a punishment equal to the offence; but we
found it very difficult since we rarely had the opportunity of seeing or meeting her. She was only a few
years older than ourselves, and therefore the affront
was the greater. With this grievance in our minds,
we were once passing her apartment, the door of
which stood open as usual. The poor thing was
seated at the time on a very light Suahely bed, which
consists of four posts only held together by ropes and
a mat, merrily singing one of her pretty national
songs. On this occasion my sister Schewâne was
our leader; a sign from her sufficed to make us at
once understand what she proposed to do. In a
trice we took hold of the connecting ropes, and,
pulling all together, we hoisted the matting upon
which she was sitting, and dropped the frightened

girl down again with a jerk. It was a very childish trick indeed, but a success in so far as it cured her effectually of her indifference to us—this was all we had wanted.

Being full of mischief, I used to play tricks quite by myself sometimes, and soon after our removal to Bet il Watoro I once nearly broke my neck. We had gone on a visit to one of our plantations. One morning I managed to escape from my attendants, and climbed up a high palm-tree as nimbly as a cat, without using the pingu, a thick rope to keep the feet together, and without which the most skilled climber cannot be prevailed upon to ascend a cocoa-tree. When about half-way up the tree, I began calling out to the people unconsciously passing below, and wishing them good morning.

What a fright I caused them all! A crowd collected, begging and entreating me to get down. It was impossible to send any one up to help me. In climbing a cocoa-tree both hands must be free, and therefore the encumbrance of a child of eight would render the feat an impossible one. I was, however, quite pleased to remain where I was, and only made up my mind to slip down when my mother, who was standing below, wringing her hands in despair, had promised me all kinds of delightful things. Everybody spoiled me that day, and loaded me with presents on account of my lucky escape, instead of soundly thrashing me as I deserved.

Such and similar pranks we played daily, and no punishment could deter us from a new one. We seven—three boys and four girls—turned the whole

house topsy-turvy, and caused no small annoyance to
our mothers.

Sometimes my dear mother kept me at home on a
week-day, and this was always an opportunity for
Madjid to spoil me thoroughly. On one of these
days he greatly frightened us. He frequently suffered
from severe spasms, and for this reason he was hardly
ever left without an attendant to render immediate
assistance. When he was in his bath-room, my
mother and Chadudj watched alternately at the door,
not trusting the slaves, and spoke to him from time
to time, and he used to tell them jokingly that he
was still alive. While Chadudj was thus walking up
and down one day at his door, she suddenly heard
the sound of a heavy fall in the room, and when she
rushed in frightened to death, she found her beloved
brother on the raised platform convulsed by a terrible
attack, the worst he had ever had. A messenger on
horseback was at once despatched to Bet il Mtoni to
fetch my father.

In all cases of sickness and disease we are unfortunately exposed to the most ignorant quacks and
mountebanks, and now that I have come to know
and to appreciate the natural and reasonable means
employed by medical men in Europe, I am induced
to think that in the majority of cases our dead have
not succumbed to their disease, but have been sacrificed to the barbarous treatment to which they were
subjected. I am sure we could not have borne the many
cases of death in our family, and among our friends
so resignedly, without being sustained by the firm
and irrefutable belief in our " destiny."

For many hours poor Madjid was lying on his bed perfectly senseless and in convulsions, inhaling all the time an atmosphere unwholesome even to any person in good health. For in spite of our predilection for fresh and pure air, the patients in our parts are hermetically shut out from the fresh air, but especially so when, as in the present instance, the evil one himself is supposed to have a hand in it, for then the sickroom and the whole house are thoroughly fumigated.

To the great surprise of everybody, my dear father arrived an hour afterwards in a mtumbi, a small fishing-boat holding only one person, and hurried into the house. The old man was deeply affected by the illness of this son, he who had more than forty children alive at the time. The tears ran down into his beard as he stood at Madjid's sick bed. " O Lord! O Lord! preserve the life of my son ! " was his incessant prayer. And God granted his prayer, for Madjid was spared to us.

My mother afterwards asked him why he had come in such a miserable vessel. " When the messenger brought the news," he replied " there was not a single boat on shore; it would have had to be signalled for, and I had no time to wait. It would also have taken too long to have a horse saddled. At that very moment I saw a fisherman pass the Bendjle in his mtumbi, so I seized my weapons, called to him to stop and to get out, and jumped into the boat to pull here by myself." I may mention here that a mtumbi is a most primitive kind of boat, made of the hollowed-out trunk of a tree, and holds hardly more than one person, who

4

has to paddle it along. It is narrow, pointed, and comparatively short, in shape somewhat like a whale-boat.

It may be thought strange, according to Western views, that a father so uneasy about the life of his child, and who sets aside all regards of etiquette in his anxiety, should find time to think of his weapons. Here, also, the saying comes true: "So many countries, so many customs." Incomprehensible as this great attachment which the Arab has for his weapons may appear to a European, so incredible are to us some of the Northern habits, as that of excessive drinking in this country, for instance. I continued to go to school daily at Bet il Sahel, and returned at night to my mother at Bet il Watoro. When I had succeeded in learning by heart about the third part of the Kurân, at the age of nine, I was considered too old for school, and after this only went to Bet il Sahel with my mother and Chadudj on Fridays to see my father.

CHAPTER V.

WE lived quietly and peacefully at Bet il Watoro for about two years. Unfortunately good times never last long, and events often arise which have been least foreseen or expected, as it was in our case. Nor is it possible to fancy a creature more lovable and of more gentle disposition than the one who unwittingly disturbed the tranquillity of our domestic life. Asche, a distant relation of ours, had only lately arrived at Zanzibar from our native country, Omàn, and shortly after she became Madjid's wife. All of us liked her very much, and rejoiced at the happiness and good fortune of our brother, all except his own sister Chadudj. It grieves me much to have to admit that, from beginning to end, Chadudj greatly wronged Asche. The latter was a truly charming person, and still very young; but, instead of instructing and training her to her new station as she ought to have done, Chadudj behaved to her in a most unsisterly fashion. She was the mistress of the house by right of her marriage, but, disregarding this, Chadudj ruled over her so tyranically, that poor, gentle Asche frequently came to my mother in tears, complaining of her troubles.

My mother now found herself, as it were, placed between two fires, and her position became more and more embarrassing. Chadudj could not be prevailed upon to give up any of her pretended rights, but continued to treat Asche as a child. My mother tried to impress Chadudj with a sense of Asche's position as Madjid's wife, and begged her to avoid, for Madjid's sake, all that might vex or cause him annoyance. It was all to no purpose, and her life at Bet il Watoro, once so agreeable and happy, grew gradually unbearable. So at last my mother decided to quit the house which was so dear to her rather than be a witness any longer to the continual discord.

But Madjid and his wife would not listen to this—Asche in particular, who never called my mother otherwise than Umma ("mamma"), was quite inconsolable. Chadudj, on the other hand, remained perfectly indifferent, and this only confirmed my mother still more in the resolve she had taken.

Asche herself could stand the life no longer. She therefore sued for and obtained a divorce from Madjid. But after this sad experience of her young life, her heart turned against Zanzibar and its inhabitants; therefore, as soon as the favourable south wind set in, which our ships had been waiting for, she came to bid us good-bye. Being an orphan, she purposed returning to an old aunt of hers in Omán, who lived somewhere in the neighbourhood of Mesket.

Our exodus from Bet il Watoro had already been effected previous to this event, and we had taken up our residence at Bet il Tani. My sister Chole was greatly pleased with this, as we now lived quite close to her, and nearly in the same place, where she had taken the trouble to select and arrange our new quarters.

It was really a difficult matter to obtain rooms in our houses, and for this reason it had gradually become a custom to give a kind of reversionary promise on the death of persons in possession, as is done in the case of charitable institutions in Europe. Sometimes it was indeed revolting to see how people would carefully watch the slightest attack of coughing, or other alarming symptoms in their neighbours, and mentally disposing of the coveted rooms. All this was very wicked, and mainly the consequence of our over-crowded condition. It was due to Chole's intercession that we obtained large and handsome apartments, without the unpleasant consciousness of being usurpers.

We saw but little of Chadudj now; she was offended at our removal, and reproached my mother very unjustly with want of affection. The latter had, however, too strong a sense of justice as to suffer quietly such unfair treatment of a defenceless and inexperienced woman, whose only offence had been that she had dared to become Madjid's wife. My brother, on the other hand, came to see us frequently, and he remained the dear and true friend he had always been.

Bet il Tani lies quite close to Bet il Sahel, and is connected, as previously mentioned, with the latter by a suspension bridge, which runs over the roof of the Turkish bath between both houses. It now retained but the shadow of its former splendour, for in the

upper floor of this palace had lived, many years ago,
a second legitimate wife of my father's, Schesade, a
Persian princess of entrancing beauty.   She is said
to have been excessively extravagant, but to have
fondly loved her step-children.   Her little retinue
was composed of one hundred and fifty cavaliers, all
Persians, who lived on the ground floor; with them
she hunted and rode in the broad day—rather contrary
to strict Arab notions.   The Persian women are subjected to quite a Spartan training in bodily exercise;
they enjoy great liberty, much more so than Arab
women, but they are also much more rude in mind
and action.

Schesade is said to have carried on her extravagant
style of life beyond bounds; her dresses, cut always
after the Persian fashion, were literally covered with
embroideries of pearls.   A great many of these were
picked up nearly every morning by the servants in her
rooms, where she had dropped them from her garments, but the princess would never take any of these
precious jewels back again.   She did not only drain
my father's exchequer most wantonly, but violated
many of our sacred laws ; in fact, she had only
married him for his high station and his wealth,
and had loved some one else all the time.   He was
about to resent her conduct one day on her return
from one of her excursions, and it was on this occasion that faithful old Nubi had saved him from committing a great crime.   Such a scene could, of course,
only end in a divorce ; fortunately Schesade had no
children of her own.   There is a rumour still current
amongst us that beautiful Schesade was observed some

years after this event, when my father carried on war in Persia, and had the good fortune of taking the fortress of Bender Abbâs, on the Persian Gulf, heading her troops, and taking aim at the members of our family herself.

In the former home of this princess I began to learn to write by myself in a very primitive way. It had to be done secretly, too, as women never receive lessons in writing, and are not even allowed to show their skill therein. Taking the Kurân as guide, I tried to copy the letters as faithfully as I could upon the shoulder-blade of a camel, which we use in place of a slate. My courage rose as I got on, and I only required at last some finishing instructions in calligraphy, for which end I appointed one of our slaves, who was notoriously proficient in the art, to the dignity of writing master.

My friends greatly ridiculed my efforts, but I did not allow my enthusiasm to be damped thereby, nor have I ever had cause to regret the hours I spent in acquiring the art of writing, since it has proved a means of communicating with the few loyal and faithful ones of my far-away home.

CHAPTER VI.

How many times have I been asked : " Do please tell me how can people in your country manage to live, with nothing to do ? " I had the pleasure of answering this question six or eight times over at a large party, and I need not say how amusing and interesting it was to me to give the same reply so many times over. Coming from a person inhabiting a Northern country, the question is quite a natural one I admit, for it is hard for such to fancy a life without work, being firmly convinced, moreover, that women in the East do nothing all day but dream away their time in a shut-up harem, or, for a change, play with some luxurious toy.

The ways of life differ everywhere ; all our views, our habits, and customs are shaped to suit our surroundings. Men and women work in the North either for an existence or for enjoyment. It is not so with people in our blessed South. I use the word "blessed" advisedly, as I look upon the contentedness of a people as a great and priceless boon ; and because the Arab, so frequently described in books as idle and lazy, is accustomed to an abstemiousness in which perhaps a Chinaman only equals him. The climate itself brings it about that the Southerner *may* work if he likes, while the Northerner is obliged to. Northern people are inclined somewhat to form opinions and prejudices in their own favour; they are accustomed to look down upon their antipodes proudly and contemptuously, which, to my taste at least, is not a very commendable quality to possess. It is but too often overlooked in this country how indispensable industry and activity are to the North to save hundreds of thousands from starvation. Are Italians, Spaniards, and Portuguese not a great deal less industrious than Englishmen or Germans? And for what reason? Simply because their summer time lasts so much longer than their winter, and because they have not to struggle so hard for existence. In the cold season so many things of the direst necessity are required, the mere name and existence of which are beyond the comprehension of people in the South.

Extravagant habits may be met with in every country. Those who possess both inclination and means will never lack the opportunity of gratifying the one and spending the other to the fullest, whereever they may be. Indeed, I do not intend to enlarge on this subject, but merely draw comparisons between the respective requirements of different countries.

Countless objects are needed in this country to protect the frail life of a newborn child against the effects of an ever-changing temperature, while the Southern baby is left almost naked, and sleeps in a draught of warm air. Here a child of two years— from the richest to the poorest—cannot do without shoes, stockings, drawers, a dress, petticoats, gloves, bonnet, ties, gaiters, fur muff, and muffatees—their sole difference being quality; whilst there, all the clothing the son of a prince requires consists of two articles—a shirt and the kofije.

Now, I ask, is the Arab mother, who wants so very little for herself and for her child, to work as hard as the European housewife? She has not the slightest idea what is meant by darning stockings or mending gloves, or of any of those numerous trifles that a nursery entails; and as for that important and troublesome domestic item, a washing-day, it is a thing to us unknown; our linen is washed daily, and dried in little more than half an hour, smoothed flat (not ironed), and put away. We do not use, and are therefore spared the anxiety of those useless ornaments called muslin curtains. The garments of an Eastern woman, those of the greatest lady included, require an incredibly small amount of attention and mending: this is easily explained, as women move very little either indoors or out, and have fewer dresses.

All this helps to render life to Eastern women, without distinction of station and rank, much less complicated. But to become properly acquainted with, and to get initiated into all these minor details of household life, it is necessary to have been in the East, and to have lived there for a considerable time. No reliance is to be placed on the reports of travellers, who stop for a short time only, who are unable to gain an insight into all these details, and maybe obtain all their information from hotel waiters. Foreign ladies even, supposing they have actually entered a harem either at Constantinople or Cairo, have never seen the inside of a real harem at all, but only its outside, represented by the state rooms decorated and furnished in European style.

Our climate, moreover, is so splendid and productive that it is hardly necessary to provide for the coming day. I do not deny that our people, taken as a whole, are averse to " flurry ; " but it will be easier to realize the effects of a tropical sun, if one only considers how very trying a hot July or August in Europe can be sometimes.

I repeat it—Arabs are by no means inclined to be industrious; they only value two things, the art of war and husbandry, and but very few settle down to a trade. Though they are obliged to do much barter trade, they are poor merchants on the whole, and have but little of the Semitic talent for trading. Very little suffices for their few wants, and the future is left to provide for itself. An Arab never thinks of making plans for the morrow, as he may expect to be called away any day. He never plants but that which he can reap himself ; and he considers him who acts otherwise to be " like the rich man who set up greater barns " (Luke xii.).

In this way life in the East is less laborious and more peaceful : it was this that I wanted particularly to point out and to prove before entering on a more minute description of the daily life in an Arab household. Let me, however, state expressly that I am only speaking here of things referring to Omán and

Zanzibar, which, in many respects, differ from those in other Eastern countries.

The hours of prayer regulate the daily life of every Mahometan; they are said five times a day, and if this be strictly observed, as is ordained by the holy book, including ablution and changing of dress, they take up three hours at the very least.

Persons of rank are roused between four and half-past five o'clock a.m. for the first prayer, and return to sleep afterwards; devout people wait for sunrise at six o'clock a.m. before doing so; the lower classes begin their daily task immediately after the first prayer. All persons in our house could live just as they pleased, provided they followed the regulations set down for devotions and for the attendance at the two principal meals.

The majority slept till eight o'clock, when the women and girls are gently roused by a slave, who begins to rub and knead them all over, which produces a very agreeable sensation. In the meantime the bath has been filled with fresh spring water, and the garments — on which jessamine and orange blossoms have been strewn during night—are fumigated with amber and musk before they are put on.

About an hour is spent with the toilet, after which everybody has to wish our father good morning before sitting down to breakfast, the first of our two daily meals. Though a very copious and abundant repast, it took us very little time to get it over, as all the dishes had been prepared and placed on the table in readiness.

After breakfast everybody is at liberty to employ

his leisure as he likes. The gentlemen get ready to go to the audience-chamber; the women, who have no work on hand, sit down at the windows to look out into the animated streets, or watch for a stealthy glance from the flashing eye of a belated noble hurrying to the *levée*, until, alas! the voice of an apprehensive mother or aunt calls the unhappy girl away from the gay scene below.

Two or three hours are thus rapidly passed away. Meanwhile the gentlemen call upon each other and send word to the ladies whom they wish to visit in the evening. The older women, who take no pleasure in all this lively stir, retire to their rooms, alone or in company, to take up some fancy work, to embroider their veils, shirts, or drawers with gold thread, or cambric shirts for their husbands and sons with red and white silk—an art which requires considerable skill. Others, again, read novels, visit the sick in their rooms, or employ themselves with their own private affairs.

At one o'clock the servants announce that it is time for the second prayer. The sun is now in full blaze, and after prayer all escape gladly to some cool place to dream away an hour or two upon handsomely plaited soft mats, into which sacred mottoes are woven, or to chat and eat cakes and fruit.

The third prayer is said at four o'clock p.m., and then we dress in our more elaborate afternoon costumes. Again we call upon our father, wishing him "good afternoon"—our grown-up brothers and sisters are allowed to call him father, the little children and their mothers only address him as hbâbi (sir).

Now followed the liveliest time of the day: we sat down to our principal meal, at which all members of our large family met together for the second time. After the meal the eunuchs placed European chairs on the grand piazza in front of my father's apartments for the grown-up people, whilst we little children remained standing in deference to old age, which is, I believe, nowhere honoured to that degree. The numerous family grouped round our usually grave father, the trim and well-armed eunuchs being ranged at some distance in rank and file along the gallery. Coffee and all kinds of French fruit-syrups were handed round, of which we children partook freely. Conversation was carried on accompanied by the tunes of a mighty barrel-organ (the largest I have ever seen), or, for a change, by some large musical box; sometimes a blind Arab woman, called Amra, who possessed an exquisite voice, was called in to sing.

An hour and a half later we all separated, and employed ourselves as we liked. Some chewed betel-nut, which is a Suahely habit, and not liked on that account by Arabs born in Arabia proper. Those, however, among us who had been born on the East coast of Africa, and were brought up together with negroes and mulattoes, rather fancied this habit, notwithstanding the disapproval of our Asiatic relations, though we never indulged in it in our father's presence.

Not long afterwards, gunshots and the beat of drums of the Indian guard announced sunset and the time for the fourth prayer. Not one of our daily devotions was performed faster, everybody seemed in a hurry to get it over. For those who did not wish to go out themselves (we and our mothers always required a special permission from our father or from his representative, which was rarely refused), or those who did not expect visitors, were sure to be invited by some one in the house, or received visits from brothers and sisters, stepmothers, stepchildren, or from other people. Coffee and lemonade, fruits and cakes were freely partaken of. There was a great deal of merry joking and laughing going on; some read aloud, others played at cards (never for money, however), or sang, or listened to negroes playing the sese, or sewed, embroidered, and made lace.

It is, therefore, quite a mistake to suppose that a great lady in the East does absolutely nothing. It is true she does not paint, nor play, nor dance (according to Western notions). But are there no other amusements to divert oneself with? People in our country are very temperate, and they are not given to a feverish pursuit of everchanging amusements and pleasures, though from the European point of view Oriental life may appear somewhat monotonous.

Our own personal attendants were, of course, all women; the menservants were dismissed every evening to their homes and families, and the eunuchs slept also outside the house.

Oil lamps are kept burning all night in the rooms and passages, but no candles are allowed after bed-time. Children above the age of two are no longer put to bed at a certain hour, they are left to themselves until they are tired. It frequently occurs that the children, overcome by fatigue, lie down anywhere and fall asleep, and then they are generally picked up carefully by some slaves and carried to their couches, sometimes a long way, without awaking to the fact.

Those people who have not gone out or received visitors generally retire about ten o'clock. On moonlight nights many take a walk on the flat housetops, which was a very delightful airing.

The fifth and last prayer ought to be said at 7.30 p.m., but as many are prevented at this time, it may be left unsaid until midnight or bedtime.

At bedtime all ladies of rank are waited upon by their female slaves, whose business it is to watch the falling asleep of their mistresses. One of them repeats the kneading process of the morning, while another fans gently, until they too may retire. I have mentioned already that all women go to bed fully dressed, and with all their jewels.

CHAPTER VII.

WE had two meals a day, as I have mentioned before. About nine a.m. we all met in the great saloon to kiss our father's hands. As a rule our brothers and nephews, even those who were married and who lived out of the house, shared our breakfast during the time our father lived in town with us. I do not remember, however, that he ever went out to take a meal with any of his sons or any one else.

The dishes were all arranged and placed by the eunuchs on the long sefra (dining-table). This sefra is made of wood, and looks somewhat like a billiard-table, only ours was twice as long, a little wider, and about three inches high, with a ledge of about a hand's breadth running round its sides. We do not have separate dining-rooms, and the sefra is carried into the gallery at mealtimes. Though we had some foreign furniture, such as couches, tables, and chairs, and sometimes wardrobes (my father's apartment contained a great deal of European furniture, which was more for show, however, than for actual use), we took our meals after the Eastern fashion, and sat down on the floor upon carpets and mats. Precedence

5

was strictly observed at table.   My father always
took his place at the upper end of the sefra ; next to
him, on his right and left, sat my elder brothers and
sisters, and the little ones (above seven years) took
the lower seats.   The fashion of taking people in to
dinner is not practised.

There was always a great variety of viands, often as
many as fifteen dishes ; rice dressed in many ways. Of
meat and poultry, mutton and fowls were liked most.
There was fish besides, and Eastern bread, and all kinds
of sweets and dainties.   As all the dishes are placed
on the table beforehand, there is no attendance required ; numerous eunuchs stand at some distance,
drawn up in line to carry out special orders.   Their
services were mostly required by my father, who
would send in portions to the smaller children who
were not yet admitted to table, or to sick people.
At Bet il Mtoni he used to make me sit in a place
where he could reach my plate. We had the same
food as the grown-up people, but it was always a pleasure to us to have our dishes selected by him, and he
himself greatly enjoyed doing so.

On sitting down to table, every one said in an
undertone, but quite audibly : " In the name of the
merciful Lord," and on rising, " Thanked be the Lord
of the universe."   My father always sat down and
rose first.

Clean plates were not handed to each person as is
the custom in Europe, but the various dishes (with
the exception of rice) were served up in small plates,
symmetrically arranged along the sefra, and two people
could always eat out of one plate.

Drinks were not taken at meals, but after them sherbet or sugared water was handed round. There was no talking, unless some one was specially addressed by my father; the greatest silence prevailed, which was very pleasant. Neither flowers nor fruit were placed on the sefra.

Shortly before and after each meal male and female slaves, smartly dressed, handed round basins to wash our hands. As a rule we used our fingers to eat with —knives and forks were deemed superfluous, and they were used only when European guests were entertained. Meats and fish were chopped up small beforehand, and we had spoons for all liquids. The upper classes perfume their hands after the washing, to remove any traces of the viands.

Fruit was never taken at meals, but either before or some time after. Each person had a certain quantity of the kinds in season sent to her rooms.

Half an hour after breakfast and dinner coffee was served by eunuchs in those well-known little Oriental cups in gold or silver casings. The coffee is very strong, boiled down to syrup, and filtered quite clear. It is taken without sugar and milk, and nothing is eaten with it, except, perhaps, a very finely chopped "areka" nut.

Coffee is always poured into the cup immediately before it is taken, and as the pouring out requires some skill, there are but few servants who can be selected for this office. The neat coffee-pot of tin, with brass clasps (china is never used), is carried in the left hand, and one of the little cups in its casing (called sarf) in the right one of the servant who pours out the beverage, an assistant following with a tray of empty cups and a large pot to fill up from. If he finds all the company still together, his work is quickly done, otherwise it is his duty to seek out each person.

It is well known that coffee is highly valued in the East, and great care is devoted to its preparation. The quantity each time required is roasted, ground and boiled immediately before use, that it may be quite fresh. Neither the surplus of roasted beans nor the boiled coffee is ever kept; what remains is either thrown away or used by the lower servants if they like.

The second and last meal is taken every afternoon at four o'clock precisely, and nothing more is served after the same until breakfast next morning, except coffee and fruits.

CHAPTER VIII.

BIRTH AND FIRST YEARS OF THE LIFE OF A PRINCE AND PRINCESS.

ALTHOUGH the birth of a prince or of a princess with us was not announced by the salute of guns, it was nevertheless always an event of importance, which caused much joy, but I regret to say much envy also. Our father and the respective mother were of course delighted at the birth of a child, and we little ones fully shared their joy. A newborn brother or sister had to go through all manners of ceremonies, and as such births occurred five or six times annually in our family, they were the welcome cause of as many family festivities to us.

No Mahometan will suffer the assistance of a medical man in such cases; midwives alone are allowed and admitted, and they are ignorance itself. The majority of them come from Hindustan, and are much preferred to native women; I do not know for what reason, for a midwife from Hindustan knows as little or less of her business than those from Arabia or from the Suahely country. In fact, mother as well as child may thank God alone, and their constitution, if they survive at all or keep well afterwards, for they owe no thanks to their stupid and foolish nurses.

After a warm water bath a kind of bandage is wound round the child's body, its neck and armpits are powdered with some strongly perfumed vegetable powder, and it is dressed in a calico shirt of an in-grain dye, or in a muslin one. The little thing is then placed on its back, its hands and feet are straightened out to the utmost, and it is swathed in a swathing-band up to the shoulders, the tiny arms and legs being thus firmly confined. In this state the child remains for forty days, except while the band is removed twice a day to give it a bath. By this process the child's body, it is thought, will be made straight and faultless for life.

The mother always watches over the child herself, and never leaves it to the care of any of her servants. Slaves are set to rock the cradle incessantly, which is of East Indian workmanship, and made of the finest wood beautifully carved. She rarely, however, nurses the child herself, except for a pastime, for each child has one or two wet nurses up to the age of two.

If it be a girl, she has holes pricked in her ears on the seventh day with a needle and thread of red silk, generally six in each ear, to which heavy gold rings are attached for ever when she is two months old. I say "for ever," because females who do not wear earrings either mourn a deceased relation or they have no holes pierced.

On the fortieth day a ceremony is performed to which European children could not be subjected : all the hair is shaved off the child's head. This may appear incredible, but many things in the South are different to what they are here. A bald-headed child would be considered as great a curiosity as a child born with a few tufts of hair is in this country. My Hamburg nurse was quite surprised when she saw my newborn daughter for the first time, whose black hair came down to her neck; nor was she satisfied until she had made my late husband bring home a small soft brush, with which she delighted in curling the baby locks two days old.

The shaving is done by the chief eunuch under certain ceremonies, in which fumigation with a species of a gum-arabic (somewhat similar to the incense used in Roman Catholic churches) plays an important part. The first hair is considered of much moment—it must not be burnt, nor carelessly thrown away, but buried in the ground, thrown into the sea, or hidden in some crevice of a wall. Twenty to thirty persons are always present during this ceremony, and the chief eunuch, who only on this occasion acts as barber, runs a great risk of crushing the soft and tender skull of the infant. He, as well as his numerous assistants, then receive a valuable present from my father.

The swathing band is removed on this day, rings are put on the arms and legs, and attached to the ears, and the child is dressed in a silk shirt and the kofije, a cap of gold stuff with ear-flaps. After this day everybody may go and look at it, for up to that time no one but the parents, the slaves on duty, and a few of the most intimate of the mother's friends were allowed to do so. This precaution is taken on account of the widespread belief in the evil eye and other dreaded species of witchcraft.

Little children of this age in the East look, beyond a doubt, much better than European ones, in whose dresses white predominates. My opinion remains unchanged on this point even after my long residence in Europe, and my own children looked hideous to me in their baby clothes when I compared them with my little brothers and sisters in their pretty attire.

The smallest children are already strongly perfumed, and everything they use and wear—dresses, sheets, bath-towels, and swathing clothes—are covered all night with jessamine (different from that known here), fumigated with amber and musk, and sprinkled all over with ottar of roses before they are used. It must be remembered that windows and doors are open nearly all day throughout the year, which mitigates to a certain extent any bad effect arising from this curious partiality for strong scents.

Several charms are also attached to the child's body on the fortieth day to protect it against the effects of the evil eye. They are called "Hamaje," or "Hafid," and consist of all sorts of things; the lower class using an onion, or a bit of garlic, or small shells, a piece of bone stitched up in leather and worn on the upper part of the left arm. In the upper classes these kinds of charms are replaced by gold or silver plates, worn on a chain round the neck, upon which sentences from the Kûran are engraved. The boys wear them only up to a certain age, the girls generally a longer period. The favourite charm consists of a gold or silver locket of pretty workmanship, likewise worn on a chain, two inches long by one inch wide, enclosing a miniature of the " hurs " (guardian). No person wearing a charm like this, bearing the holy name of the Lord, may enter an unclean place—a proof surely of the great reverence of a true Mahometan for his Lord and Creator !

From a very early age the child is fed (besides mother's milk) from a long spouted cup several times a day with milk soup, boiled with rice flour and sugar ; the sucking bottle was quite unknown in my time. It receives no other kind of food until it teethes ; after that it may eat anything. It is not customary to carry the children about, they are put on the carpet and then left to their own devices.

Another festivity follows at the first attempt of the child to sit up by itself, for the exclusive benefit of its little brothers and sisters. To celebrate this festive event in befitting style, extra cakes and other good things are provided. The mother, the nurses, and the child are dressed in their best, and wear their finest jewels. The child is then put into a small square carriage on low wheels, stuffed with cushions. The little legs are steadied upon a board fixed perpendicularly to the poles, and the other children gather all round.

Grains of Indian corn, which have been roasted in a peculiar way, till they get as large as a thimble and soft as wadding, are then mixed with a quantity of small silver coin, and this compound is poured over the child's head ; this done, the children rush upon their little brother or sister to obtain the coins, not seldom endangering the infant's life. The children of friends are sometimes invited on this occasion.

The child runs about barefooted until it is strong enough to wear sandals. Those worn by boys (watje) are much lighter than the kubkâb of the girls, and the latter are generally allowed to wear boys' sandals until they are able to put on the kubkâb. Stockings are not worn by either sex; ladies of rank use them at times upon riding excursions, as custom requires the ankles to be covered.

Besides the nurses, two or three slaves are appointed as personal attendants to each child when three months old, after which they are its property. The number of slaves is gradually increased as the child gets older, and in the case of death of any of them the vacant place is filled up by another, or a certain sum of money is paid instead by my father. The little girls wear boys' caps in the house up to a certain age.

Until their seventh year the princes live among the women; they then solemnly embrace the Mosaic faith, the ceremony being followed by great festivities, in which the state dignitaries and all high officials take part. This, if possible, is enacted in the country and in the presence of our father, and ends in public rejoicings of three days' duration.

On this occasion the boy is presented with a quiet mare, and with mounted attendants. The boys are thus taught to ride from early youth, and in time attain the dexterity of circus riders. It requires, of course, a great deal more skill to gain a firm seat on horseback without the good saddles and stirrups used

in this country. So great was the importance my
father attached to perfect horsemanship, that the
slightest mishap while out riding would call forth a
severe reprimand not only on his sons, but on their
incompetent riding masters.

Indeed not one of us was spoiled in the least. My
father's high sense of justice and unparalleled
generosity was combined with great and firm con-
sistency. We were expected to obey strictly our tutors
and teachers, be they Arabs, Abyssinians, or Negroes.
He was deaf to our entreaties or complaints if ever we
made any—a severity which taught us to respect those
in authority over us, and to appreciate that authority
when we had come to years of discretion.

The nurses, even those whose term of service had
been but short, were highly esteemed and honoured
as long as they lived. They are always slaves by
birth, but as a rule they are freed in reward of their
fidelity and devotion. Especially the black nurses
distinguish themselves by their great attachment to
their charges; the most anxious mother may quietly
leave her child with such an one who considers
herself a second mother to the child and treats it
accordingly. What a difference there is between
them and the half-hearted interest shown by the
nurses in this country! Many a time have I been
unable to resist interceding in behalf of poor little
nurslings when some flagrant carelessness forced
itself upon my notice.

The contrast which exists between the wet nurses of
these parts and our Arab nurses may possibly be
explained by the fact that in most cases the former are

compelled to forsake their own children in exchange
for a perfect little stranger—a sacrifice for which,
every mother will admit, no consideration of mere
money will compensate.

The position of a black wet nurse with regard to
the child entrusted to her by her mistress is quite a
different one. She has been in the latter's service for
years, may even have been born in her house : thus her
own interests and those of her master's are closely
knitted together. And further, there may be added a
circumstance of much weight—a black nurse is not
required to part with her child, but frequently, if not
always, she retains it. The child of the nurse receives
the same nourishment as its little foster brother or
sister, shares its pap, its fowl, its bath, wears its old
dresses, and by and by shares its toys. The child
grows up into a slave, but always preferred to others
except by very badly disposed people who can forget
their foster relation.

This patriarchal state of things generates more
faithful and devoted nurses than any European system
could achieve. I have often reflected how very hard
it must be for these poor women to part with their
own children for the sake of lucre, though I have
repeatedly been told that they are by no means so
sensible of this as I supposed. This, however, I cannot
understand. Could I ever entrust my poor helpless
child to a perfect stranger, and with the greatest indifference too ? Not for the world !

These black nurses, however, have *one* very bad
habit: they are acquainted with all sorts of dreadful
and absurd stories, which they tell the little children of

three to five years to amuse and to keep them quiet.
The lion (simba), the leopard (tschni), the elephant
(tembo), and numberless witches * (watchawi) of course
play a prominent part in these fairy tales, some of
which are really blood-curdling. It is perfectly impossible to break them of this noxious habit.

~ Rearing children is unquestionably much easier in
the South than in Northern countries : colds, coughs,
and the other numerous assailants of European
children are unknown there ; yet although the climate
is very hot, and indoor life is replete with enticing
comforts, the children are not given to sluggishness
and indolence ; they are allowed to roam in full liberty,
and from the mode of their garments their limbs are
nowise fettered. Gymnastics are unknown, but boys
from ten to twelve go in greatly for high jumping,
some of their flying leaps taking them over two horses.

Swimming in the sea is practised as eagerly, and
the boys teach themselves. At an early age they learn
to shoot, and very passionately too, sham fights being
very favourite pastimes. In spite of boys always
going about armed to the teeth, provided with as much
ammunition as grown-up men, one hardly ever hears
of an accident arising from want of precaution.

I have already mentioned that the young princes
live in their fathers' houses up to a certain age, after
which a residence of their own is assigned to each, in
which they generally keep house with their mother if
she be living. They have a certain monthly allowance,
fully sufficient to supply all their wants. In the event
of marriage or an increase to the family, or even after

* A Suahely word, the singular of which is mtschawi.

a time of irreproachable conduct, an extra allowance may be looked for, but in no other case. However, on the arrival of our father's ships once a year with new goods, all our brothers and sisters living by themselves appeared with the whole of their family to claim their individual share, whether they required it or not. If any of them had the misfortune of exceeding their allowance they found it no easy matter to extricate themselves, as my father never countenanced the fact, and none would transgress more than once if he could help it.

In case of war, which was unfortunately rather frequent in Omân, all the princes, the half-grown included, were expected to join and take their part in the fight like the common soldier.

They were subjected to a very strict discipline, but this only caused the sons to look up to their father with greater respect and veneration. I often watched, as a child, how my elder brothers would hurry to the door, in advance of the slaves, to put the sandals my father had left there in readiness for him.

There is but little to say about the education of a princess: the first years of her life resembles that of her brothers, with the exception that the latter were allowed much more liberty out of the house after completing their seventh year. The only thing which deserves mention is, that at the birth of a princess—to suit the hairdress in our country—a broad comb, generally of silver, is placed under the back of the newborn child's head, to give it a flat shape. When a princess is married to one of her numerous cousins, either in Omân or in Zanzibar,

she quits her paternal home, of course, in exchange
for that of her husband. The former, however, remains open to her at all times, as the sole and real
place of shelter against any vicissitudes of life,
though she may go and live with a brother if she
prefers it.   Each sister has her favourite brother,
and *vice versâ ;* they maintain a fast friendship in
good and in bad times, and advise and help each
other to their utmost.   Though this might prove
a source of deep joy in one way, it often gave rise
to bitter jealousies which the stoutest heart had
difficulty in overcoming—neither were the opportunities very rare in so large a family as ours.

It often happened, too, that a sister would intercede
with our father in mitigation of some foolish deed of a
favourite brother, and succeed entirely on the strength
of his evident preference for his daughters, and his
usual inability to refuse any of their requests.   He
was particularly kind and courteous to his elder
daughters, walking towards them and seating them
by his side on a sofa, while the elder sons and the
little people stood by respectfully.

CHAPTER IX.

On the whole the school (mdarse) is considered by Eastern people, and likewise by us, as of little moment and consequence. School in Europe is the centre of life in Church and State, alike to prince and to citizen; from its efficiency depends essentially the cultivation of mind and knowledge as well as most future prospects. In the East the "mdarse" is altogether a matter of secondary consideration, and for a good many people it does not exist at all. Before discussing this point further I wish to say something about what we called "school" at our house.

Between the age of six or seven all children—boys and girls—had to enter the mdarse; the latter were only required to learn to read, the former both to write and read. At Bet il Mtoni and at Bet il Sahel there was only one lady teacher, respectively, specially imported by our father from Omán. I need not say that unforeseen holidays, brought about by our teacher's occasional sickness, did not meet with proper regret on our part.

We had no separate schoolroom; our lessons were

said in an open gallery, to which pigeons and parrots, peacocks and ricebirds, found free ingress. We also had an uninterrupted view of the courtyard and its busy life there. All the furniture of the schoolroom consisted of a single large mat. Our school property was equally simple—all we required was a Kurân on a stand (marfâ), a small inkstand containing homemade ink and the well-bleached shoulder-blade of a camel for a slate, on which the writing with ink is easy, without the irritating, jarring noise produced on the slate. Slaves have to see to the cleaning of these blades.

The first thing we learned was the very complicated Arab A B C, after which, for want of any other spelling-book, reading was taught from the Kurân, and the boys copied from it. Those who could read pretty fluently read in a chorus, and rather loudly too. But this was the extent of our schooling, for we never got any explanation of *what* we were reading about. Hence the fact that perhaps one only amongst a thousand really understands and is able to explain the sense and the precepts of the Mahometan holy book, though there may be eighty in every hundred who have learned at least half of it by heart. To meditate or to speculate upon its contents is considered irreligious and condemnatory; people are simply to believe what they are taught, and this maxim is rigorously carried out.

After a repast of fruit we assembled at seven o'clock in the morning on our mat, and there awaited the arrival of our teacher, whiling away the time with wrestling, boxing, jumping, and with perilous

6

attempts at climbing the railings, &c. A watch was set at a corner of the gallery to inform us, by a cough, of the teacher's approach, upon which we would promptly seat ourselves, looking extremely demure, only to rebound, like so many indiarubber balls, respectfully to shake hands with the dreaded one and to wish her good morning. She always carried the much detested bamboo cane in one hand, and a large brass inkstand in the other. Until she had taken her seat we had to stand up before her in file, and were finally allowed to sit down ourselves cross-legged around her on the matting.

She now began to recite the first Sura of the Kurân, which may be called the Mahometan Lord's Prayer, echoed in chorus by us and concluded with Amîn (not Amen). Then we repeated what we had learned the day before, and took a new piece in reading and writing. Lessons lasted till nine o'clock precisely, and were resumed after breakfast up to second prayers at noon.

Each of us was allowed to bring some slaves to school to join in our lessons; they sat at some distance behind us, while we grouped ourselves as we pleased. There were neither fixed places nor a division into forms. Reports which are looked forward to with such feverish anxiety in European schools were unknown to us. Our respective mothers and our fathers received only a verbal report if any of us made very good progress, and in the reverse case, or if very good or bad conduct called for comment. Our teacher had received special orders to punish us severely whenever she deemed it necessary, and we gave her often enough occasion to make use of her cane.

Besides reading and writing, we were taught a little arithmetic, that is, ciphering in writing up to 100, and up to 1000 mentally; everything beyond that was thought to be of evil. No pains were taken with either grammar or orthography; the very complicated " Ilnahu " can only be acquired by much reading in after years. Of such sciences as history, geography, mathematics, physics, and others I never heard—I only was made acquainted with these branches of science when I came to Europe. I am not sure, however, that I am so much better off now for the smattering I have acquired of these things at great pains, than the people on the other side. This only I know, that my increased knowledge has not saved me from being repeatedly deceived and swindled. Oh, ye happy ones at home who are spared the inevitable sorrows which lie beneath the dazzling gauze of civilization !

The style of our tuition did not admit of home tasks of course, which take up so many hours in this country.

The teacher, feared as she may be, is treated with great respect by everybody, and by her pupils especially is treated with veneration in after life.

One thing, however, schoolchildren in the East and in Europe have in common—the natural instinct of gaining the teacher's favour by means of little bribes. When my children used to ask me for a few pence to buy a nosegay or a flower-pot for Miss So-and-so, I was always reminded of my own schooldays. This trait belongs, I believe, to every race and nation. Before we ever dreamt of the existence of foreign countries or of their schools and school-children, my brothers and sisters and myself tried to ingratiate ourselves with our teacher by taking her all sorts of things, sweets in preference; every day she received a goodly portion of the French goodies our father gave us. I know not whether the other effect of this kind of present was a premeditated one, but certain it is that a repeated result was a violent toothache—and a holiday for us.

There was no fixed term for attending school. What was considered necessary to know had to be learned in any case; but it depended entirely upon the capacity of each individual if this knowledge was acquired in one year, in two, or more.

Fancy work was not taught at school, it was from our mothers that we acquired the art of sewing, embroidery, and lace-making, at which most of them were very proficient, though we were not expected to attain any particular standard. Some of my sisters, for instance, who had acquired great skill in such work, could easily have made a living by it, had they ever needed; others, again, never got beyond sewing on a button.

There exist some schools, but only for children of poor parents. Every one who is at all able to afford it, keeps a private tutor or a governess. Sometimes the secretary of the master of the house undertook to give lessons to the girls—however, only as long as they were quite young.

This brief mention is all I have to say of our

schools. It is but natural that I should sometimes be tempted to draw comparisons between them and European ones, between the over-cultured hero and the ignorance of the children there. I myself was born, bred, and educated there, and my judgment, which is based upon my experience both in Arabia and Europe, and which I feel to be quite free from any prejudice whatever, may perhaps be of interest.

In general I am of opinion that Europeans exact just *that* too much from a school, as the Arabs demand too little. As yet no people has discovered the right middle course, nor will it ever be found; contrasts like these will exist as long as the world lasts.

There is hardly any science which the children are *not* taught here, and to such an extent that the childish understanding cannot possibly retain all. With the beginning of school life parents see hardly anything of their children. The latter are so much overtasked, even after their regular school-hours, that home life and influence are almost at an end. There is a continued race and chase all day from task to task, and how much of these studies will be of lasting value to them? How much of it is crammed, only to be forgotten again as quickly! To my idea, a few extra hours spent in their home would leave a healthier impression on their minds and memories by and by.

For five or more hours daily the poor children are cooped up in a schoolroom which is insufferably hot and stifling. In one school, with more than two hundred children, I remarked that there were only four tumblers. Can any one be surprised under such circumstances if a child sickens? However much care and pains may be taken for its welfare at home, they are rendered quite useless by the effect of the foul school air. You need only look at some of these children to make your heart ache ! Was not our large, lofty gallery a much fitter place ? What is the use of all accomplishments if they are acquired by ruining health ?

Of that feeling of respect which was inculcated into us in early youth for our parents, teachers, and tutors, and old age in general, there is not much to be perceived here. The lessons in religion also seem to me to miss their aim ; the children are overburdened with learning numberless dates of ecclesiastical history, while their hearts remain a barren soil.

The word of God and His holy commandments should be taught more, and less time be bestowed on subtle inquiries into indifferent matter. It will surely always remain a vain longing of the short-sighted human mind to fathom the innermost secrets of nature and creation. I once read a beautiful and impressive simile. Man's short life was there compared with that of a moth, which first saw the light of day within the walls of a large cathedral ; the moth's short span of life expired long long before it could realize one hundredth part of all the beauty and mystery surrounding it—such is the life of man amid the wonders of the universe. Let wise men continue their investigations and their broodings ; but let them cease cramming children's minds with dry unprofitable stuff that the brain cannot digest and the soul sickens with and dies.

I was shocked, in looking over some statistics on

lunacy, to find that the majority of these deplorable cases were returned from former students of high schools and universities. A good many of these surely were the victims of overpressure. I could not help thinking of my native home, where lunatic asylums are not needed, where I never saw but two maniacs, and never heard of any others—and of these two, one was a negress, the other a native of Hindustan.

As I previously said, I have no desire to criticise European culture, nor am I able to do so; I only wished to speak of my own observations, which convinced me that there are many sad failures in the European educational system. But at all events, I shall be pardoned if I question the right which Europeans take upon themselves in deploring the fate of a people as yet "unenlightened," and their justification in forcibly imparting their civilization on the same. I am firmly convinced, Arab born and bred as I am, that all efforts on the part of Europeans to do away, at a sweep, with the incarnate ignorance of Mahometans, and to fly the flag of science and learning, with even the smallest amount of precipitation, will meet with barren effect.

Other nations, like the Japanese for instance, whose creed and precepts are less binding than the Mahometan, probably offer a more grateful soil—the more so as they are naturally more desirous of stepping into the footprints of Europeans.

People frequently deride the Turkish half-culture, and yet the Turks have striven much harder to become civilized than is at all good for them. They have only weakened themselves without achieving the desired end, because foreign culture is contrary and opposed to their fundamental views. Civilization cannot be obtruded by force, and it will only be just to concede to every nation the right of adhering without hindrance to their views and institutions, which have in the course of centuries been founded under the influence of ripened experience and practical worldly wisdom. Above all, the pious Arab would be deeply shocked if his civilization were to begin with lessons on natural science, of which, according to the European code of education, people are supposed to know something. What would be his bewilderment if any one were to talk to him of the laws of nature, who sees in all the universe, down to its most infinitesimal details, but one source of creation—the all-guiding and all-directing hand of God!

CHAPTER X.

In Europe the father of a family generally makes his wife and his unmarried daughters a certain monthly or quarterly allowance for their dresses. This, however, is not the case with us. Zanzibar has no manufacture of any kind, therefore all the clothing and materials required for the entire population have to be imported from foreign lands.

My father carried on an extensive barter trade for the immense requirements of his various households. Several of his large sailing ships were annually despatched laden with produce (principally cloves) to England, Marseilles, Persia, to the East Indies and to China, and the net proceeds of these cargoes was reinvested by our agents in these countries in such goods as they had instructions to purchase. The master of each vessel took an endless list of the goods to be brought back, most of them being articles of dress and fashion.

The day for the yearly distribution of these goods depended, of course, upon the return of the ships. It is but natural that this event was impatiently looked forward to ; it signified to us the beginning of a new season of fashion, and the style and quality of our finery for a whole year depended upon the contents of the ships lying in our ports.

To us children this time also had an especial charm : it brought all our beautiful toys from Europe. I remember my frantic joy on one of these occasions at being presented with a beautifully dressed doll—my first one—a doll that cried and had teeth !

Soon after the vessels had arrived in port, a day was fixed on which the distribution of the cargo was to take place to old and young, high and low, in the house. Our younger brothers generally tried to find out beforehand from the captains what toys they had brought back. There were always twenty to thirty cases, containing nothing but horses, carriages, dolls, whips, fishes, and ducks, with magnets, musical boxes of all sizes, concertinas, flutes, trumpets, guns, and what not ! Woe to the captain whose goods did not give satisfaction, for he was responsible for all he brought back, having full power and positive orders to buy only the best of everything, wherever he could get it, without regard to price.

The distribution took place at Bet il Mtoni and at Bet il Sahel, and it always took three to four days before each of the hundreds of recipients had received his share. The eunuchs had to do the unpacking, and my elder brothers and sisters were entrusted with the general apportioning. I regret to say, however, that this time never went by without a good deal of heart-burning and real or imaginary grievances.

The materials for clothing, costly and plain, were

delivered to each member of the family, after which a lively exchange was carried on in the house for the next fortnight—resulting in a general satisfaction all round. There were musk, ambergris, numerous Oriental oils, ottar of roses and rosewater, saffron (which, mixed with other ingredients, is used for dressing the hair), silks of all colours, gold and silver thread for fancy work, gilt and silver buttons—in short, every article an Arab lady could desire—besides which, to refund the outlay for various trifles, a certain sum of money (in Maria Theresia dollars) was paid over to each, varying according to rank and age.

Sometimes it happened that an extravagantly fashionable lady spent more in the course of a year than she could well afford—in which case she would have to appeal to father or husband for help. Such requests were always kept very secret, for the lords of Arabian households are as averse to recklessness as their Northern brethren, and although the petitioner's request was generally granted, it was also accompanied with a wholesome reprimand.

Of course there were also people of economical propensities among the members of our household, and these were of opinion that keeping slaves for mere show—a custom with people of rank and wealth—is a great piece of extravagance. They, therefore, had their young women-slaves instructed in different branches of trade, such as dressmaking, embroidering, and lace-making, while the boys were employed in saddlery, carpentering, and so on. The owners of such slaves managed thus to greatly reduce their expenditure, whilst those who were less provident gave

their work out to be done, and paid heavily in proportion.   The slaves who had been brought up to some
kind of trade were more highly valued than those who
had not had this advantage, and were better able to
make a living when freed.   In Omân, where but few
slaves are kept, it is a standing rule to have them
taught a trade that will be of use to their masters as
well as to themselves.   For this reason, slaves are
frequently sent from Zanzibar to Omân for a practical
education.   A negro or a negress of this class always
obtained a higher price.

If any visitors happened to be staying with us at
the time of distribution, they always received, by my
father's orders, a share of the presents, and even of
money—the residue of the cargoes being put aside in
store for our numerous relatives that came to see us
from Omân in the course of the year.

Our yearly outfit was of course adapted to, and very
much simplified by, our close proximity to the equator,
where we only know the four seasons by name.   It
would have been rather a difficult matter to provide
garments for autumn, winter, and spring wear all at the
same time.   The only winter we have is the rainy
season for some six or eight weeks, with a temperature
as low as 70° F.   During this more wet than cold
season, velvets and stouter materials are worn.

All clothing was hand-made, as sewing-machines
were unknown in my time.   All dresses rejoice in a
uniformly simple cut, alike for men and women,
differing only in materials and trimmings.   The
abomination of tight-lacing, or lacing of any kind, has
not yet found its way into the elegant world of the

East—neither that fickle goddess, at whose shrine there is so much blind and reckless worship in these enlightened lands of Europe.

Of whatever rank or station an Arab woman may be, her dress consists only of a shirt reaching down to the ankles, trousers (*not* drawers), and a kerchief for the head. The material varies, of course. Rich people have gold brocades of many patterns, velvets and silks richly trimmed. During the hot season plain light calicoes or muslins are worn. Shirt and trousers are never of the same pattern. The shirt must not be too long, that it may not hide the rich embroidery of the trousers or the two anklets; a number of little golden bells are suspended from one of these, which make a pretty tinkling sound at every step. Two long tasselled ribbons hang loosely over the back or on both sides of the head, from the band that is worn round the forehead. The silk kerchief reaches down to the ankles.

In her walks an Arab lady puts on the "schele," which is shawl, waterproof, and cloak, all in one. The schele is a large shawl or mantilla of black silk, more or less richly trimmed with gold or silver borders, according to the wealth and taste of its owner. This is the only wrapper an Arab lady uses until it is completely worn out, its fashion never changing; even the greatest and richest ladies do not possess more than one schele at a time.

That an Oriental lady, in the idle indolence of her exotic home, and in the uncultured condition of her mind, should give her finery a good deal of thought, does not seem so very unpardonable. But what struck me, years ago, before I became accustomed to the fact, was that the ladies I came into contact with in my new European home, and who had, I knew, from their childhood up, received the most thorough and comprehensive mental training—that these ladies, I say, should never find any other topic of conversation but the one all-important, all-engrossing— dress.

During the rainy season the great Arab ladies wear indoors the "djocha," a kind of cloak of cloth trimmed with gold and silver embroidery. It is worn open in front, only held together over the breast with gold lacing. The elder ladies prefer a Persian shawl to the djocha. This is the only covering to protect us against the comparative coolness of winter or rainy season.

I may mention that we had, in cases of emergency, a kind of heating apparatus. It consisted of a brass bowl, some 8 inches deep by 12 inches wide, on a three-legged stand, which was filled with burning charcoal, and placed in the centre of the room, the charcoal fire producing a very pleasant and mild heat. This "mankah" served at the same time to roast the green, freshly-gathered cobs of Indian corn. Doors and windows were, however, always left open, even when we had such a fire in the room.

CHAPTER XI.

A PLANTATION.

My father owned forty-five plantations, scattered all over the island. Fifty to sixty slaves were employed as labourers on most of these estates, and as many as five hundred on the larger ones, with an Arab overseer to each estate. Two only of the plantations had real palaces, six to eight had villas, and the remainder merely had houses for the officials, and farm-buildings. For a stay of any length we could only visit one of the first.

During my father's lifetime we could but seldom leave the town, and then for a short time only, as he was always too busily engaged, and preferred staying at home. But as we all very much enjoyed such visits to a plantation, we generally teased him till he granted us permission to go.

These excursions always required great preparations, since it was no easy matter to provide properly for so many people on a plantation some eight miles distant, to which all the provisions had to be conveyed upon the heads of negro slaves. Several hundred of these came some days prior to our departure to carry off all that was requisite. To the great annoyance of our cooks and chief eunuchs, into whose management it was given, so much was destroyed and lost on the road, that double the quantity actually required had to be sent out. The overseers of the plantations we visited always came off very well on these occasions, for they were allowed to keep for their own use what we left behind.

The night before the start most of us were too excited to retire to rest, so instead we went and inspected our lovely white asses which were to carry us, their tails having been dyed red with henna.

But those who happened to have no ass of their own had either to stay at home, or to borrow one— my father having no time to trouble himself with such matters.

Matters were, however, greatly simplified when our destination was a plantation on the seashore, for there were plenty of boats to convey us and our provisions.

These excursions offered the welcome opportunity to all the ladies for showing off their finery. How they vied to outdo each other in splendour! Indeed, if one of these " belles " had set her heart upon wearing a particular new garment, which did not come home in time, she would bemoan her disappointment by staying behind.

Our start was generally fixed for half-past five in the morning, immediately after the first prayer. For hours there has been noise and confusion in the courtyard below—half-a-dozen voices calling down the stairs, and as many shouting back; slaves tumbling over each other, and vociferating loudly—sometimes even cutting their arguments short by kicks and cuffs. And mingled with all these various sounds you heard the bray of the asses, intended, no doubt, to remind you that they have been saddled for the last hour.

Everything is ready at last, and the animals are led into the road, and mounted. The slender and weak eunuchs are likewise on horseback; the black slaves, however, are on foot. During the very pleasant ride which now begins, many harmless tricks are played and enjoyed to while away the hour.

The whole cavalcade looks very picturesque: the white donkeys with their rich trappings of gold and silver plates, jingling at every step, their high saddles and splendid saddle-cloths, as well as our sturdy runners in their clean white robes and their glittering muskets. As the sun gets hotter, one of these slaves runs by the side of each lady's animal with a large parasol to protect the rider from the glare. Some of the slaves trot along with one of the smaller children, while the bigger ones, who cannot yet ride by themselves, are placed on the saddle with a eunuch.

We passed through the town at dawn, and kept close together as long as we were within the city walls; but as soon as we had emerged into the open country, all restraint was over, and we hurried along as best we could. However much the eunuchs might try to keep the procession together by calling out in their thin voices to the riders of very fiery animals, we generally arrived at the end of our journey in separate small detachments.

The first and oldest of our slaves and the family of the overseer, if he was married, were in attendance to

7

receive us. But the overseer himself, conformably
with Eastern etiquette, did not show himself during
our whole stay.

Fruits of all kinds were handed round immediately
after our arrival, and we sat down to breakfast at
once in the same order of rank as at home. After
breakfast we separated to amuse ourselves as we
might, quite unrestrainedly, for here we could wander
wherever we pleased, since no strangers were likely to
surprise us in the grounds. Only at meals and at
prayers the whole company met again.

Invitations from the adjoining estates soon followed,
and the ladies from the neighbourhood sent word to
announce their visits. Invitations and calls were
always intended for all the family; while our guests
were received and entertained only by our elder brothers
and sisters, every member of the family was at liberty
to accept an invitation.

As it was impossible to provide the necessary
bedding for so many people, everybody lay down to
sleep on horse and saddle-cloths, their arm for a
pillow.

The quantities of eatables consumed on these excursions were really astounding. I have already said
that these were conveyed by many hundred slaves for
several days; besides all this, our kind neighbours
insisted upon replenishing our store daily, in proof of
their friendly feeling. I need not say that many
cases of sickness occurred in consequence of this
bountiful feasting.

Dear old Ledda, the head of the customs, had
always shown, though a Banjan, rare loyalty and

great personal attachment to our family, and nothing pleased the grey-haired star-worshipper more than to think of some new amusement for us children. He never forgot to send us pretty and curious presents, ordered from his Indian home, which invariably included, besides sweetmeats, several baskets of fire-works (fetâk). He always sent an extra relay of these latter when we made an excursion into the country, so that our evenings were made very pleasant, watching the effect of the beautiful Indian pyrotechnical con-structions. But, failing those, we spent our evenings in the gardens, looking on at the games and dancing of the negroes. The negro dances are not nearly as ugly and uncouth as some African travellers describe them. When I first saw Europeans dance I did not admire the art either, for the continual turning round of the dancers made me feel giddy only to look. We generally took them with us to the plantations for our evening's entertainment. Their performances are very clever, and they are well paid for them. They may not receive the fabulous sums that are lavished on great dancers in Europe, still they are sufficiently well paid to enable them to return to their Indian homes in gladness, notwithstanding their extravagant habits. They are, however, held in little esteem in our country.

Such evenings in the East are truly romantic. Fancy a numerous company of all complexions, elegantly dressed—though somewhat fantastically and gaudily—standing, sitting, and squatting in all direc-tions, laughing and making harmless fun with all the unconventional ease of Southerners — the whole framed in with the foliage of the most magnificent trees, and bathed in the silvery light of an intensive tropical moon! Description fails me to do justice to a scene which, however, once beheld, can never be forgotten.

But the hour came at last, though not before the greater part of the night was spent, when we felt it was time to break the charm and retire to our rest.

On these excursions we often took a funny little French girl and her two wild brothers, fourteen and fifteen years old, the children of the French Consular doctor. They all three talked Suahely very well, and sang most amusing songs. The first time Claire came with us, she caused a general burst of laughter at bed-time, when she appeared in her white European nightgown. We had never heard of such a thing before, for everybody in the East lies down to sleep in the dress worn during the day—at least, in washing dresses, not in a costume made of velvet or gold brocade.

During a protracted stay, our father used to pay us flying visits of a few hours at a time, for he always returned to town in the evening. On such occasions mounted couriers kept up an uninterrupted communication between the town and our plantation.

We rarely undertook these excursions at harvest-time, so as not to interrupt the slaves in their labour. Cloves have a peculiarity of ripening quite suddenly, so that it requires the greatest exertions to gather in the crops at the right moment. Rice, too, makes a quick harvest, while more time can be taken over gathering in the sugar-cane, cocoanuts, sweet potatoes,

and other produce. Cattle is never used for farming
purposes, and scarcely any agricultural implements,
not even the most simple plough, is known. All the
work is performed by hand; the ground is dug with
spades, and the rice cut in sheaves with a common
little straight knife. The master or the mistress of
the estate frequently joins in the work during the clove
harvest, to stimulate their negro slaves, whose inborn
idleness requires a great deal of shaking up; but since
this cannot be done individually, they have a task set
them, proportionate with their age and strength.
Anything in excess of this task is rewarded, and the
shortcomings are punished. The only really busy time
of the year, then, is the harvest. The ground in that
gracious clime almost takes care of itself. No manure
is ever used, except the straw that is sometimes
burnt.

The length of our stay was determined by my
father, and he fixed the day on which, between half-
past six and half-past seven o'clock, p.m., we had to
be back in town. The family of the overseer received
suitable gifts on our departure, which my father himself selected, and we were always accompanied some
distance by our lady friends from the neighbouring
estates. An escort of about one hundred and fifty
soldiers were sent to meet and conduct us into the
city. In spite of their heavy accoutrements (every
man carried musket, shield, lance, sword, and dagger)
they always managed to keep pace with our beasts.

We were not allowed to neglect our evening prayers,
even during the journey. The company halted somewhere near the town, generally at Ngambo, or at

Muasimodja, and prayers were said in the open air on mats which everybody carried for the purpose. Supposing a mat was lost or left behind, the worshipper would kneel on the giant leaf of a moz tree (plantain), as none other but a vegetable substance may be used.

When it was dark a number of very large lanterns were lighted; then we once more resumed our saddles and entered through the gates like a procession from fairyland.

CHAPTER XII

MY FATHER'S VOYAGE.

I WAS about nine years old when my father determined to visit his old empire of Omân, on a tour of inspection, as was his wont in the course of every three to four years, my eldest brother, Tuêni (incorrectly called Suêni at times) acting as regent and head of the family at Mesket.

There was besides an urgent reason this time for my father's voyage. The Persians had made several incursions in the neighbourhood of Bender Abbas, which, though of little account in themselves, might easily have caused complications of a more serious nature. This small territory in Persia, rather important from the fact of its commanding the entrance to the Persian Gulf, had not only given infinite trouble, but proved a great expense to my father ever since his occupation of it. We were deprived of it again by the Persians at a later date, which was hardly a matter for regret; there was no peace for us till they had succeeded, neither could we blame their efforts.

We owned no steamers at the time I speak of, and the departure of our sailing-ships was retarded by the absence of fair wind. It took at least eight or ten weeks before all preparations were completed and all the provisions put on board ; the baking of the captain biscuits alone took up much time, as about one thousand persons had to be provided for ten weeks. Salt beef we did not know, and preserves were of no use, as they were " háram " (*i.e.*, unclean, according to our dietary laws) ; it was therefore necessary to ship an immense quantity of live stock, and a dozen milk cows ; it is impossible to state what were the quantities of fruit supplied by our forty-five plantations for the voyage, but they amply account for the many cases of dysentery which occurred.

All sons had permission to join in an expedition of this kind ; but only few of the daughters, on account of the inconveniences caused by women in travelling ; and only a couple of the most favoured Sarari.

Few of us cared much about going to Omân, as the proud Omân ladies rather regarded Zanzibar women as uncivilized creatures. Even our brothers and sisters there were not free from this conceit, and all the members of our family born in Omân thought themselves much better and of higher rank than any of their African relations. In their opinion we were somewhat like negroes, as we had been brought up amongst these ; and our speaking any other language but Arabic was the greatest proof of barbarity in their eyes.

A great number of my brothers and sisters and countless relations lived in Omân, most of the latter in reduced circumstances, and supported by my father's bounty. All these expected presents on his

arrival, and, in consequence, his luggage was somewhat formidable.

It was also a welcome opportunity for sending
messages to friends in distant Asia, with whom none
but the feeblest correspondence had been kept up.
The general ignorance in writing was a great hindrance to this, and it can hardly be conceived to what
straits most people were put to meet this difficulty.
They had to get their letters written by strangers, and
strangers again were employed to read them. The
services of my brothers and of all the male slaves
conversant with the art where at such times in great
demand ; but if, from pressure of work or from un-
willingness, not an unfrequent case, these services
could not be secured, then the compositions were entrusted into the hands of utter strangers. Needless
to say that such epistles must have greatly fallen short
of what would be considered private and confidential
in this country.

The following may, for instance, prove a case in
point. A fine lady calls up her body-servant and says,
" Feruz, go to such or such a Kadi, and ask him to
write a beautiful letter to my friend in Omán for me ;
pay him whatever he asks for it." Then Feruz is told
quite a number of things which the Kadi is to put into
the letter. The Kadi, however, may be greatly pressed
for time, as he has a dozen such letters or more on
hand, therefore it can hardly be a matter of surprise
that he jumbles up the different orders. And Feruz
returns in triumph to his mistress : " Here are your
letters, Bibi ! " The lady, however, being of a cautious
turn of mind, goes to some literate person, and desires

to know what the letter contains. But picture to yourself her amazement and indignation when she hears that the letter, which was intended to convey her congratulations upon some joyful event, is couched in terms of the deepest condolence. Or in another instance the case may have been exactly reversed. Consequently nearly every letter has to be written over several times and by different people, until it contains at last something of the desired meaning.

Everything was ready at last. The ship *Kitorie*, *i.e.*, Victoria (in honour of Her Majesty Queen Victoria), was to convey my father and his family; and two or three other vessels took on board his retinue, the servants, and the luggage. This was but a small fleet to carry such a crowd of passengers. However, Eastern travellers require very little room and no cabin of their own; everybody looks out for a place on deck at night where he can lie down and go to sleep on his mat.

The retinue and the slaves embarked first; next followed the women about five o'clock in the morning; and, lastly, my father with his sons at noon. My brothers Châlid and Madjid, with some of the younger ones, accompanied the travellers on board, and remained there until the ships weighed anchor, the *Kitorie* firing a last parting salute of twenty-one guns to the country and to the family collected on the shore.

The house settled down now to great quiet, though it was as crowded as before. Every one felt the absence of the head of the family, and we led henceforth a somewhat retired life. My brother Châlid, as the eldest of the remaining sons, now reigned in Zanzibar in my father's place ; several times a week he came to see us to assure himself of our welfare, and he went as often to Bet il Mtoni to look after its inmates there, but especially to receive any orders our exalted step-mother might wish to give.

As head of the family, Châlid was very strict, and we often had reason to complain of his harsh measures. It may suffice to mention two instances here. A fire broke out at Bet il Sahel once, which was fortunately soon extinguished. When it began we all rushed to the gates in our terror, but found them locked and guarded by soldiers, who had been ordered there by Châlid, to prevent our being recklessly exposed to public view in the broad daylight.

Another time he rudely turned a distant relation of ours, who possessed great influence in Zanzibar, out of the mosque because he had dared to propose for one of my sisters in that building, nor was the poor suitor permitted to show himself for months after, either in the daily assembly or in the mosque to which Châlid went to prayers. It however came to pass that the rejected suitor married another sister of ours some years later, after Châlid's and my father's decease.

The latter had appointed my sister Chole to act as lady superintendent during his absence both in Bet il Sahel and Bet il Mtoni, to the great annoyance of many. It may well be conceived that this " bright star " of our house felt anything but comfortable in her new position, reaping nothing but ingratitude and jealousy from her office, since, notwithstanding her sweetness of temper, she found it impossible to please

everybody; few only were reasonable enough to consider that hers was but a limited power.   It was no
fault of hers that she was so much preferred by my
father; unfortunately, however, envy was too strong—
it positively blinded all reason in her opponents.

In the meantime our vessels had sailed several
times between Omân and Zanzibar, and brought news
and presents from our father, which always created
much joy and pleasure in our midst.

Unfortunately, our brother Châlid was shortly
after called away by our Lord.   Madjid, the son next
in age, now succeeded in the regency, and contrived
to gain the goodwill of all by his kind and gentle
manners.

A vessel arrived at last one day from Mesket with
the joyful news that our father was about to leave
Omân for Zanzibar.   It soon spread all over the
country, and caused great satisfaction everywhere, as
he had now been absent three years, and had been
missed very much.   Those even who were not personally attached to him looked forward to his return
with pleasure on account of the many presents he was
expected to bring back with him from Omân for young
and old, and preparations for his reception were made
everywhere, just as if we were about to celebrate one
of our great holy days.

However, the time which was generally allowed for
the voyage from Omân to Zanzibar passed away, and
no ships arrived, which caused great uneasiness to us
and to the whole country.   The Arabs are fond of
consulting so-called seers in the future, and nowhere
this habit prevails so much as in Zanzibar.   I verily

believe no gipsies in Europe can in any way equal the
craftiness and mendacity of their Suahelian brethren;
but, then, where else would one find such unbounded
and foolish credulity to encourage their wiles.

No means were left untried which possibly might
help to throw a light on the whereabouts of the three
overdue ships; some of the oracles then were fetched
many miles off from the most remote nooks in the
country, most of them belonging to the tribe of the
Wachadimu—if old, they were brought in triumph
riding on donkeys.

The most remarkable of all these diviners was supposed to be a woman, of whom the story went that
she, or rather her unborn child, could look into the
future. Such a monster was quite beyond anything
that had ever been heard of before, and had, therefore, to be procured at whatever cost it might be. One
afternoon (I have never forgotten the scene) this
prophetess, appalling and unwieldy in size, arrived.
Her unborn child was said to be omniscient—it could
tell what things were on the highest mountain tops as
well as in the nethermost depths of the sea. Now it
was to tell us how our father was, and why his return
was so much delayed. In quite an audible, squeaking
voice the monster reported its observations, while the
company stood around spellbound. It pretended to
see several three-mast vessels far away on the high
seas steering for Zanzibar; then it proposed getting
on one of the mast-tops of my father's ship to see
what was going on on board. After a while it reported with full details what every one there was
doing. Finally it ordered sacrifices to be brought to

the spirits of the sea to secure their future favour with which to shield the travellers from possible evil. As a matter of course the commands of this mysterious voice were obeyed to the letter, and the legion of professional beggars with which our beautiful island is infested could for several days indulge to their hearts' content in plenteousness of meat, fowls, and rice, which were distributed amongst them, together with clothing and money, as acts of propitiation.

I was not a little ashamed at a later time to perceive that we had simply been duped by a ventriloquist. At that time, however, we all firmly believed in the wonderful child that could reveal the invisible and read the secrets of the future as from a book. Even now it is not quite clear to me whether the woman was really a conscious imposter or a dupe herself. No one had ever heard of a ventriloquist in our country, so that, as no denunciation was forthcoming in the shape of a satisfactory explanation, we went on implicitly believing.

In our parts people are fond of everything supernatural; the more mysterious and incomprehensible it appears the more faith it receives. Everybody believes in spirits, good and evil. At the decease of any one the chamber of death is for days fumigated with incense, and as it is a general belief that the soul of the departed has a longing to return to and especially prefers to stay in its former abode, no person cares to enter the same in the daytime, and flies from it at night.

Superstition rules supreme. In cases of sickness, of betrothal, of pregnancy, on all possible occasions, the help of female prophets is called in—they are required to know and to tell if the disease can be cured, and how long it is to last, if the betrothal may be considered a happy one, whether the expected child will be a boy or a girl, and so on. If, as on frequent occasions, the very contrary happens, the prophetess screens herself behind numerous subterfuges and excuses. She declares herself to have been under the effects of an evil star that day, and trusts to be more successful next time; and this explanation is made to do—and does do. Certain it is they prosper and grow very rich.

CHAPTER XIII.

DEATH-NEWS.

DAY after day and week after week passed away without my father's return; the only pastime we had was
to listen to prophecies of the kind I have just described, and which, if they did no other good, at least
shortened our suspense. One afternoon at last, while
most of us were engaged at prayers, the gladdening
news spread that a fisherman had seen several ships
bearing our flag on the high sea, but that he had not
dared to approach them on account of the stormy
weather. That could be no one but our father!
All hurried away to dress in their best, which had
been kept in readiness for weeks. We always expressed
our pleasure at the return of a dear relation from a
voyage or from a victorious campaign in this way,
while we showed our regret at parting by putting
on our plainest and most simple garments.

While the fisherman was still repeating over and
over again that he had reported the truth, a mounted
courier had been despatched to our high step-mother
at Bet il Mtoni to inform her of the news. Cattle
were slaughtered, the cooks had plenty of work in the
kitchen, and the rooms were freshly perfumed. By

the fisherman's report the vessels might be expected to arrive within two to three hours.

Madjid and his retinue hastened to join his father on board. They started in two cutters, battling against a heavy sea, which threatened to swamp them every moment. They hoped to be back again by seven o'clock in the evening with our father; but man proposes and God disposes.

Time went on. Seven o'clock had long since gone by and the vessels were not yet in sight. The whole town was in a fever of excitement—we in the house were of course the most restless of all. Many of us had forebodings of coming evil; still, we never dreamt of what we were to hear so soon. It was feared that Madjid and his companions had perished in the raging storm, and that my father's arrival had been retarded by witnessing this terrible accident. By degrees the belief gained ground that all the ships, both large and small ones, had foundered in the hurricane. Conjectures upon conjectures were made, and nobody, not even the smallest children, cared to go to bed, until the absent ones had arrived safe.

News suddenly spread, which at first no one would credit. The whole palace was said to be surrounded, and to be strongly guarded, by several hundred soldiers. We rushed to the windows in hopes to get at the truth of this report. The night was pitch dark, and we could distinguish nothing but the gleaming matches of the soldiers, a sight which did not help to pacify us; moreover, it was said that the soldiers allowed no one to pass in or out of our doors.

What had occurred? why were we locked in? of

course everybody wanted to know. Who, it was asked, had ordered such a measure? As far as we knew, Madjid had not returned; his house was likewise surrounded by the same gloomy, silent guard watching ours, and we could discern his people anxiously running about the house with lights.

We were the worse off, as all the eunuchs and male slaves slept out of the house, so there were but women and children left. A few of the stoutest hearted gained the front hall of the ground floor, separated only by a door from the large guard-room on the other side of the portal, where they could easily speak to the soldiers through the hall windows. They, however, sternly refused all information, in obedience to their orders; and at last, when the slaves, one and all, lifted up their voices in wailing and lamentation, the soldiers threatened to fire on them.

The whole place was in a dreadful state of confusion; some women cried and abused the invisible evil power that kept us locked up, the most devout ones said their prayers, and the children shrieked and screamed on all sides and could not be pacified. Any one suddenly dropped in on this wild scene might easily have taken it for a lunatic asylum.

Morning dawned at last, and still we had not learned why we were kept prisoners and where Madjid could be. In spite, however, of the general excitement and anxiety, everybody grew orderly at the time fixed for morning prayer. But who can fancy our horror when, after prayers, we observed our fleet at anchor, and mourning flags flying in the breeze! How can I describe our grief when the gates were opened early in the morning and our brothers entered the house without our father!

Then only did we realize that the black flags were flying for him, and that we and the whole country had sustained an irreparable loss. Our dear father was no more! On the passage from Omân to Zanzibar, surrounded only by a few of his children and followers, he had been called away by the Lord, whom he had faithfully and humbly served all his life. The wound in his leg, from which he had so long suffered, had put an end to his existence.

He had not only been the most loving and devoted head of his own family, but also a most conscientious king, and a true father to his people. The general mourning on his death proved how sincerely he had been loved by all. Black flags hung from every house, and even the smallest hut fastened up a piece of black stuff.

We soon learned from Bargasch, who had been on the same ship, and who had been present at our father's death, all particulars of his illness and of his end. To him we were indebted that the dear remains had not been sunk into the sea, as is ordained by the Mahometan law. It was at his urgent request they were placed in a coffin and brought on to Zanzibar. His great love and respect for our dear father had prompted him to take this course, though he thereby seriously trespassed against our customs and our religion. Our law does not permit the use of a coffin either to prince or to beggar—the body is to be placed into the earth, and so return to it once more.

We were also informed now of the reason why we had been so strongly guarded the night before. Madjid and his companions had suffered severely from the storm, and had given themselves up as lost. Their small boats were only built for coasting service, so they stood in great peril of their lives before they reached the ships they were in search for. When they did at last board their father's vessel they found Bargasch gone. As eldest son he had taken the command of the fleet, and when in sight of the land had quietly gone on shore with the body, to have it interred secretly and unobserved in our burial-place.

There is an old tradition that, disputes on the succession to the throne must be settled in presence of the body of the deceased ruler, under the supposition that the veneration paid to the deceased will always assist the legitimate successor. Bargasch wanted to be ruler, but knowing that his elder brother's claims were better supported, he resolved to act before he could be met with opposition. He relied upon carrying out his plan by the force of arms, and above all by the suddenness of his operations.

He had, therefore, on landing, ordered the troops to surround our house and Madjid's. But his plan miscarried, principally because he failed in taking Madjid prisoner. Bargasch afterwards tried to plead in excuse of his conduct that he had been desirous to avoid a revolution.

Madjid, who had carried on the government of Zanzibar since Chálid's death, maintained it now, and proclaimed himself sovereign on the following morning. But doubts still prevailed whether he really were our legitimate chief, or whether our eldest brother, who always resided in Omân, would not endeavour forcibly to obtain the power to which he was entitled by birth.

CHAPTER XIV.

OUR MOURNING.

MANY formalities had to be observed during our time of mourning. In the first place, old and young people had to put aside their costly garments, to replace them by coarse black cotton dresses, and plain black stuff instead of the richly-embroidered veils. Ointments and all kinds of perfumery were strictly avoided, and the woman who tried to remove the smell arising from the dye of her black dress by sprinkling over it some drops of rosewater or ottar of roses was called heartless, or at least frivolous. During the first few days none of the grown-up people slept in their beds, in proof of their love for our departed father, whose body was lying wrapped in the cold ground.

For more than a fortnight our house resembled a large hotel. All persons, prince as well as beggar, were at liberty to enter and eat. It is an old custom to have the favourite dish of the deceased prepared on such occasions for distribution amongst the poor.

The wives of the departed, the legitimate and those purchased as slaves, submit to a special religious mourning for a period of four months. These unfortunate widows have to mourn their husband and master in a dark room all the time, nor are they allowed to step out into the light of day, much less into sunlight. A Terike (widow), who is compelled to leave her darkened apartment and to pass the gallery, throws a thick black cloak over her veil, and covers herself up in such a manner that she can just see her way. In consequence the eyes get quite unused to the light, and it requires always great caution to re-accustom them gradually to daylight after the expiration of the term of mourning.

The widows are formally bound over to their state of widowhood by the Kadi, before whom they appear deeply veiled, and are released again by the same person under like formalities after the lapse of four months. On the day on which the widows receive back their liberty they pass through a great many ceremonies founded on dark superstition. Firstly, they wash themselves all at the same time from head to foot, while the women slaves stand behind their mistresses beating together two sword blades over their heads (poor people use nails as a rattle, for it must be an iron substance). The number of my father's widows being too large to enable the performance of this ceremony within the baths, it had to be done on the beach, and a very curious spectacle it was.

The widow now puts on other clothing, and not till then is she free to marry again. All the male members of our family and our slaves had had free access to the house up till then, but after the lapse of these four months our mothers were only visible to our brothers alone.

During the first year of our mourning some of us regularly visited our father's tomb every Thursday, on the eve of the Mahometan Sunday. The tomb was a square building supported by a cupola, in which several of our brothers and sisters had been buried before. After saying the first Sura of the Kurân (the Mahometan Lord's Prayer) and other prayers, and after calling upon the Almighty to have mercy upon the departed, and to forgive their sins, ottar of roses and other essences are sprinkled over the graves, which are also fumigated with amber and musk amidst loud lamentations.

The Mahometan has an implicit faith in immortality, and believes that the soul of the dead is allowed, unobserved of course, occasionally to revisit its former abode. For this reason people like to visit the graves of their dead, to keep up intercourse with their immortal souls by imparting to them all their own joys and griefs. Their memory is honoured in every way; and a Mahometan who swears by the head or by the name of his dead, would sooner perish than turn false to his oath.

During the mourning of our mothers, everything in our house remained unchanged, and no business was allowed to be transacted. Moreover, everything had first to be settled with our relations in Omán, to whom a vessel had been despatched with the news of our loss. Of course we discussed the question every day how Tuéni would act, who, as the eldest son, was the legitimate successor to the government: whether he would come to some amicable arrangement with Madjid, or involve us in a family feud.

Some months later our brother Mhammed arrived as the representative of all our brothers and sisters in Omân, to arrange about the division of the inheritance. He returned to Mesket immediately after having settled this matter. Mhammed was considered the most pious of our whole family, who from his early youth had never cared for worldly things. Averse to all show and splendour, and perfectly indifferent to worldly goods, he had never been happy in his station as prince. Disdainful of wealth, he had always dressed very plainly, and nothing vexed him more than the luxury and extravagance he met with at Zanzibar, to which he was quite unaccustomed in Omân; he never got over it all the time he was with us—indeed, his aversion to his surroundings made him hasten his departure to the utmost. In that primitive home of ours at Omân he could once more resume the life that was suited to his tastes and habits.

The question of the succession was still pending. Madjid, who had the power in his hands in Zanzibar, did not seem to trouble himself as to what Tuêni, who had succeeded in the government of Omân, might have to say about his usurped rights; but certainly Tuêni never acknowledged him as Sultan of Zanzibar. An agreement was afterwards entered into between them through the mediation of the English, in which the payment of an annual sum by Madjid to his elder brother was stipulated. The former, however, did not keep to the terms of the treaty, for he discontinued the payment, which he was afraid might be regarded as a tribute, and himself as a vassa of Omán. Tuêni had no means of defending his rights. He had more fighting than enough in the one territory of Omán, without engaging in a war with his wealthy brother, which must have resulted in the utter ruin of his country's resources. Thus, in the absence of a satisfactory compact between the two powers, Omán and Zanzibar have since remained two distinct and independent sovereignties.

No difficulty had arisen, on the other hand, in the division of our late father's private property between Mhammed and ourselves. Unlike European nations, we do not keep up a State with public funds, or with an inland revenue. Neither is there a public exchequer. All the proceeds arising from customs duties are paid into the sovereign's treasury, as also those accruing from his plantations, he being the largest landowner in the island. From this source alone all public expenses are paid.

In my time there were no income or other taxes, nor ground rents, of which there is such a plentiful crop in Europe.

The whole of this private property was divided between the brothers and sisters; even the men-of-war were included and accounted for in Madjid's and Tuêni's shares, who took them over at a certain valuation. The Mahometan law of inheritance favours sons much more than daughters, for the reason that a man has to maintain a family, which a woman has not. Each of the sisters received in consequence only half of what fell to the share of our brothers.

My brother Ralub, my old playmate at Bet il Mtoni,

and myself were declared of age at the same time, though we were neither quite twelve years old. This was rather early, even with our customs, but the times were exceptional ones, and many unlooked-for changes took place in our family. Both of us received our share of the inheritance, and we had now to manage for ourselves, young as we still were. Madjid acted as guardian to our younger brothers and sisters, whose property he undertook to manage.

In his last will my father had directed that those of his widows who had no children should receive an annuity for life, while those who had children were to have a capital paid down, which, however, was comparatively small. It was no doubt his intention that the children should make a home for their mothers, whose limited incomes made this dependence absolutely necessary. But our father had judged us correctly. I am happy to state, to the honour of all (there were thirty-six of us alive at the time of his death), that none failed in their trust. Our mothers were loved and honoured as before, and not one of us ever took undue advantage of the favoured position in which we found ourselves. Indeed, such an act would have justly deserved condemnation—for may she have been a born princess or a purchased slave, no one can replace our mother; she needs neither rank nor wealth with her child; with love and respect alone can we in a measure repay the sacred debt we owe her.

Shortly after the division of the inheritance our house, so crowded up to this time, became rather lonely and empty. A number of my brothers and sisters, with their mothers and their personal slaves, removed from Bet il Sahel to set up house for themselves. As my sisters Chole, Schewâne, and Asche were still staying on, I continued to live with my mother at Bet il Tani for some time more.

There were also many changes at Bet il Mtoni. Zemzem removed to her estate until she married, and Metle went to hers. It was indeed high time that those of us who were now independent left the large houses to make room for our younger brothers and sisters.

During our father's lifetime we had all, figuratively speaking, helped ourselves out of one dish, but things were now completely changed. Those who had received their share of the inheritance were supposed to manage for themselves henceforth; the old aspect remained the same only for the little ones, their mothers and slaves, and for the widows without children. It was Madjid's business to look after these now, for which purpose their allowances were given into his keeping.

CHAPTER XV.

In the course of my narrative I have already spoken of several of my brothers and sisters. I do not know how many I had in all, as a great number died before my father, but I have reason to think that their total was about one hundred. Thirty-six of them were alive when my father died, eighteen sons and eighteen daughters. It would hardly be interesting to the reader to be told the history of each one. But I cannot refrain from describing some of them, feeling convinced that I shall thereby be able to invest the picture of my old home with some life and colouring.

1. *Scharîfe.*

My father, who was the head of and personally conducted all the affairs of government, found little leisure to occupy himself with his younger children, but to the grown-up ones he was all the more lovable. It made the little ones very jealous to have to remain standing before him like little waxworks while the elder sisters were allowed to sit on the sofa by his side. The object of my bitterest envy was my sister Scharîfe, and the thorn in my brother's side was Hilâl.

Scharife, the daughter of a Circassian, was of dazzling beauty, with a complexion fair as a European's. She was very clever besides, and a much trusted adviser of my father's, who consulted her on every important matter, and, as I was told afterwards, he never once regretted having followed her advice. This surely proves that woman in the East is not quite a cipher.

For a short period only they had a slight disagreement. Following her own inclination, Scharife had married a cousin of ours who did not appear to my father to possess those qualities of character which he desired in the husband of his darling daughter. At first she kept aloof from her paternal home until my father's displeasure had subsided. She had, however, made a happy choice, and remained the only wife of her husband; her one child, Schaun, a very beautiful boy, whom she passionately loved, but brought up very strictly, was my playmate. Every Friday he came to us with his mother, always bringing me some trifling gift, in particular when the ships came from Mesket with the Monsoon (Arab, Mossem). Scharife had many relations there, and was very fond of Mesket, where she died, having accompanied our father on his last trip to that place.

2. Chole.

When I went to Bet il Sahel first, Chole became my favourite in place of Scharife. She was also a special pet of my father's, whom she had won by her charming manners, her grace and bright spirits. I have never met with a more perfectly moulded figure.

She dressed with great taste, and everything seemed to suit her. In plain cotton dresses she eclipsed all others wearing the most costly garments. Her opinion on all matters of fashion was considered as infallible as that of the Empress Eugénie in her time.

Her mother, who was from Mesopotamia, was so clever and circumspect, that my father appointed her superintendent of the household at Bet il Sahel. Chole had much to suffer from her sister Asche, who was considerably older, but she bore all with meek patience. She always turned a deaf ear on those people who wanted to slander Asche in her presence. It was only I who knew how deeply pained she was by her sister's conduct, for in spite of my youth she confided all her sorrows to me, and I knew all her secrets. She often said to me with tears : "O, Salme, what have I done, and how can I help it that my father is pleased to favour me? Do I not share with her all the presents he gives me? And am I to blame that he always requires my services?"

I am sorry to say there were many in the house who regarded her with the same envious feeling. Sweet words were not wanting to court her intercession with my father, but as soon as the desired end was attained her ungrateful suppliants again resumed their unloving attitude. She assisted her mother in superintending the household, and later on was herself called to fill this office, and, as it was impossible to please and satisfy everybody in such an overcrowded palace, there were opportunities enough for complaints. If among our huge supplies of provisions there should be found a flaw in either fish, flesh, fowl, or fruit, it

was Chole's fault; if some of the purchases made for
the house and distributed failed to give unequivocal
satisfaction, the fault was laid at Chole's door; or
even if the crop of roses in Turkey had failed, causing
a short supply of rose-water and of ottar of roses,
Chole was blamed and held responsible for it.

But the greatest soreness of all was caused by my
father taking her with him into the treasure-chamber,
or by sending her there by herself. So spiteful were
her enemies that I verily believe they would have
liked to have her searched on leaving it, as they do
the pearl fishers in the Persian Gulf. Her numerous
antagonists were very much startled one day by the
news that my father had made her a present of a
splendid and very precious crown, which he had expressly ordered from Persia for her. This magnificent
diadem was made of golden palm leaves, richly set
with diamonds, decreasing in size from the large
centre stone. It was of a shape that could not be
worn with our head-dress, and it was intended more
as a valuable investment in case of need. It may be
conceived that the possession of so splendid an ornament only increased the number of her adversaries.
My father's marked preference was greatly censured
and resented; and yet not even his great loving
heart could have distributed such love among all his
children in equal shares.

All this bitter feeling it would seem only brought
out the goodness and sweetness of Chole's disposition
—the most cruel shafts she turned off with a gentle,
forgiving hand. As for revenge or retaliation, they
never entered her head. She used merely to say:

"Well, I shall be content if only my father approves of my doings."

Chole took care of me faithfully, as long as I was a child, and afterwards she was my dearest friend. Our friendship became closer still when she removed to Bet il Tani after my father's death. We lived and dined together, talked till late at night, and then retired to rest by each other's side. It will be shown further on how great an influence she had gained over me. After my reconciliation with Madjid our intimacy was troubled for a short time only, but after that she loved me all her life. After my husband's death in 1871, she had a letter written to me (she could not write herself), in which she asked me to send her one of my children for adoption, to which I could not accede, as the child would have had to become a Mahometan.

Her liberality and kindness had grown quite proverbial. She treated her servants very well, pardoned all their faults, and always interceded for other people's slaves. I had a Nubian slave from Mesket, who was a splendid cook, and who gave me great satisfaction in that respect; but I soon found it impossible to keep her, as every article she could lay hands upon vanished. No admonitions or even convictions of her guilt could alter her propensities, so that at last I decided to sell the thief. No sooner had Zafrâne, as she was called, heard this, than she escaped one night to Chole's estate, to beg and pray her to intercede. Indeed, she managed so well to touch my sister's heart, that I had to keep the dangerous person out of regard for Chole.

9

Chole, who had not inherited more than any of us, bought with her share one of our finest plantations, which my father had been in the habit of visiting most. There was a beautiful palace, splendidly furnished, on the estate, which, however, was not a valuable property, though she had to pay a high price for it. But in memory of the great love our father had always shown to her she was willing to make any sacrifice in order to possess herself of his favourite resort. She went every year to her plantation, called Sebe, for the clove harvest. I look back with great delight on those days, when we used to walk about the fragrant gardens hand in hand, talking to the numerous children of the slaves, or looking out from the windows to watch the people at work.

My father's richly-furnished room was never occupied, and was only opened and shown to distinguished visitors at their special request.

Chole was very hospitable to the many people who were attracted by the beautiful situation of Sebe. She had some of the rarest exotic plants in her gardens, which were kept by her faithful overseer in the same state as in my father's time.

A very pretty stone building had been put up just outside the high garden-wall, overshadowed by a magnificent tree, higher than the tallest oak-trees in Europe. This building contained one saloon only, paved with marble, mirrors covering the walls up to the ceiling; and it was furnished with bamboo chairs and numerous coloured lamps. When at Sebe, my father used to receive his visitors and take coffee in this place. We could now quietly visit this beautiful

shady spot, enjoy ourselves like children, and talk of
our dear departed parent.

My dearly beloved Chole, she, the object of such
great love and such bitter hate, is of this world no
more ; I lost her in the year 1875. It is said that
she fell a victim to a dastardly act of poisoning, but
that belief is too much shrouded in mystery to give
it foundation. She will always be with me in spirit.

3. *Asche.*

It rarely happens that two real sisters are more
whimsically endowed by nature, than were Chole and
Asche. The latter was small and dark, Chole tall
and fair ; Asche was pockmarked, while her sister
possessed a countenance of perfect Oriental beauty.
Asche was reserved and even cold in manner, Chole
a radiant sunbeam, though perhaps she was not so
clever as her sister. A greater contrast could not
well be conceived, and it was difficult sometimes to
convince our Asiatic relations that they were really
sisters.

Poor Asche was very well aware of her plainness,
and the marred expression of her features ; and for this
reason she never appeared unveiled, even to her
relations and servants. For the same reason she did
not pay much attention to her outward appearance,
and, for her station, she dressed very plainly and
even meanly. One Abyssinian female slave, very
clever as a hairdresser, attended her in this capacity,
also as milliner and lady's-maid all in one.

She was, however, reputed far and wide as a person
of refined culinary taste, and she kept, indeed, the

best table for miles round. Young people were frequently sent to learn the secrets of cookery from her cooks, and my brother Madjid partly boarded with her, getting five or six dishes daily from her place, for which he paid a fixed sum monthly.

On account of her good common-sense she was often chosen to settle disputes, and very clear her judgment was, too. She was a capital manager, and kept her financial affairs in exemplary order, for which few of us deserved praise. Her exchequer was never at an ebb, not even before harvest-time, which we always looked forward to as the tide in our purses. It is true that persons of extravagant habits put a very uncharitable construction on her possessions: they said she was miserly and selfish.

Poor Hilâl was her favourite brother. She was devotedly attached to him and took a motherly care of his eldest son, Sund, after his death.

4. *Chadudj.*

Chadudj, Madjid's sister, is already known to the reader. She was much better liked than Asche, but she did not often come to see us, as she lived with her brother, whom she very fondly loved.

In later years she took the mother's place with our youngest brother Nasor. With him she went to Mecca, weary of life, after Madjid's· death, as the last refuge of the Mahometan, and both died there within a short time after their arrival.

5. *Schewâne.*

When I went to Bet il Sahel, Schewâne, though

older than myself, became my playmate. She was very sensible, and possessed a power of expression in her eyes that might have subdued a lion; these qualities combined made her play an important part in our house. She installed me at once as her errand-boy, thrashed me every day, and under fortunate circumstances requited my services with the doubtful compliment: "You white ape!" For she was the daughter of an Abyssinian, a race well known with us for rudeness and violence as well as for cunning. I had a "white" mother, and this fact exposed me to a good many attacks from my dark-complexioned relations. My brother Djemschid had still more to suffer from them, for he had not only his mother's fair hair, but also her blue eyes.

In early youth she had lost her only brother Ali, who was much more good-natured and more generally liked in consequence; her father and mother died within a short time of each other; and thus, still quite young, she found herself alone in a world totally different from what she wished it to be. Madjid was the only one of her numerous brothers whom she cared for a little out of regard for Ali, who had been his intimate friend.

Her majestic figure and the almost classic beauty of her features made her a very dignified and even imposing personage. She possessed a strong spirit of self-reliance, and would never take advice from any one, or betray by word or look what she intended to do. Thus she fell into the hands of a crafty negro slave, who took advantage of her inability to write, and robbed her right and left. With all her rough manners, however, she was very charitable, and a severe but just mistress to her servants.

She always tried to pick out and to own the handsomest slaves, whom she loaded with the most costly weapons and jewels. Everything about her showed a fairy-like display of riches and splendour.

I was the only one of all her sisters who managed to get on with her, notwithstanding the bad treatment I had suffered at her hands in early years. Once when I seized a favourable moment to represent to her how much she was blamed for her extravagant habits, and especially for keeping such a great number of slaves, she quietly replied, that she was sure she would not live long, and that she intended partly to spend her money on the poor, partly on herself, as fast as she could, so as to leave us nothing. She was very rich, having inherited a considerable fortune from Ali, besides her own share, but she always continued to live in our paternal home, regardless of the general feeling of dislike entertained for her.

The opinion of her fellow-creatures troubled her very little. Though residing under the same roof with several hundred people, she took no notice whatever of any of them, and only lived for and among her slaves. Thus it came to pass that we were informed too late of her severe illness. Exasperated at what she considered want of sympathy on Chole's part and on mine, she refused to receive our visits, and much as we were grieved we could not force ourselves upon her and violate that firm will of hers. When she felt she was dying from rapid consumption, she made all her servants swear solemnly that no one should

see her in death, except the woman who would per-
form the last offices. Her commands were carried
out to the letter, for the moment she expired her
rooms were locked. We were only admitted after the
body had been laid out, covered with camphor and
wrapped in a sevenfold winding-sheet, the face included, as prescribed by our religious rites. Overwhelmed with grief, I knelt down by the body and
embraced it, unmindful of the scared bystanders, who
wanted to drag me away, and who warned me of the
danger of infection.

In spite of the difference of our characters, I really
had liked Schewâne ; I always took her part, for she
deserved to be loved by all who could overlook her
rough manner and her eccentricities. Pride and
ambition were her besetting sins—no wonder she
made many enemies, especially among her elders.

Before her death she made ample provision for her
town slaves and for the upper slaves on her estates.
She not only set them free, but bequeathed all their
costly arms and jewels to them, besides one whole
estate for their maintenance. She did not wish that
those who had worked for her so long should have to
begin life again among strangers.

6. Metle.

Like Schewâne, Metle was the daughter of an
Abyssinian ; but she had so fair a complexion that
nobody could have guessed her descent. She and
her brother Ralub were my playmates during my
stay at Bet il Mtoni. Her mother was totally para-
lyzed, and could not devote herself much to the

rearing of her children; nevertheless, they turned
out excellent and worthy persons.

The poor sufferer was obliged to live on the ground-
floor, which was intended only for store-rooms, and
naturally very damp and unsuitable for an invalid
like her.

A sheltered place had been erected in front of her
room, close to the banks of the Mtoni, about a yard
in height, to which the sick one was carried in the
day, and where she was attended on by her children
and her slaves. Her step-children and their mothers
frequently came to keep her company; and my
mother in particular used to read to her from the
Kurân and other holy books, for, like most of the
other women who became members of our family after
they were grown up, she could not read herself.

Metle and Ralub were a dear little couple; they
loved their mother fondly, and only thought of
pleasing her. Metle especially, my senior by some
years, was very sweet, and a most unselfish playmate.

After my father's death she was my nearest neighbour on her estate, and during our stay in the
country we met daily. Ralub delighted to break in
upon us unawares with his friends, and so cause a
great deal of confusion, as we were not allowed to
show ourselves to strangers; and I am bound to say
he always succeeded!

After her mother's death, Metle used to spend the
rest of the year at Bet il Mtoni, until she married a
distant cousin in the town. She was very happy
with her two charming boys, whom she always carried

about or had on her knees when I came to see her. She was the most unassuming and contented person in the whole house, the very opposite to Schewâne. But even this did not please everybody—her tastes, they said, were far too simple for a princess; to which she replied that nothing would change her, nor did she consider it at all derogative to her dignity or to her station, to treat prince and beggar with the same kindness. "What matters it," she said, "if I do not choose to be always dressed in silks and velvets— am I worth less on that account than my brothers or sisters? Do I not remain my father's daughter at all times?" I must own to my shame that I had not sufficient good sense then to understand this kind of philosophy, which I only learned to appreciate properly afterwards.

7. Zejâne.

Zejâne and Zemzem are sisters by an Abyssinian mother. I have already mentioned, that during our stay at Bet il Mtoni an intimate friendship existed between my mother and Zejâne, who had a great weakness for me, and spoiled me more than my mother approved of. Our apartments were far apart, and as it took me a long time to get to their rooms, I often stayed there all day, to my mother's annoyance, who vainly sent messenger after messenger to bring me back, until she came herself, and in her turn stayed all the evening with my sisters.

Zejâne was the first to teach me pillow-lace making, at which she was very clever. Alone, or with my mother, she invented the prettiest designs, which no

one was permitted to see until they had been success-
fully completed. She made many friends by her
kindness, and was never tired nursing the sick and
helpless.

The days that my father did not spend at Bet il
Mtoni, the women had permission to go out ; and on
these occasions Zejâne could always be seen in company with some slaves, loaded with many presents,
which she distributed amongst the families of officials.

It was a very sad parting when we removed from
Bet il Mtoni, for both Zejâne and my mother knew
well that they would now see but little of each other,
for Zejâne rarely went into the town, which she disliked. Before we left, I was much with her, and she
gave me many keepsakes, at the same time exhorting
me to be always good to my mother.

I was the more strongly impressed with our sad
leave-taking, as we had to go immediately afterwards
to our overbearing stepmother, Azze bint Sef, to bid
her a cool good-bye.

8. *Zemzem.*

Much prettier than Zejâne, Zemzem possessed all
the good and noble qualities of her sister, who was
taken away from us much too soon. I only knew her
more intimately at a later date, when we had become
neighbours on our estates. She was very practical,
not given to extravagance, and fond of simplicity and
solidity—and things prospered more under her management than in any other Arab household. I may
say that, taken on the whole, she came nearest to the
ideal of a good European housewife.

She was very motherly to me, as I had been her dear sister's favourite. When I did wrong, she looked at me with her large, expressive eyes, and said: "What a pity that your mother had to leave you behind so young in this wretched world! Zejâne would have been a second mother to you, if she were alive, and you would have remained a child much longer. For after all you are a child yet, with very little common sense." And to appease me, she added: "Don't be angry with me for speaking to you thus, if I do it is only for love of Zejâne, to whom you were so dear. Others, you see, commit the same follies, but I never take the trouble to reprove them!"

She was of great assistance to me in my farming—she rode with me over the plantations for hours, and pointed out any improvements she considered necessary. Once she turned to my " Nakora," or overseer, and said: " Your mistress is a mere child still (in Suahely, *mhoto*) and does not understand these matters; you must therefore look after her interests, and my Nakora will always be ready to advise you." This was not very flattering to my self-esteem, but as she meant well I could not be angry with her.

Zemzem married rather late in life our distant cousin Humud. (It is the custom with us to marry as much as possible in the family, so as not to be linked with people of lower rank.) Humud was the same who had once dared to ask Châlid in the mosque for another sister of ours, and had been so harshly repulsed on that occasion. After Châlid's death he made personal advances to the lady, but with no

better success—and when he had recovered from
his great disappointment, he proposed to Zemzem
and was accepted. They were married immediately
after, but very quietly, for Humud was exceedingly
stingy, and not even hospitable, as all Arabs tradi-
tionally are, though he was one of the richest men in
Zanzibar. He was fanatically orthodox, and made a
great display of rigorous devoutness; but this mantle
of hypocrisy was seen through by most people, since
he did not hesitate to commit the greatest cruelties
on the slightest provocation. For this reason he was
almost universally despised—and yet no one ventured
to show open hostility to so rich and influential a
person.

After her marriage I saw but little of Zemzem.
She seemed to live happily with her unpopular husband
—in her practical way I suppose she managed to get
on even with him.

9. Nunu.

I will say a few words about a sister, treated badly
by nature, who deserved to be greatly pitied. Nunu
was the daughter of a Circassian, who received the
name of Tadj (crown) on account of her marvellous
beauty. She had been greatly distinguished by our
father, and became the object of much envy and
jealousy. When her child, as beautiful as herself, was
born blind, many looked upon it as a punishment to
the mother, who had been guilty of being my father's
favourite. This misfortune bitterly distressed her,
and only the firm belief that God had so willed it
made her bear it. Nor was she spared long to her

blind child, for soon after she died of a kind of dropsy.

Poor blind Nunu was now quite alone. But in her case also the old saying proved true, "that God's help is nighest in our extremity." A trustworthy Abyssinian slave had solemnly vowed to the dying Tadj to look after Nunu and never to desert her as long as she lived. She kept her promise in an exemplary manner, and shielded her little mistress from all mischances of life, though she had often more than just cause to complain of her. She took orders from no one but my father, who in his love for the poor blind child took more care of her than he had been able to do of his other children, and this again gave rise to much envious talk.

Nunu was the wildest and most unruly child I have ever seen, and the terror of all mothers with little children. From the age of six until she was ten years old, she waylaid all her younger brothers and sisters, on purpose—incredible as it may appear—to scratch out their eyes! When told of the birth of one, her first question was whether it could see and had sound eyes. After a time it was deemed advisable not to tell her the truth, and it then pleased her much to know that there were others also who would never be able to see the sun or the moon. Her little soul was filled with the most bitter envy. A very pretty little brother of ours was greatly admired for his beautiful long eyelashes. His mother having gone to dinner one day, and the nurse having turned her back for a moment, the child was heard to scream fearfully; and upon their rushing back, they found that Nunu had cut off the eyebrows and eyelashes of the child with a pair of scissors!

No child in the house was from that time left ungarded for a single moment. Nunu possessed a knowledge of locality hardly credible in a blind person, and she moved about with the greatest ease and quickness. She was to be found everywhere, and as busy as a wicked little fairy. Her greatest pleasure was to smash whatever she could lay hold of, china, glassware, and particularly our pretty Asiatic water-coolers.

One of her peculiarities was that she insisted on being treated as though she could see. When the guns announced sunset, she ordered her room to be lighted up. She insisted upon selecting her wardrobe herself, and when she was being dressed by her servants she always stood before a looking-glass. When she heard that any one had fine hair, or beautiful eyes and brows, she subjected those parts to a critical examination, only to observe that she was either disappointed or pleased.

To the great satisfaction of all, Nunu became more reasonable and sedate as she grew up, and in consequence she was no longer regarded with such horror; indeed, she gained on everyone's affection as her good qualities began to shine more prominently. The poor unfortunate girl lost her faithful nurse soon after her parents, and as she could not live by herself without some help and supervision, our sister Asche took charge of her and kept house together with her.

10. *Schembûa and Farschu.*

I must not omit to mention in this place two nieces of mine, Schembûa and Farschu, who were at school with me and who afterwards had the same party views as myself. They lived opposite our place, and as the streets in Zanzibar are very narrow, we could easily talk together from our windows without deaf and dumb language—discuss fashions, household matters, and politics. In the last case we observed the precaution of stationing such servants at the corner as would not be likely to attract attention, who would warn us of the approach of an enemy by dropping a stick, by coughing, or by a low whistle. About these times I shall have to say more further on.

Schembûa and Farschu were my brother Châlid's only children, and from their earliest youth they had been so fond of each other that they were almost inseparable. This brought them frequently into conflict with their mothers, who were exceedingly jealous of each other. Schembûa, some years older than her sister, was gentle and modest, just the reverse of Farschu, and so sensible that she took exciting almost a mother's care of her.

They were both very rich, having inherited the whole of their father's large fortune. In their love for each other they resolved not to divide their property, but to live together and share their possessions. But this arrangement greatly displeased Farschu's mother, an Abyssinian, who wanted her daughter to shake herself free. Farschu, who was very determined, refused to accede to this

demand, and declared she was firmly resolved not to
divide the fortune as long as she and her sister
remained unmarried.   Her mother, deeply hurt by
this refusal, and finding that things in other respects,
too, were getting unbearable, left her home and her
child secretly one day, taking with her only a small
parcel and a very small sum of money.   At first no
one knew where she had gone, and it was generally
believed she would return to her daughter after a
while.   But it was soon discovered that she neither
intended returning to her child nor living by her
bounty—and would, therefore, gain her living by her
own work.   I have previously alluded to the circumstance that at the death of her husband the widow is
made almost entirely dependent on her children, and
that in some cases, as for instance in this, the law
proves a disaster instead of a protection.

The place of the unhappy mother's concealment
remained perfectly unknown as long as her scanty
means lasted; and she only came to Bet il Mtoni,
after having spend her last "Pesa," to see my elder
sister Zuênē, who had formerly been on very friendly
terms with Châlid.   With her she continued to live
on condition that Zuênē would never attempt to bring
her and her daughter together, unless the latter came
of her own accord to acknowledge her wrong.   Farschu,
however, remained perfectly indifferent to this state
of affairs, nor did she take any steps to be reconciled
when her mother began to sicken.   Neither entreaties
nor even the severest censure took the least effect on
her.   Repeatedly, but in vain, I tried to remind her of
a child's duty—she remained obdurate.   It was almost

impossible to believe in so much unrelenting hardness in so small and pretty a being; but from the flash of her dark eyes one might have guessed how inflexible was her resolution. Soon after my departure from Zanzibar, Farschu died of consumption, and I have never been able to learn whether she was ever reconciled to her mother before her death.

The finest estate that belonged to my neices was the grand and superb plantation "Marseilles;" Châlid's predilection for France and for everything French had made him select this name. The walls of all the rooms, except those set apart for prayers, were covered with large mirrors, which had a wonderful effect when lighted up. The floors were inlaid with black and white marble slabs, producing a pleasant freshness much appreciated in a southern clime. A large collection—such as a clock of very ingenious construction, from which dancing and playing figures stepped out at the striking hours; glass globes reflecting the most grotesque distortions; large round quicksilver balls like those put up sometimes in gardens, and a variety of other works of art—gave the palace quite the look of a museum, especially to all simple and uncivilized persons and to our relations from Omân. Frequently I heard expressions of wonder and surprise, such as "Truly, the Christians are real devils!" At "Marseilles," perhaps the best insight into the real ways of Eastern life was to be gained.

I have spent many a happy day on this estate. The house was always full of guests, and as my nieces were rather emancipated and very tolerant in religious matters there was no constraint put upon intercourse. The cries of the runners and outriders : " Sumila! sumila!" (make room), and the announcing of visitors by slaves never ceased. All people here were gay and merry, and seemed to know of no care. The amiable hostesses often induced ladies to stay for more than a fortnight who had only come for three days, much to the displeasure of their respective fathers and husbands.

Everybody could spend the day as he or she pleased best, without being considered impolite, for it is only true hospitality that grants full liberty to guests. In the evening about sunset the whole company met to stay till one or two o'clock in the splendidly lighted saloons, or, on moonlight nights, in the park. When there was no moon, piled up stacks of wood saturated with palm oil were kept burning in various spots all the time.

Unfortunately, this splendid and pleasant place was soon after destroyed. My brothers Bargasch and Abd il Aziz fortified themselves in the castle during our rebellion against Madjid, and the closing and decisive battle was fought here. The estate was totally ruined in consequence, and my neices were great losers thereby. But their great wealth made them soon get over this loss, nor did they like to have it much talked about, " as it was not worth while losing a word about the matter ! "

11. *Hilâl.*

I will speak of two of my brothers only in this place, of Hilâl and of Tuèni, both of them unhappy men ; the one by his own faults, the other a victim to his own son.

It is well that the Mahometan religion forbids the use of all spirituous liquors, and our sect, which does not even sanction smoking, is in this respect much more rigorous than the Turks or Persians. By degrees a sad report began to gain credence that our brother Hilâl, (Newmoon), seduced by Christians and in particular by the then French consul, had taken to drinking. He then had frequent attacks of giddiness, the smell of wine was noticeable about him, and the unfortunate man had not the strength of mind to conquer the evil spirit that possessed him. Hilâl was the favourite son of our father, to whom this caused a bitter anguish. He tried to reform the seduced son by having him at first confined to the house, but soon found himself compelled to banish him altogether from our family circle.

Our sister Chadudj suffered most of all, as she was very fond of Hilâl. He still visited her at our paternal home after his banishment, but could only gain admitance under the greatest difficulties and dangers, and when he stayed over-night with her and some others, who had remained faithful to him, the room was kept dark so that his lights might not betray him. No one ever found the heart to apprise our father of these visits. He kept him very short to prevent him from indulging his vice, but Chadudj assisted him largely, though greatly to his own ruin.

Hilâl sank deeper and deeper under his evil passion, until he was scarcely ever sober, and he was soon released from this misery by death. In spite of all that had occurred, our father's grief for his favourite son was unspeakable.   He often locked himself up in his chamber, and the traces of tears could be seen afterwards in the place where he had knelt down to pray.   Something which had never happened before : he gave vent to his grief even in words like these : "How great is my despair and my grief for thee, oh, Hilâl ! "

Hilâl left three sons, Suud, Fesal, and Mhammed. The last and youngest was adopted by my stepmother Azze bint Sêf, who was childless.   The boy completely won her over, an attempt in which none of us had ever succeeded.   She had always been reported to be mean and ungenerous, and nobody could believe their eyes when Mhammed commenced living very extravagantly, with her money of course.   No one had ever before dreamt of keeping dogs—he ordered a whole pack of hounds from Europe, amongst them such splendid beasts as had never been seen in our country. His whole time was taken up with these dogs and some really beautiful horses.   He would not allow his favourites to be fed on garbage, but had a separate kitchen put up for them, where a variety of food was prepared.   The fattest fowls, the best joints of meat, and the largest fish, were picked out for them.   Report even had it, that his dogs and horses got no water to drink, but only champagne.   I cannot say whether this was true ; at all events people said a great many bad things of Mhammed, that were probably not entirely without foundation, for his was the refinement of extravagance.

Suud had a great weakness for European habits and

style of life ; in his manners he resembled his father most.

The third of Hilâl's sons was very different from his brothers. Gentle Fesal, who had not the luxurious habits of Mhammed and Suud, was always so modestly dressed that he might sooner have been taken for a plain citizen than for a prince. He was of a philosophical turn of mind, very averse to all material pleasures, and always remained a puzzle to his brothers. In after years he bought a small estate near my own and often came to see me. He went hardly ever to the town without bringing me back some small present, if it was only a bundle of fireworks, which I liked very much.

Misunderstood by his brothers, the poor fellow was very unhappy ; he had a gentle and noble disposition, which is thought much too lightly of in this world. But by his gentle and amiable manners he won the friendship of all who saw more of him. He had lost his mother when very young and had hardly ever known true love. "It pains me the more," he used to say to me, who, though I was his aunt, was much his junior, "that my brothers look on me as quite superfluous, and care not one jot for me. I care not whether I live or die, for no one will ever miss me." My heart ached when I heard him talk so, for he really deserved to be loved. How truly happy a monastic life would have made this man, who felt a stranger in his own land and an alien in the world !

No one regretted more than poor Fesal, when I yielded to my brother Madjid's request to return to the town. In the course of time he had become quite

accustomed to telling me of all his thoughts and
sorrows, as if I had really been a sensible aunt, and
not what I was, a wild and inexperienced girl.

12. *Tuêni.*

Our eldest brother Tuêni was born at Mesket, and
spent all his life in Omân. He never came to Zanzibar, and could not be shaken in his prejudice against
that birthplace of most of his brothers and sisters.
Since a Mahometan is not allowed to have his portrait
painted, a commandment which is strengthened, if
possible, by superstition, and as photographs were not
yet known with us at that time, Tuêni always remained
a perfect stranger to those of us who had not been to
Mesket. We had only heard a good deal of his gentle
manners, of his courage, and his bravery in war. His
soldiers idolized him, and his presence alone inspired
them with confidence. Like our father, he was very
fond of warfare, and a more accomplished soldier than
any of my brothers. He had spent the best part of his
life in the camp, to the great sorrow of his legitimate
wife Ralie, our cousin, by whom he had several
children. During my father's residence in Zanzibar,
Tuêni acted as his representative in Omân, but having
enough to do to look after the defence of the frontiers of
the empire, he left the real government in the hands of
our pious second brother Mhammed, who was possessed
of the same prejudice against Zanzibar. Tuêni would
either fight about Bender Abbas with the Persians, or
resist the invasions of the wandering tribes of central
Arabia. These numerous tribes are very poor, and
most of them live only by pillage. An Arab of the

desert seldom possesses more than a camel, some indispensable arms (such as musket, sword, dagger, lance, and shield), one or two iron cooking pots, a bag of dates, and at best a milk-goat. The men, young and old, carry their arms into battle, followed at some distance by their wives and daughters on foot, and met after the fight with cool water, milk, and viands. Omân was invaded every year by larger or smaller hordes, and the country was kept in a continual state of activity by them. None but the most resolute and energetic ruler could hold his own against their incursions.

Such was the state of affairs at the time my father died on his return to Zanzibar. Had his death taken place at Mesket, Tuêni might have been in a position to possess himself of the government of Zanzibar, instead of Madjid, our fourth brother, who, taking advantage of favourable circumstances, caused himself to be proclaimed Sultan of Zanzibar. I have already stated that Madjid agreed to pay an annual sum to Tuêni, but that he soon afterwards withdrew from this engagement. His conduct was universally condemned, the more so as Tuêni's position became daily more difficult. The continued campaigns were a heavy drain on the country's resources, and just at the worst time the supplies from Zanzibar began to fail. Money at last became so scarce that he saw himself compelled to levy duties on various articles of merchandize. Luckily for Omân, public loans, which have been the ruin of more than one Eastern State, were then unthought of. But even these light taxes raised a spirit of discontent, and the malcontents unfortunately succeeded in gaining great influence over Tuêni's eldest son, Sâlum, who at last became guilty of the heaviest crime man can commit.

One day when Tuêni, after having been to an assembly, had thrown himself, greatly fatigued, upon a couch, to take a little rest, his son stepped up, and peremptorily demanded the suspension of all taxes and duties, for which unjustifiable proceedings he was naturally called to order. Whereupon this unnatural, cowardly son drew a revolver, which he had kept hidden until then, and shot down his father where he lay!

But the misguided youth did not long enjoy the fruits of his evil deed—a speedy retribution was in store for him. He had hardly installed himself as ruler of Omân, when his brother-in-law Azzan determined to depose him. He surprised Mesket one night, and put the capital to massacre and pillage. His action was much facilitated by the great exasperation of the people against Sâlum, as no righteous man would take up arms on behalf of a parricide. The wild invaders met with little resistance—they carried off all they could, and destroyed the rest. Sâlum's palace in particular was sadly wrecked, and he succeeded under great peril in escaping on board one of his men-of-war, saving nothing but bare life.

His unfortunate mother and her other children just managed to save themselves on board a ship, and she, too, lost her all. A young Indian merchant, called Abd il Rad (servant of the Lord), had the good fortune to buy the greater part of her precious jewels for a mere trifle from a Bedouin (it was said for about three

hundred dollars), and the honest fellow restored the
lost property to the unfortunate princess as a gift!

Azzan, the invader, was himself soon after turned
out by my third brother Turki, and he again suffered
the same fate at the hands of my younger brother, Abd
il Aziz (also servant of the Lord). The latter, Chole's
ward, was much distinguished by intelligence, courage,
and energy. At the age of twelve he had already
taken our side in the conspiracy and conflict with
Madjid, and he lived afterwards for a time in Beloo-
chistan, whence most of our soldiers used to be
drafted. He succeeded in the end to restore peace in
Omàn for a short period, but was not able to maintain
himself in power for long. Turki returned, and
possessed himself anew of the government, whereupon Abd il Aziz sought a refuge again in Beloochis-
tan, where he still lives.

Surely a sad page, these family feuds! They can
only be understood by those who are personally acquainted with the ambition of Eastern princes and
with the passionate dealings of Eastern people in
general. I, myself, was not to remain a stranger to
these, indeed among the first I was to be a sufferer
by them!

CHAPTER XVI.

BEFORE proceeding with the account of my personal adventures, I desire in this place to include some chapters describing various phases of Eastern life. I do not intend enumerating all our customs and habits, as I am not writing strictly for instruction; I only wish to enable the European reader to form a more correct idea of the prominent features on the general aspect of Eastern life. I hope I may not be led away to speak of matters wholly uninteresting—though I would like to come as near as possible to completing a picture that will impress itself on the mind.

I will turn at once to the most momentous of all these questions, to the description of woman's position in the East. I find it rather difficult to speak of this matter. I am convinced that, as a woman born in the East, people will be apt to think me partial, and I fear I shall not succeed in eradicating altogether the false and preposterous views existing in Europe, and especially in Germany, on the position of the Arab wife to her husband. In spite of the easier ways of communication in these days, the East is still too much considered the land of fairy-tales, about which all sorts of stories may be told with impunity. A traveller making a few weeks' tour to Constantinople, to Syria, Egypt, Tunis, or Morocco, sets about at once to write a big book on the life and the customs of the East. He has been able to judge only quite superficially of these, and has seen absolutely nothing of domestic life. He contents himself with setting down the distorted stories and second-hand accounts of the French or German waiters at his hotel, or from sailors and donkey boys, and considers these sources of information perfectly reliable and trustworthy. But even from these there is not much to learn, and accordingly he throws the reins over the neck of his imagination, and gallops away into fable-land. The only necessary merit of his book, he thinks, is amusement and entertainment, which are the sugar-plums between the pages, and lure the reader on, and his production is pronounced " such a success ! "

My own experience, I admit, was somewhat similar —for I myself judged things in Europe at first by their outward appearance only. When I first met in European society faces beaming all over with smiles, I was, of course, led to believe that the condition of husband and wife must be much better regulated, and that connubial happiness was a thing much more frequently met here than in the Mahometan East. When, however, my children had outgrown the age when a mother's continual presence is more desirable than her absence, and I was able to go more into society, I soon perceived that I had completely misjudged men as well as the general state of affairs. I have watched many cases of what is called "wedded life," in which the parties seemed to be chained together expressly to make each other suffer excruciating torments. I have seen too many of such unhappy cases to make me believe that Christian wedlock stands on a higher level or renders people much happier than the Mahometan. To my mind married life, in the first instance, cannot be made more or less happy by any particular religion, or by existing views or habits alone; matrimonial happiness can alone depend upon real congeniality and harmony between husband and wife. Where these exist, happiness and peace will always predominate, and from them will spring in time that harmonious sympathy which wedlock truly ought, and is intended to be.

Taught by this experience I will try not so much to give my own opinion, but to define simply the position of women—and of married women in particular—in the East. I admit that I know intimately only the state of affairs in Zanzibar, and tolerably well that existing in Omân. But it is just in Arabia, and with the Arab people, that the true Mahometan spirit, upon which the views of other Eastern nations are founded, has maintained itself most pure, and for this reason my description may claim to be applicable to the entire Mahometan East, with the exception, of course, of such cases of degeneracy which have arisen from, and grown out of, a closer connection with the Christian occident.

In the first instance, it is quite a fallacy to think that woman in the East is placed socially on a lower

level than man. The legitimate wife—the purchased
Sarari are of course to be excepted—stands in all
respects on a par with her husband, and she always
retains her rank, and all rights and titles emanating
from it, to their full extent.

The mere circumstance of her retired way of life
makes the Arab woman appear more helpless and
possessing fewer rights. But this is a custom existing with all Mahometan (and also with many non-
Mahometan) nations in the East, and the higher the
rank the more rigorously it is observed. Only her
father, her sons, brothers, uncles and nephews, and
her slaves are allowed to see her. When she appears
before a stranger, or has to speak to him, the law
requires her to be shrouded and veiled; part of the
face, the neck and chin, and, above all, the ankles,
must be completely covered. As long as she keeps to
this rule she may move about freely, and walk
abroad in open day. Poor people, who have but
few or no slaves at all, are obliged, on this account
alone, to go abroad more in the daylight, and consequently enjoy more liberty. Ask a woman of this
class whether she does not mind exposing herself so
freely, and she will reply: "Such laws are only
made for the rich, and not for poor women!" I must
say that ladies of higher rank often envy their poorer
sisters on account of their advantages, of which
especially the women in Omân avail themselves,
who, owing to the poverty of their country, are prevented from keeping many slaves.

I have already stated that the lady of rank too
may walk abroad in the daytime. For instance, if

one of her near relations falls sick she may visit the invalid veiled; in the same way she may appear before a judge to plead her cause in person, for luckily we know nothing of lawyers. But custom requires that this right be only put into force in most urgent cases, and vanity has a good share in upholding it, as the veil disfigures women to a degree, and makes them look like walking mummies.

I fully admit now that this swaddling in the East is carried too far, though I cannot say that I find the European customs any better. In my opinion the *want* of dress in the ball costume of a fashionable lady is carried much further still.

It is true that a single woman is an object deserving pity. Shut out completely by precept and custom from any intercourse with men, and without any protection, her position frequently becomes a painful one. As she is not allowed to see or speak to her own officials and managers, if these be Arabs, she is often robbed by them; and I am myself acquainted with several ladies who only married to save themselves from being at the mercy of these frauds and impostures. This proves that the seclusion of women has its unmistakable drawbacks, and that this also is carried too far. There is, on the other hand, a great deal of sentimental pity wasted on the Eastern woman. She is perfectly unaware that any constraint is put upon her, and habit makes the greatest inconveniences bearable after a time.

Pity is also lavished upon her because she has to share her husband's love with one or many others. By law the Moslem is permitted to have four legitimate wives at one time, and to marry a fifth if one of the former dies or gets divorced from him. Sarari, or concubines, he may buy as many as he pleases, and can pay for. But I have never met with any man who really had four wives at once. Of course a poor man can only afford to have one; the rich man restricts himself to two at most, who live apart and keep house separately.

In the East there are, of course, women too who know how to take care of themselves; who first take the precaution to inquire whether the suitor to their hand has a wife already, and who stipulate the clause of a formal promise in the marriage-contract that he will wed no other wife or purchase a Surîe.

Practically, and in most cases, monogamy predominates. Whenever a man avails himself of the full liberty granted to him by law, the relations between the different wives become rather uncomfortable. Ruffled tempers and envy soon turn into raging jealousy with the hot-tempered southern women. Apathy and indifference do not create jealousy; this comes only when we have reason to doubt our power over the object we love and want to keep to ourselves alone. Do not these frequent outbursts of passion sufficiently prove the fact that women in the East can love more deeply than her cooler northern sister?

By jealousy polygamy is turned into a source of great vexation and torment—and that is well. Many a man of sufficient wealth to facilitate this has a horror of daily scenes, and therefore he prefers monogamy, which acts as a further check to this bad custom. No

sensible man, and surely no woman, can excuse or
defend polygamy.   But now comes another question.
How is it with Christians ? how about wedded life in
civilized Europe ?   I will say nothing of the fact that
in a Christian state the Mormons, a sect who call
themselves Christians, are publicly and openly avowed
polygamists.   Is wedlock always considered a sacred
nstitution in moral Europe ?   Is it not bitter irony
and delusion to talk of only " one " wife ? The Christian may, of course, marry one woman only, and that
is the great superiority of Christianity ; the Christian
law requires the just and the good, the Mahometan
allows the evil ; but custom and practice mitigate to
a great extent in the East the evil consequences of the
law, while sin is rampant here in spite of it.   I should
say the only difference in the position of a married
woman in the East and in Europe to be, that the
former knows the number as well as the characters of
her rivals, while the latter is kept in a state of con-
siderate ignorance about them.

Of course only a wealthy man can purchase Sarari.
Slaves by birth, they become free as soon as they
have children.   It happens very rarely, and then
only in the case of very hard-hearted men, that
the Surîe is resold by her master after the death of
her child, from necessity or because he is weary of
her.   In case of the husband's death, his Sarari are
absolutely free and have no other master.   And if
they are married again to a brother or to any relation
of the deceased, they become, as free women, the legitimate wives of such.

It is an absolute myth that the Arab husband treats

his wife with less regard than is the case here. This is already provided for by religion, which, though neglecting the wife in some points, recommends her, like a helpless child, to the protection of the husband. The believing and pious Mahometan has as much humane feeling as any highly-civilized and moral European; he is perhaps even more strict and rigorous to himself, believing in the ubiquity of the Lord, who made the laws, and carrying the firm conviction to the grave that his good acts and his bad will by and by meet with just retribution.

Certainly there exists in Zanzibar as well as in this country the uncomfortable character known as the domestic tyrant. But I may state upon my conscience that I have heard here a good deal more of loving husbands who sometimes think fit to establish their argument by physical manipulation. Any decent Arab would feel ashamed and dishonoured by such an action. It is different with negroes, for I have frequently had to separate couples fighting on my plantations and make peace between them.

Neither is the wife obliged to submit unconditionally and for ever to all the whims and humours of her husband; in such cases she always finds shelter with her relations, or, if she stands alone, she has the right to make a complaint to the Kadi in person. Frequently, too, she has recourse to the law.

A lady, with whom I was very intimate, married at the age of sixteen a cousin of hers, who was many years her senior, but by no means worthy of her. Continuing to lead his former gay life, he thought he could treat her as he pleased; but he was not a little

11

surprised when he found one evening on his return home a very strongly-termed letter instead of his wife. I had always been accustomed to go to my friend's estate without being first announced, as I knew that her amiable husband was never at home, and preferred the pleasures of the town to his wife's company. After the above-mentioned occurrence, however, my friend called upon me one day to tell me that I could no longer visit her without being announced, as her husband was again living with her on the estate. Remorseful and repenting, he had followed and implored her pardon; and having once learned what a determined little wife he possessed, he took good care to mend his ways. I could speak of many instances of this kind.

When married people meet they kiss each other's hands, and they take their meals in company with their children. The wife performs all kinds of friendly services for her husband. She fastens on his weapons when he goes out, and takes them off again on his return; she refreshes him with cool drinks; in fact, shows him all those trifling acts of attention which make life more pleasant and affectionate. But all these services are voluntary, and by no means the duties of bondage.

The household stands entirely under the control of the wife, and there she is absolute mistress. She does not receive a certain sum for house-keeping, as is customary in Europe—she has full liberty to dispose of her husband's funds. When the latter has two wives living apart, his income is equally divided between them.

Of course much depends upon the individual disposition of husband and wife, how far the latter may venture in using her authority. I had once invited a large party to one of my plantations, but the invitations had been issued too late to allow all the ladies to order their riding donkeys in time, and I was afraid, therefore, many of them would have to decline. In this plight a young married lady, a friend of mine, at once placed a large number of fine donkeys, fully harnessed, at my disposal. Before accepting her generous offer I wanted her to ask her husband's permission first—upon which she very quietly replied that she was not accustomed to let her husband interfere in such trifles as these.

Another lady of my acquaintance in Zanzibar had still greater control over the household and all the property. She managed quite by herself all her husband's large estates and his town-houses. The latter was not even aware of the extent of his income, nor did he consider it derogatory to his dignity to ask her for money whenever he wanted any; he knew well enough that he could not do better than leave the entire management of his affairs to his prudent and sensible wife.

The education of the children is left entirely to the mother, whether she be legitimate wife or purchased slave, and it constitutes her chief happiness. Some fashionable mothers in Europe shift this duty on to the nurse, and by and by on the governess, and are quite satisfied with looking up their children or receiving their visits, once a day. In France the child is sent to be nursed in the country, and left to the care of strangers. An Arab mother, on the other hand, looks continually after her children. She watches and nurses them with the greatest affection, and never leaves them as long as they may stand in need of her motherly care; for which she is rewarded by the fondest filial love. Her children repay her in a great measure for all the disadvantages of polygamy, and their affection renders her life more happy and contented.

If foreigners had more frequent opportunities to observe the cheerfulness, the exuberance of spirits, even, of Eastern women, they would soon and more easily be convinced of the untruth of all those stories afloat about the degraded, oppressed, and listless state of their life. It is impossible to gain a true insight into the actual domesticity in a few moments' visit. And the conversation carried on on those formal occasions hardly deserves that name; there is barely more than the exchange of a few commonplace remarks—and it is questionable if even these have been correctly interpreted.

Notwithstanding his innate hospitality, the Arab has the greatest possible objection to having his home pried into by those of another land and creed. Whenever, therefore, a European lady called upon us, the enormous circumference of her hoops (which were the fashion then, and took up the entire width of the stairs) was the first thing to strike us dumb with wonder; after which the very meagre conversation generally confined itself on both sides to the mysteries of the different costumes; and the lady retired as wise as she was when she came, after having been sprinkled over by the Eunuchs with ottar of roses, and being the richer for some parting presents. It is true, she had been to and entered a Harêm, she had seen the much-pitied oriental ladies (though only through their veils), she had with her own eyes seen our dresses, our jewellery, the nimbleness with which we sat down on the floor—and that was all. She could not boast of having seen more than any other foreign lady who had called before her. She is conducted upstairs and downstairs again by the Eunuchs, and is watched all the time. Rarely she sees more than the reception room, and more rarely still can she guess or find out who the veiled lady is with whom she conversed. In short, she has had no opportunity whatsoever of learning anything of domestic life or the position of Eastern women.

It is essential to know another fact in order to understand oriental wedded life properly. The marriage of a girl neither changes her name nor the rank she has held previously. The wife of a prince, descended from the family of a simple citizen, will never think of demanding equality of rank with her husband —she remains always the daughter (bint) of N. or M. On the other hand, an Arab prince or chief often allows his daughter or sister to marry one of his slaves. He reasons thus: "My servant will remain her servant, and she will always be his mistress." Only he ceases to be a slave after marriage, but he, of course, addresses his wife as "Highness" or "mistress."

If a man has occasion to mention his wife in the course of conversation, which he avoids doing if he can, he never calls her, "my wife," but always "the daughter of N. N." At best he uses the expression, "Um Ijali," i.e., "mother of my family," whether she has children or none.

It stands to reason that people who marry, being previously unacquainted with each other, do not always agree; or there may arise difficult and painful circumstances from other causes, such as I mentioned in the cases of my father and Schesade and of Madjid and Asche. In cases like these the Mahometan law has the great advantage of facilitating a divorce. It is decidedly preferable that two people completely at variance in their views and disposition should be able to separate in peace, to being compelled to remain chained together—often a cause for crime. In such a case the wife has her whole dowry returned, the disposal of which also rests with her during her wedded state. If the divorce has been moved by the husband, she also retains the marriage settlement made by him, which, however, she cancels on suing herself for the divorce.

I trust the above will suffice to demonstrate that woman in the East is not at all the degraded or oppressed and outlawed being she is generally believed; she is by no means a cypher. What power and how great an influence some women may gain I have already pointed out in speaking of my step-mother, Azze bint Sêf. She ruled our father completely, and court and public affairs depended in most cases on her verdict. All attempts on the part of her step-children to weaken her influence completely failed, although their efforts were, if at no other time, perfectly united in this aim. Any request of ours, made

to our father in person, was invariably referred to her
final decision, even in matters that might be thought
to have been beneath her consideration. While my
father lived she ruled with a rod of iron.

Here is a case in point: The daughter of the commanding officer of one of our fortresses in Omân came
over to Zanzibar with her husband. They were pretty
well off, and had no children—"fortunately," as the
lady told me herself. She was very clever and witty
(wit is nowhere more valued than with us) but fright-
fully ugly. Her husband, nevertheless, adored her,
and bore all her whims and humours with an angelic
patience. When she walked out he had to accompany her, whether he liked it or not. He could never
dispose of his time himself, and in the morning after
prayers he had to wait for orders from mistress Asche,
to know if she deigned to remain at home with him
or intended to go out for the day. He was altogether
her slave.

I will only speak of one more member of our family,
whose history contradicts better than anything else
all the fabrications about the inferiority of Eastern
women. My great-aunt, my grandfather's sister, is
to this day held up as the model of a clever, courageous, and energetic woman. The history of her life
and of her deeds is told over and over again to old
and young, and listened to with awe.

My grandfather, the Sultan Imâm, of Mesket, in
Omân, left at his death three children: my father
Said, my uncle Sâlum, and my aunt Asche. My
father was only nine years old at the time, and a
regency had to be established. Contrary to all

custom, my great-aunt at once declared in the most
decided manner that she would carry on the government herself until her nephew was of age, and she
suffered no opposition. The ministers, who had never
anticipated such a thing, and who had already in
secret congratulated themselves on the prospect of
ruling the country for some years, could do nothing
but submit. They had to make their reports to her,
and to receive her instructions and commands every
day. She closely watched and knew everything, and
nothing could remain concealed from her, to the great
vexation and annoyance of all the disloyal and idle
officials.

Personally, she put aside all rules of etiquette ; regardless of what people might say, she merely wore
her schele in the presence of the ministers, and went
her own way with energy and firmness..

Her courage was soon put to a very severe test.
Not long after she had taken up the reins of government a very serious war broke out—unfortunately, a
frequent occurrence in Omân. Some of our next of
kin had thought it an easy affair to overthrow the
government of a woman, to extinguish our house, and
possess themselves of power. Their hordes ravaged
the country with fire and sword, and advanced close
to the gates of Mesket. Thousands of country people
from the sacked provinces had already fled for shelter
and protection into the city, leaving all their goods
and chattels behind. Mesket is strongly fortified, and
well able to stand a siege, but of what use are the
strongest walls when provisions and ammunition are
exhausted ?

But in this terrible distress my great-aunt proved herself equal to the occasion, and she even gained the admiration of the enemy. Dressed in man's clothes, she inspected the outposts herself at night, she watched and encouraged the soldiers in all exposed places, and was saved several times only by the speed of her horse in unforeseen attacks. One night she rode out, oppressed with care, having just received information that the enemy was about to attempt an entrance into the city by means of bribery that night, and with intent to massacre all, and now she went to convince herself of the loyalty of her troops. Very cautiously she rode up to a guard, requesting to speak to the "Akîd" (the officer in charge), and did all in her power to seduce him from his duty by great offers of reward on the part of the besiegers. The indignation of the brave man, however, completely allayed her fears as to the fidelity of the troops, but the experiment nearly cost her her own life. The soldiers were about to massacre the supposed spy on the spot, and it required all her presence of mind to make good her escape.

The situation, grew, however, to be very critical at Mesket. Famine at last broke out, and the people were well-nigh distracted, as no assistance or relief could be expected from without. It was, therefore, decided to attempt a last sortie in order to die at least with glory. There was just sufficient powder left for one more attack, but there was no more lead for either guns or muskets. In this emergency the regent ordered iron nails and pebbles to be used in place of balls, the guns were loaded with all the old iron and brass that

could be collected, and she opened her treasury to
have bullets made out of her own silver dollars. Every
nerve was strained, and the sally succeeded beyond all
hope.   The enemy was completely taken by surprise,
and fled in all directions, leaving more than half their
men dead and wounded on the field.   Mesket was
saved, and, delivered out of her deep distress, the
brave woman knelt down on the battle field and
thanked God in fervent prayer.

From that time her government was a peaceful one,
and she ruled so wisely that she was able to transfer
to her nephew, my father, an empire so unimpaired
as to place him in a position to extend the empire by
the conquest of Zanzibar.   It is to my great-aunt,
therefore, that we owe, and not to an inconsiderable
degree, the acquisition of this second empire.

She, *too*, was an Eastern woman!

CHAPTER XVII.

In Arabia matches are generally arranged by the father, or by the head of the family. There is nothing peculiar in this, as the same is done even in Europe, where man and woman are allowed to meet freely. Does it not often happen here that a reckless father who has run deeply into debt sees no way out of his difficulties but by the sacrifice of his pretty daughter to some creditor; or that a fashionable, pleasure-loving mother hurries her child into marriage for the sole purpose of obtaining an undisputed sway?

Amongst the Arabs there are just as many despotic parents, who care as little for the happiness of their children, or listen to the voice of conscience. But it is not abuse of power alone which makes parents in those parts choose for their children; they are compelled to do so by the retired life of the women; though even by this seclusion a meeting with men cannot always be prevented. But it is a general rule that a girl must not see (except perhaps from the window) nor talk to her future husband before the evening of her wedding. Yet he has not been quite a stranger to her—his mother, his sisters and aunts have had frequent opportunities of describing him, and telling her everything about him that may be of interest.

Sometimes the young couple have been acquainted in early youth, as girls are permitted, up to their ninth year, to associate freely with boys of the same age. In such a case the young man goes to the father of his old playmate to ask for her hand, after having secured her own consent through the mediation of his mother or sister.

In all such cases the cautious father asks: "But where have you been able to see my daughter?" To which the reply is made: "As yet I have never had the good fortune to see your honoured (makschume) daughter—but I have heard a great deal about her charms and virtues from my own people."

If the candidate does not suit, he is straightway refused by the father, though, as a rule, the latter asks for some little time to take the matter into consideration. He does not mention a word at home about what has occurred—but secretly and rigorously he watches the conversation between his wife and daughter. Occasionally, and in quite an indifferent manner, he will speak of his intention to give a small gentlemen's party in a few days, mentioning the names of his friends with as little concern as possible if the women require to be told them. If they appear to be pleased at hearing the suitor's name mentioned, he knows that some understanding exists already between the two families. Then only he informs his daughter that N. N. has asked for her hand, and asks her opinion. Her yes or no are almost always decisive—only a despotic father takes the decision upon himself without waiting for his daughter's acceptance or refusal.

Our father, too, showed in such questions his sense of justice, and left his children to decide their own lot. A distant cousin of ours, Sund, proposed for my elder sister Zuêne when she was barely twelve years old. My father disapproved of his proposal on account of her youth, but did not like to decline it altogether without having first consulted his daughter. Zuêne had lost her mother, and having no one to advise her, she was so pleased with the idea of being a married woman soon, that she insisted upon accepting him, and my father gave his consent.

There are cases, it is true, in which children are affianced and married in very early youth. Two brothers had agreed upon the intermarriage of their children, and, as it happened, they had only one child each, the one a son, the other a daughter. The marriage was already talked of when the boy was seventeen, and the girl seven. The boy's mother, who lived on an estate not far from my own, a very prudent and sensible woman, often complained to me of her husband and her brother-in-law, who insisted upon her accepting a little child as daughter-in-law, whom she would have to nurse and educate first, while on the other hand the girl's mother was inconsolable at having so soon to part with her daughter. But they both only so far succeeded as to have the wedding postponed for two years. I do not know how the matter was finally settled, as I left Zanzibar soon after.

All friends and acquaintances are formally informed of the engagement by handsomely-dressed female slaves, who, sometimes to the number of twenty, go from house to house with the announcement and the invitation to the wedding, for which message they are richly rewarded at each house.

The paternal home of the bride is now the scene of much life and bustle, for the wedding generally takes place within four weeks. Under any circumstances the betrothal never lasts long, as but few arrangements are necessary in our blessed South. There we know nothing of the hundred and one things considered indispensable to Northern people on such occasions, and an Eastern bride would become speechless with surprise at the sight of a European trousseau. Why are people in these parts so very fond of loading their new bark with such a quantity of unnecessary ballast?

The dowry of an Arab bride is comparatively a small one; according to her rank and wealth it consists of rich dresses, jewellery, male and female slaves, of houses, plantations, and ready money. She gets presents from her parents, from those of her affianced husband, and from the latter himself. All this remains her personal and private property, and the cost of her dowry is never deducted from her share of the patrimony.

The making of the bride's dresses takes some time, for a lady of rank has to change her toilet twice or thrice a day during the first week after her marriage. A bridal dress, like the white robe and veil here, is not worn in the East, but the bride must put on perfectly new garments from head to foot—the colour of the dress is left to her taste. Some appear in all the colours of the rainbow, yet their costume is neither ugly nor without taste.

Special perfumes are prepared, which play an important part at the wedding feast—the Rhia, a costly mixture of powdered sandal-wood, musk, saffron, and plenty of ottar of roses, is used as an ointment for the hair, and a pleasant incense, made of the wood of the "ud" (a species of the aloe), of the finest amber, and of a great deal of musk. An Eastern lady never can get too many perfumes.

Then comes the baking, the preparing of sweetmeats, and the slaughtering of cattle, which occupies all hands fully.

The bride herself has yet to go through several unpleasant and tiresome ceremonies. During the last eight days she has to stay in a dark room, nor must she put on any of her finery, so that she may appear all the more resplendent on her wedding-day. All this time she is a much-to-be-pitied creature—visit follows upon visit, all the old women whom she knows, and her nurses foremost of all, whom perhaps she has not seen for years, come to her with hands open ready to receive. The chief of the eunuchs, who has shaved off her first hair, who is very proud of this service of honour rendered to her once, begs to offer his congratulations, and returns his way with a souvenir—either a costly shawl, a ring for the little finger of the left hand, a watch, or some guineas.

The bridegroom is spared this imprisonment in a dark room, but otherwise he has to undergo quite as many trials. All those who have ever been in his service or in that of his bride come to him before calling upon her, and in this way they obtain double presents.

The bridegroom stays at home during the last three days, and only his most intimate friends visit him. But there is a lively intercourse between the two families—for there is no end to the interchange of compliments and of presents between bridegroom and bride.

The great day appears at last. Generally the nuptial ceremony is performed in the evening at the bride's house, and not in the mosque. The act is performed by a Kadi, or, if no such is to be had, by a reputedly devout man. It may appear strange to a European, that the principal person, the bride, is not present herself during the solemn act; she is represented by her father, her brother, or some other near male relation.

She only appears before the Kadi in person if she has no male relations at all, to be united to her bridegroom with the customary ceremonies. In this case, she enters the empty room first, completely muffled, after which the Kadi, the bridegroom, and the witnesses are admitted. After the conclusion of the ceremony, in which the voice of the bride is barely audible, the gentlemen leave first to let the newly-married wife retire to her apartments.

All the gentlemen, the bridegroom included, partake of a sumptuous feast. Whilst this lasts, the room in which it takes place is richly perfumed with incense of ud and of ottar of roses.

The surrender of the bride to the bridegroom does not always follow upon the ceremony, but in most cases three days later. Numerous persons are now engaged in dressing her in her finest garments, and at about nine or ten in the evening of the third day she is conducted by her female relations to her new abode, where the bridegroom receives her in company with his male relations. Before the entrance to the private rooms, leave is taken with many congratulations and blessings, and the company then retire to the reception-rooms on the ground floor, to celebrate the marriage by merrily feasting for several days.

Some rules of etiquette are always to be observed when the bridegroom has entered the bride's apartment. If her rank is higher than his, she remains quietly seated, nor deigns to speak to him until he has first addressed her, and meanwhile still retains her costly mask, which covers her features. Then, to prove his affection, and as a bribe for the removal of the mask, the young husband places at her feet such presents as his means can afford. A few pence will suffice with poor people—but by rich ones large sums are spent on these offerings.

On the same evening, a general entertainment commences in the house of the young husband, which lasts three, seven, and even fourteen days. Friends, acquaintances, strangers—all are welcome, and may eat and drink as long as they will. There is, of course, neither wine nor beer, and even smoking is not allowed with the sect of the " Abadites," to which we belong —but that does not prevent people from being very merry and jolly. There are plenty of good things to

12

eat, and almond milk, lemonade, &c.; songs are sung, warlike dances are performed, and stories are listened to. Eunuchs perfume the rooms with ud and sprinkle rose-water over the guests, out of silver dishes.

The ladies always remain together till midnight, but the gentlemen stop all night till they are called away to prayers in the morning.

Wedding tours are not known in the East. The young couple spend their honeymoon quietly at home the first week or fortnight, invisible to the outer world. After this time, the young wife receives visitors, and in the evenings her apartments are filled with her female friends, who have come to offer their congratulations.

CHAPTER XVIII.

AN ARAB LADY'S CALL.

I have repeatedly mentioned that we made many visits to, and received as many from, our friends and acquaintances. It may be interesting to the reader to learn a little more of such calls, and also about the etiquette observed and the conversation on such occasions.

If we wished to call upon any one, we had ourselves announced on the same day by well-dressed female slaves; we rarely ventured to go without having done so. In town our visits were made on foot, in the country we rode. The finest dresses are, of course, worn on such occasions, not only in honour of the friend to be visited, but also to exhibit our costumes and jewellery—just as it is done here!

An Arab lady is not permitted to show her face; at home it is generally, and walking abroad it is always, covered by a mask, which is not like those worn by Egyptian women, which are ugly, and render respiration difficult. Our masks are nicely made of black satin, trimmed with splendid lace of coloured silk, and of gold and silver thread. They are in two parts, the upper portion covering the forehead, the lower hiding the nose and part of the cheeks. The eyes, the tip

of the nose, mouth, neck, and half of the cheeks
remain free.   The mask is fastened with long chains,
twisted several times round the head, serving at the
same time to keep the head-dress in its place.

Generally, Mahometan ladies do not walk abroad
into the public streets during the day—they mostly
do so early in the morning or in the evening, after
sunset.   The streets in Zanzibar were not lit up at my
time ; we took lights with us to walk through the narrow, uneven, and dirty streets.   A great deal of luxury
was carried on with these lanterns, of which the larger
ones sometimes were more than two yards in circumference.   The prettiest were sometimes small fac-similes
of a Russian church, a big cupola in the centre and
four smaller ones at the corners.   The light in each
of these towers was reflected through glass windows,
white, red, green, yellow, or blue.   A lady of rank
always had two or three such lanterns carried before
her, and it required very strong slaves for that.
Common citizens use one lantern only.

Rainy days, though they occur rarely, hang heavily,
as they admit of no sociability out of the house, and
prevent all intercourse with the outer world.   Umbrellas, these indispensable companions in the North,
are not owned by every one in the East, nor is it easy
to get one borrowed for a walk.   The middle classes,
and sometimes the negroes, carry immense umbrellas
of Indian make, covered with yellow, green, or black
oil-skin.

Ladies of rank are accompanied by a large troop of
armed slaves, who look more martial however than
they really are.   These attendants are very expensive,

as their weapons, with the exception of musket and
revolver, are always very costly and richly inlaid with
gold and silver. But that did not prevent the rogues
from selling their arms for a mere trifle, or pawning
them at some usurer's (these nice fellows are generally
Hindoos or Banyans) for the mere sake of quenching
their thirst for once in "Pombe" (palm wine). In
such cases the mistress can do nothing but redeem
the weapons at a tenfold rate, or equip the rascal
anew, and let a well-deserved, severe chastisement be
administered to him at the same time. Nothing,
however, could break them of their equanimity in
disposing of their masters' property, which was
always a heavier item than the buying of the
slaves.

The vanguard was led by ten to twenty of these
armed fellows, two or three in a line carrying lanterns; the mistress, with an Arab companion, followed; and a number of well-dressed female slaves
closed the procession.

The slaves turned all people, high or low, passing
the street at the same time, out of the way; and to
let the procession pass, they were obliged to take
refuge in a by-street or in some open doorway. This
measure, however, could only be carried through by
members of the reigning family—other great ladies
were not so easily obeyed, and the lower classes rarely
disposed themselves with alacrity to clear the way.

It was a very pretty spectacle to see such a long
procession move on with lanterns; and although
Southern custom prescribes that perfect decorum be
observed in the public streets, it would be almost too

much to expect that such a merry party could proceed many yards in total silence—and there is a general rush to doors and windows to see it pass. If a sister or lady friend was met in the street, the processions joined and formed into a large one.

Having arrived at the place of destination, we were at once announced; after which, we followed the servants into the reception rooms, or, on moonlight nights, up to the clean paved roof.

The hostess is seated on her "Medde," a seat some six inches high above the ground, which is covered with rich cloth of gold, reclining against a "Tekje," a cushion put against the wall. It is not customary for her to rise and meet her visitors as courtesy requires in this country; she only rises to express her pleasure, or in honour of the rank and station of the calling lady.

Arab women are very reserved to strangers, whether of high or low station; but whenever they meet you as friends the difference in birth and rank disappears at once. It is true that Southern women are more easily inclined to be jealous, but they also love more intensely than the children of the cold North; there the heart is allowed to speak for itself, while here the cool, calculating mind rules alone—which no doubt is as well, considering the different mode of life.

The visitors kiss the hands of the hostess, her head, and the hem of her shawl (persons of equal rank only shake hands), and they then seat themselves. Only a lady of the same rank can sit down on the Medde—those of an inferior station in life have to sit at some distance.

The mask is retained; with the exception of the shoes no part of the dress is removed, not even the Schele. In walking, the wooden sandals are replaced by the richly-embroidered " Kosch," a kind of leather slipper with broad heel. The shoes are slipped off before entering the room, and this custom is followed from the sovereign down to the slave. It is the business of the attending slaves to place these shoes, which are all much alike, in such a way that the owner on leaving can at once step into them. Even in this there is a strict rule of etiquette maintained : the slippers of the lady highest in rank are placed in the centre, and all the others round in a circle.

Coffee is then handed round in little cups, and this is repeated whenever a new visitor appears; fruits and sweetmeats are served besides.

The hostess is not required to keep up the conversation, and certainly not such a formal one as in these parts, from mere politeness. People are perfectly natural, and talk about everything they can think of. There are no theatres or concerts, balls or circuses, that can be talked about; nor are there any bright remarks made on the state of the weather. The conversation turns mostly on personal affairs and on agricultural pursuits, for which every lady of rank has a taste. There is nothing to check or restrain good spirits, and jests are exchanged without anxious regard to dignity. It is one of the greatest blessings Southern people enjoy, that they are nearly always bright and merry. Why should they not be so, when their serene and bright sky at all times sets them so good an example? And how should they have fits of the blues when Nature grants them so bountifully all they need and can wish for?

During visiting hours the master of the house does not come into the rooms of his wife, daughter, or mother. The sovereign only, and his nearest male relations, are dispensed from this rule; but whenever a lady cousin of equal rank from Omán was present, even our brothers and nephews were not allowed to enter without being announced. The husband of a married sister, upon whom I call, remains in his reception room until I have departed. If the master of the house is compelled to talk about some matter of moment to one of his female relations, he has her called into another room. The same is done by ladies who wish to speak to their male relations, when these are engaged with their friends. This custom is rigorously observed even if a lady stays with her friend all day, say from half-past five a.m. to seven o'clock p.m.; and the gentlemen are frequently put to a great deal of inconvenience to avoid coming across strange ladies.

Still the Oriental bears the inevitable with incredible patience; for he has been reared in these views, and has lived no other life. The force of habit and its influence remains alike everywhere. I do not at all deny that many things in the East are exaggerated, and may appear superfluous. But are people in Europe quite free from such conventional tyranny and foolish customs? In one country the strictest reserve is observed in the intercourse between men and women; the most licentious liberty prevails in the other. There, a state of muffling up and wearing of masks in spite of the heat ; here, in the cold North, the fashion of low dresses, and so on. All these are extremes; both things are overdone, and the happy medium has not, as yet, been put into practice anywhere.

Amidst very lively conversation these calls generally last from three to four hours. At last the time has come to part. The slaves must be roused to get into order for the procession ; the lanterns are always kept lighted during the visit—a perfectly useless extravagance—but it is "swell" to do so.

Before separating, the hostess presents each visitor with a parting gift, however trifling, and the same compliments are exchanged as at the arrival. It always takes some time before the different processions form into proper order to return home ; but home must be reached by midnight, this being the hour for night prayers.

The Arab ladies possess another great advantage over their European sisters : they are never required to thank their hostess at parting for their entertainment, and make pretty, hypocritical speeches. It is bad enough to be compelled to go to a tiresome party, it is worse still to have to express thanks for it afterwards. I have often heard ladies in this part of the world highly complimenting their hostess on the great success of her delightful party, and immediately afterwards picking them both to pieces. What degrading hypocrisy ! Would it not bring us nearer to our Creator if everybody endeavoured to meet his neighbour in a kindly, yet a straightforward, spirit ? Why carry on such an eternal masquerade ?

CHAPTER XIX.

TWICE a day, by an old-established custom, all the male relations, the ministers and officials—in fact, all those who wish to see or speak to him—are allowed free access to the sovereign in the morning after breakfast and later in the day, after fourth prayer. The audience chamber (barze) was on the ground-floor, in a wing of the palace, built close to the sea-shore, and at high tide the water came right up to its walls; there was a magnificent view far out into the sea from its windows. It was a very large chamber, and yet not sufficiently so to contain, at times, all persons who appeared. The furniture was in the same plain style as in all Arab rooms, consisting only of some carpets, of tall looking-glasses, some clocks, and of a number of chairs ranged along the walls.

As no Arab of rank goes out by himself, there was always a crowd of some hundreds of followers outside the doors waiting for the return of their masters and friends. As many of them as could find a place sat down on the stone seats provided, the remainder stood about in the open court of the palace.

To us this was always a very interesting spectacle—
for the gentlemen appeared at the audiences in their
state-dresses, that is to say, with turbans, and in the
long overcoat (djocha) reaching down to the ankles,
with their scarves girt round.

At home the Arab covers his shaven head with a
white skull-cap, which is sometimes very handsomely
embroidered, but whenever he walks abroad he puts
on his turban (amame). It requires a great deal of
skill to twist it up, and takes some people more than
half an hour to arrange it properly. It must be taken
off very carefully, so that it may not collapse; but, as
a rule, it is built up afresh every time it is worn.
The cloth used for it is not expensive, and only costs
some five to eight dollars; much more costly, however, is the material for the scarves (mahsem), their
price varying from twenty to two hundred dollars
each; it is of silk richly interwoven with gold and
silver thread. A man of rank possesses a great many
scarves, and changes them as frequently as people in
this country change ties; old and devout men, who
no longer care for fashion, wear only mahsems of
plain white or black silk. The Arab's full dress is
not complete without his weapons, as I already
mentioned before. They are generally handed to him
by his wife or daughter, or by his son, when he is
about to leave the house.

Before entering the audience-chamber, the gentlemen slip off their shoes, and by the manner in which
this is done the different ranks can be easily distinguished. The common people, for instance, take
off their "watjes" some distance from the door;

those of rank and station just in front of it. This is not ordered by some "despotic" law, it is an established and voluntary action. The Arab is accustomed of old to pay respect to every station, and his sentiments to his sovereign and to his house are instinctively loyal.

As soon as the audience-chamber is full, the sultan opens the proceedings. During my father's life, the procession was formed in the following manner: A detachment of negro guards came first; then a number of young eunuchs headed by the chief eunuchs; behind these my father, followed by his sons, the youngest closing up the column. In front of the entrance to the barze the guards and eunuchs formed into double line, through which my father, with his sons, passed into the chamber. All rose to salute him, and the same order of procession was repeated when he retired from the assembly. If a man of rank wished to leave the room before the audience was over, my father used to walk with him a few steps, and the whole company rose. To Europeans this may appear peculiar, and the liberty allowed to every one to come in and go without being dismissed by the monarch, or until the latter had left himself, is to a certain extent quite in opposition to the usual ceremonious bearing of the Arab.

At the morning audiences coffee was rarely served, but this was always done at those of the evening, after which business began. Everybody had a right to come forward and prefer a request, or to bring in a complaint, and to ask for a decision in his case. Nearly all the proceedings were verbal ones—either to settle affairs or give judgments in writing is much disliked. Petty business was mostly referred to the ministers or to the kadis (judges), and even to the chief eunuchs. The audience continued for two to three hours; people who had not got their business settled within this time, or who had come in too late, were ordered by the chief eunuchs to let the arbitration stand over till next day.

From the age of fourteen to sixteen the princes are permitted to assist at the assembly; afterwards they are even obliged to. In the same way every notable is obliged to put in an appearance, to show his loyalty and respect to his sovereign, unless he be prevented by some urgent reason. If any such notable absent himself for several days running, the reason for his absence is at once inquired into at his house, and in case of sickness he may count upon a speedy visit from his master; not even the most contagious diseases, such as cholera or smallpox, will prove a hindrance— indeed, this will prevent no one from going near him, for all things are predestined and ordered by God. The nurses of the sick man, his wife, mother, or other females, of course leave the sick-room while other men are present.

Every Arab of standing has such a barze on the ground floor of his house, quite apart from the ladies' rooms, and there he generally lives and re- ceives his friends. In most cases, the floor is paved with black and white slabs of French marble, and to keep the chamber cool there are neither carpets nor mats in it.

The gentlemen have the same visiting hours as the

ladies, after seven o'clock in the evening. The Arab never goes out without a certain aim or object; he never dreams of taking the so-called constitutional walk, and if he sees a European pacing up and down on the roof of his house in the evening, he thinks he is saying his prayers in a fashion peculiar to Christians.

I need not add anything about the ceremonials or the conversation carried on at these gentlemen's calls; they are much the same as with the ladies, only there are more topics to be talked about, such as the affairs of town and country, the features of the last audience, the petitions and various lawsuits either pending or settled. To all these parties, and to the audiences especially, Europeans are freely admitted, and thus the patriarchal way of living with us, its advantages and disadvantages, are much better known in the North than anything connected with an Eastern woman's secluded life.

CHAPTER XX.

THE LONG FAST.

MOST people may have heard that the Mahometans have to fast some time every day for a whole month, until the sun has sunk below the horizon, but the Mahometan fasting is not like that of the Roman Catholics, which is very easy in comparison. Every Moslim fasts himself and makes his children do so after their twelfth year. My mother being very devout, I had to keep the month of the Rumdân (thus pronounced by us, and not as it is here generally, Ramadân) from the time when I was nine years old.

It is indeed no easy matter for a child of that age to eat and drink nothing whatever for fourteen hours and a half every day. Thirst being much more trying in the tropics than hunger, and having very little conception of religious duties at that age, I admit I more than once quenched my thirst secretly with water. When questioned by my mother, I ruefully confessed my sin, and was only forgiven after promising not to trespass again. The rules are so strict, that it is even considered wrong to swallow the saliva, and for the first few days I was in such a drooping state, that I was sent away to sleep, to get over the time.

The beginning of the fast is signalled at four o'clock in the morning by firing from the ship; from that very moment you cease eating, you put down the cup untouched that you were about to raise to your lips. After these shots no grown-up person in sound health touches either meat or drink; people sleep, however, a good deal during the day, to enable them to enjoy the pleasures of the table at night.

The sun sets at six o'clock; at half-past six, after prayers, the fast is broken. Beautiful fruit and cool water are taken as first refreshment, and then the whole family meets, and with every conceivable variety of delicacies makes up for lost time.

During the month of Rumdán, the Arab completely puts aside his ordinary simple habits, and devotes himself completely to sumptuous feasting.

On the whole, it is a very social time—hymns are sung throughout the evenings and nights, stories are told, while eating and drinking go on uninterruptedly. At midnight a gun gives the signal for those who have gone to sleep, to get up for the night meal (Suhur), which is taken between three and four in the morning, and even the little children who have been put to bed at ten o'clock, are roused to take part in it. The Suhur is generally served to all persons separately in their own rooms.

In this manner the whole month is passed. Fainting fits occur frequently at its commencement, and people grow visibly thin and slender—but gradually they get more accustomed to this mode of life, and they sleep less in the daytime than they did at first.

The fast is kept very strictly, and the head of the house keeps his slaves to it, especially those engaged in the household and the personal attendants. An exception is only made with slaves working on the plantations, who, having for the most part no religion at all, are at liberty to fast or not.

Children and all invalids are dispensed, of course, but the latter have to make up, after recovery, for the days missed, by an equal number of unbroken fastings in the course of the year. The same rule is valid for people travelling at this time.

The fasting season is not meant to be a mere probation to the outer man—it is intended to be a time of serious reflection to the devout Mahometan. He endeavours to discover his own deficiencies, and prays for forgiveness of his sins, in the same way as a good Christian spends Lent and the Holy Week. Even dangerous beasts are spared during this holy time, and every one endeavours to do as much good as he can. Thus the Rumdân is intended to be, as far as possible, a time of " Peace on earth, and goodwill towards men." Those who may at all other times lead a heedless life, are in this month's rigid service of their Lord brought nearer and raised to Him.

The traditional hospitality of the Arab never shows itself more than in this period, when it is considered a religious duty. All those who have a family or a household of their own, entertain as many strangers as they can find, often without inquiring their names. They request the warden of the mosque they habitually attend to send them a certain number of poor to their evening meals. The persons

13

invited are not necessarily poor people, they are often rich men of high rank, who, being strangers in the place, have no home of their own during this holy season, and the true and hospitable Arab is only too happy to supply this want. No one considers it derogatory to be entertained by a man poorer than himself, nor would he in that case think of offering to pay for the hospitality received. Selfishness cannot become a national sin where such principles prevail. Happy those nations where charity is practised as a sacred duty.

The Rumdân is in some respects like Christmas-time. A great many presents are distributed on the first day of the following month, Schewâl, which is one of the great feast days of the Mahometans. These presents consist but rarely of ladies' fancy work; in general they are articles purchased ready made. The best business is done by goldsmiths and jewellers—nearly all of these are Hindoos and Banyans, and they are without exception the most mendacious crew. They are, however, very clever workmen, and have succeeded in driving all the Arab goldsmiths out of the field. They have plenty to do before the feast; they get more orders than they can execute, but undertake them nevertheless. To insure our orders being executed in time, we had to send a couple of armed slaves to the workshop to watch our work being done, and to prevent other orders being finished first. These may seem rather strong measures, but we had no choice else. One of my sisters first suggested this expedient.

The presents most preferred consisted of arms. To

European ladies it may sound odd that a woman makes a present of weapons to her husband, her brother, her son, or her bridegroom. But it must be remembered that these are not ordinary arms, but perfect gems of workmanship, and Arabs do not mind paying fabulous sums for them—when they are intended as presents.

Many other things are bestowed besides jewels and arms, such as beautiful horses, white riding donkeys, and—it will shock the civilized European to hear it—even slaves!

The last week of the Rumdân is spent with great preparations in every household for this feast, and as the first day of Schewâl draws nearer, there is much bustling in getting the presents and everything else ready in time. The night of the twenty-seventh day is considered the most holy one, it being the "night of value," in which Mhamed received the Kurân from heaven. The prayers on this particular night are uttered with the full conviction of their being granted.

On the last day of the month, the twenty-ninth or thirtieth (our months have only twenty-nine or thirty days, and our year three hundred and fifty-five days), all try to be the first to discover the new moon. In our country only scholars are initiated into the use of the almanacs—but on this occasion its prognostications alone would not avail, as the new moon must be clearly seen before the fast can be said to be at an end—a discovery which is rarely retarded by clouds in our deep blue southern vault.

Opera and field-glasses are passed from hand to hand—friends and acquaintances from a long distance send to get the loan of one for a short time. Keen-eyed men are sent up to the roof of the fort (a remnant of the Portuguese dominion) and to the mastheads of our ships to signal the first approach of the silvery crook.

The greatest excitement always prevailed in our palace. Forgetting that a shot fired off on board the ships right in front of us could hardly have passed unnoticed some one cries out every now and then, "There's the signal," "Hark!" all of which of course are false alarms, till at last a crash shakes our building from roof to basement, and immediately on that follow cries of joy from every soul in the town, with the words, "Id mbarak" (a happy feast to you). People on distant plantations despatch mounted messengers into the town to learn and bring back the longed-for news, or they send slaves up into high trees to watch the horizon; but should any false alarm cause the fast to be broken before its lawful termination, then the shortcoming must be made up, which is a harder trial while it lasts than the whole month put together.

CHAPTER XXI.

THE LITTLE FESTIVAL.

As I have already said, the preparations for the celebration of this feast begin a week beforehand. A
large supply of bullocks, sheep, goats, gazelles, fowls,
and ducks, has been provided (veal is not used, and
pork forbidden to Mahometans), and the stalls are
barely large enough to hold all the beasts. The
eunuchs of rich people are very busy changing gold
pieces and guineas for silver dollars, to be distributed
during the festival among the poor, especially among
the numerous poor from Omân.

Immediately after the signal, announcing that the
celebration of the so-called "little festival" is to take
place on the morrow, a very picturesque and lively
spectacle is enacted in every Arab house. People,
whose usual demeanour is staid and dignified, rush
about hurriedly to offer congratulations to all their
dear ones, and in this high-water-mark state of
general brotherhood inveterate enemies are frequently
seen to shake hands. There is such hurrying and
scurrying, such talking in various languages, and
such quarrelling among the slaves, who have yet to
get through some work, all through the night, that it
is impossible to get any rest whatever.

The butchers (slaves) rush upon their bellowing and squeaking victims, and despatch them with the words, "In the name of the Lord, the merciful;" the throats of the animals are cut in a strictly ritual manner, the heads quickly severed from the body, and after being skinned the animals are sent into the kitchens at once to be prepared for the festive meal of the morrow. On such an evening our slaughtering yard was changed into a lake of blood; for this reason all the Banyans at Zanzibar, who are vegetarians, looked upon our feasts with much horror, and took care not to come near any such places at this time. I have already spoken of these Banyans as the principal traders and money-lenders in the town, and in the last capacity they are, beyond a doubt, the greatest cut-throats imaginable; they are bitterly hated on this account, and on occasions like these there is a splendid opportunity for their victims to take revenge upon them. Among the lower-class people it is a standing joke to entice the Banyans, who never allow any chance of business to slip out of their grasp, under pretence of some important order, into these blood-streaming yards, which is the greatest insult that can be offered to the star-worshippers, of whom it can be said, however, in spite of their low, moral standing, that they adhere religiously to their code in being strict vegetarians.

In some of the ladies' chambers the burning question of dress is still being gone into or revived before the morning. Every fair one desires to surpass the other. Three complete costumes are required for the three feast days, every item of which must be brand new. Incredible quantities of fresh roses, jessamine, orange-blossom, musk, amber, and all kinds of the finest Oriental perfumes and essences are used during this time. Many an Arab lady spends more than five hundred dollars on perfumery alone, and no nerves could stand these conglomerate strong scents if the doors and windows were not always kept open.

The henna is an important article of an Eastern lady's toilet, particularly on festive occasions; it is prepared from the leaves of a medium-sized tree, and serves to dye the feet of the women and children red. This henna, so indispensable to Eastern ladies, is used for two purposes—as a remedy for boils, prickly heat, itching, and the like, and as an ointment for the hands and feet. The leaves, resembling those of the myrtle, are not efficacious if used alone; they are dried, pulverized, and mixed with some lemon-juice and water. A stiff paste is made of this, which must be exposed to the sun for several hours, when used it is again softened with lemon juice.

The lady who is about to undergo the dying process is stretched out full length on her back, and is not allowed to stir. The paste is put on the sole of the feet, the toes included, about an inch thick—the upper part of the feet is never dyed; soft leaves are then applied as a covering, and the whole is tightly wrapped in linen. The same process is gone through with the palm of the hand and the fingers. To keep the application in its place, she must remain all night perfectly still without moving; for no other parts but those named must have the dye, and a smudge on the back of the hand or on the finger-joints is considered a great disfigurement.

All this time she is dreadfully teazed by the swarms of mosquitoes and flies, but she dare not move to drive them away. In the upper classes women slaves have to watch all night by their mistress, to keep these plagues off with fans until the paste can be removed in the morning. The same process must be gone through three nights running, to obtain the desired dark red tint; then it sticks for about four weeks, and resists all washing.

I remember reading once about a fashion that prevailed in France at one time, of employing only one particular hairdresser who was very clever, and that this man, in order to satisfy on festive occasions his numerous customers, had to begin his work on the previous day, and that the ladies were compelled to pass all night seated in their high-backed chairs without stirring, so as not to disarrange their fashionable head-dress. This story reminded me very much of my youth in the East, though the sufferings we had to undergo for vanity's sake were even worse.

Middle-aged ladies and little children are not subjected to this tormenting process; they only employ the henna as a cooling ointment, and wash their hands with a liquid solution thereof.

The festive day has at last arrived; as early as four o'clock all are in full dress. More time is spent over prayers, and more fervently this morning than usual. At half-past five some ladies may be met already hurrying along the gallery in all their magnificent finery, showing their new dresses and jewels to

particular friends. It would not do to postpone this
to a later hour, for the general splendour by and by
would preclude any close and individual inspection,
and swallow up the due share of admiration. The
scene is something like that in a European ball-room,
with the difference that quieter colours or white
dresses prevail there. I wonder what a European
belle would think of an Arab lady's "full dress,"
and whether she would care to exchange her gauzy
and delicately tinted ball costume for the following
combination: a loose red silk dress, richly embroidered with gold thread in different patterns,
elaborately trimmed with gold or silver lace, and
satin trousers of bright green. It sounds odd, I own,
but habit soon does away with a great many of
our scruples.. I was struck with something of the
same feeling, but from a perfectly opposite cause
when for the first time I saw people in Europe
dressed in sober grey and black. I was far from over-
joyed at having to adopt these dark shades myself,
and being told that they were conformable with good
taste and breeding.

The first gun is fired at six o'clock, to be followed
by the firing of a succession of shots in honour of
the Feast of the Faithful; if there are any foreign
men-of-war in port, they also fire a salute of twenty-
one guns. Every Arab shows his joy on such a day
by letting off as many fireworks as he can—a
stranger might almost fancy himself in a bombarded
city. Every ship in port runs up whatever flags she
has, as do our own men-of-war.

An hour later all the mosques are crowded to

excess—no Arab stays at home on this day—and those
who cannot find a place within say their prayers in
the open street. Mahometan worship is attended
with a great deal of bodily exertion; it prescribes
bowing down very low, and touching the ground with
the forehead repeatedly. To have to do this in a
dirty ill-paved street is decidedly unpleasant. The
faithful must not let their prayers be interrupted by
rain or thunderstorm, and on festive occasions, it is
specially ordained to say them either inside or close
to a mosque. Our father always went to the nearest
mosque on such days shortly before the hour for
prayers, followed by his numerous sons, and by a
very large retinue.

Meanwhile, there is a great deal of bustle in our
house to get everything ready for the entertainment
of the numerous people, who come to offer their congratulations on the return of the gentlemen from the
mosque. As soon as the conclusion of the worship
is made known by the guns, everybody is free to
enjoy the good cheer offered, for the fast only closes
when the prayers in the mosque are over.

We waited for our father's return in his apartments,
from where we could see the crowds of visitors arrive.
On his entering the room, we all rose to congratulate
him, and to kiss his hands. This kissing of hands
continues all day, only, however, between people of
high rank; the middle class kiss the head, or rather
the cloth on the head of those superior in station, and
common people kiss the feet.

The moment for the distribution of the presents
had now arrived. Accompanied by my sister Chole

and by Djohar, the chief of the upper eunuchs, both
of whom were not a little envied for this proof of
confidence, my father went into his treasury, which
contained a great variety of precious objects, such as
costly arms inlaid with precious stones, all kinds of
women's trinkets, from the plainest to the most expensive, rare materials for dresses, ordered expressly
from Persia, Turkey, or from China, ottar of roses
and other varieties of fine essences in large jars, from
which smaller bottles were filled, and any amount of
glittering gold pieces.

It was impossible to expect that our father should
know how much and what kinds of jewellery each of
his wives or daughters possessed, or what they desired
to have ; he generally inquired a few days beforehand
.to learn the wishes of each, but Chole would again
refresh his memory when he selected the gifts.

The sorting was done by the eunuchs in our father's
presence, the name of the recipient was attached to
each article, and handed over by the eunuchs. The
presents were of course inspected at once, and it
occurred frequently that they were returned to our
father with the request to change them for something
else, which was granted in most cases, as he was extremely good-natured. He was always very liberal,
but never received anything in return. It is a beautiful custom in Europe for children to offer presents to
their parents on their birthdays or at Christmas—
the head of an Eastern family does not fare so well.
Arab children never give a present to their father.

Hitherto, I have only spoken of the presents made
by my father to his family ; his obligations did not,

however, end there.   On this day everybody expected
something ; he had to remember all high African or
Asiatic chiefs who happened to be in Zanzibar at the
time, his officials, the soldiers and their officers, the
captains of his ships and the crews, the managers of
his forty-five estates, and last, but not least, all his
slaves, exceeding 8,000 in number. The various gifts
were, of course, suited to the rank of the receiver ;
the slaves, for instance, merely received materials for
dresses.   To all these many hundreds of poor may be
added, who sometimes came a fortnight afterwards
to claim a present ; on the whole, it was not a bad
time for the poor, who received rich donations from
all the wealthy people.

A similar and quite as comprehensive a distribution
of presents took place at Bet il Mtoni.   I often
wondered at the inexhaustible productiveness of the
treasure chamber to withstand such a drain, particularly on ready money, as was made upon it during
these three days, which proves, I think, that our
father was an excellent manager, and a clever business
man.

CHAPTER XXII.

THE GREAT FESTIVAL.

THE Mahometan celebrates only two great festivals in the course of the year, and to a Roman Catholic with his numerous saints' days this may seem very strange. Two months intervene between the little and the great feasts, called Id il hadj generally known in Turkey and in Europe by the name of the great Beiram feast.

It is a repetition of the one I have just described, with the difference only that it is celebrated in a still more beautiful and grander style, and is altogether of a more solemn order. It is the time of the great pilgrimage to Mekke,* which is the dearest wish of every one of the Faithful to undertake at least once during life. The devout Muslim cannot be deterred by the danger of cholera and other epidemics, which carry off many thousands of the pilgrims at times; countless crowds join every year to seek forgiveness of their sins in the holy city of the Prophet. These poor people have to travel on foot over long distances; and the manner in which they are conveyed in over-crowded ships is really dreadful. Still they go,

* The word is pronounced as written above, and not Mekka.

putting their trust in the Lord, in whose hands their life is. Truly, such faith, which knows not fear, and shuns no hardship to carry out this religious duty, may well hope for mercy.

This, the greatest feast of the Mahometans, falls on the tenth day of the twelfth month of the year, and lasts from three to seven days. Many hallow the same by a nine days' fast, beginning on the first day of the month, in the same way as is done by the devout pilgrims to Mekke.

Whoever can possibly afford it, procures a sheep, which is killed on the first holiday, and distributed among the poor. The law prescribes, that the sheep, intended for this purpose, be of the very best quality, and perfectly sound ; it must not have lost even a single tooth. It is, of course, next to impossible to procure so faultless a sheep, and we used to send slaves all over the island a fortnight and more before to obtain what we required, but if none were to be had near home, the slaves crossed over to the African continent, where there is a greater abundance. The owners knew that Arabs of high rank were ready to pay any price for really fine sheep, and made their charges according ; so that, added to the other expenses incurred in the purchase, each specimen represented a somewhat disproportionate value.

No part, however, of the immolated animal may be consumed by any of the family nor by the slaves— every particle must be given away to the poor.

To them, the great feast is the most important event of the whole year, as on this occasion one of the most commendable of all Mahometan customs is made manifest, viz., the self-taxation in favour of the poor.

With the exception of such half-cultured States as Turkey, Egypt, and Tunis, public funds and shares are things quite unknown in the true East; nobody understands the meaning of the word investment. All the property consists in plantations, houses, slaves, jewels, and ready money. Religious law exhorts every Mahometan to give to the poor a tithe of the yearly profit on his crops, the rental of his houses, or any other source of income. At the same time he must get all his property, consisting of precious stones and gold and silver, valued by experts, and relinquish the tenth part for the same purpose.

All this is done without any authorized civic supervision or control. Alone the voice of conscience prompts to the performance of this duty. This law of the Prophet is kept particularly sacred, and none but people of really bad character ever try to elude it. Moreover, this act of charity is never talked about or inquired into, but is carried out on the precept that the left hand shall not know what the right hand doeth.

This may account for the fact that such a great number of beggars, if I may say so, are quite an indispensable institution in every Mahometan state, and also for the reason of this self-taxation. But these poor people must not be compared with the poor in these parts, who have far better claims on our charity. For one-half of the Oriental beggars possess more perhaps than they want. Begging is their trade—it has become their second nature, and

they would never be fit for anything else. Their craft
is more often than not a heritage, and you may
happen to be accosted thus : "Why, don't you know
me ? I am the daughter (or the son, the sister-in-
law, &c.,) of So-and-so, to whom you always used to
give so much, when they were alive. Now I have
taken their place, and if you have any alms to give,
please be good enough to send them to such or such
a place."

Hundreds of such poor used to assemble for their
share of the alms we distributed in fulfilment of certain vows we made during the year. They gather
also under the windows of sick people, and alms given
in such cases are called "Satka." No Mahometan
will refuse the poor on such occasions, even if he has
to part with all he has. Whatever his motive may be
—real charity or the hope of being acceptable in the
eyes of God, I think it a beautiful custom.

Many of these beggars are covered with wounds
and sores—some go about minus some feature, and
otherwise horribly maimed and disfigured. They are
the victims of a very bad disease called Belas, which
attacks hands and feet first, and leaves these snow-
white ever after. Everybody flies from them, as the
taint is thought to be contagious. I cannot say
whether this is leprosy or not, but these unfortunates
always receive rich alms.

The giving away of presents does not, however,
stop with the feast itself. For those who may have
been ill or absent at the time do not forego their
right to their share of the alms. Weeks and months
may have passed away—the new feast may already

be close at hand—still they come and claim their overdue present.

There is no other religious holiday for the next nine or ten months—nothing to interrupt the even and regular course of life, unless it be by some such festivities already described or about to be described in the next chapter. Birthdays are not celebrated in our country.

CHAPTER XXIII.

AN OFFERING AT THE SPRING TSCHEMSCHEM.

WHEN I was about fifteen years old, I wore one day for the first time a red dress of silk brocade; and on the very next day some kind of inflammation spread over my whole body. Old and experienced people declared at once that I was bewitched, or that some jealous being had cast an evil eye on the pretty dress. I had, however, always been a great sceptic in this respect, and declined to part with my new dress, which, in spite of all warnings, I put on again. Perhaps the dye really contained some poisonous substance—or from some other unexplained reason—I was taken ill again, and had to stay in bed. The matter was now perfectly clear—I was not allowed to wear the dress any more; therefore, to settle the point, I gave it to a courageous citizen's wife, who believed no more in witchcraft than I did. Had I acted strictly in accordance with the prescribed precaution in such cases, I should have ordered a "spell" to be said over it, or had it burnt so as to completely destroy its evil effect.

The above may serve as a little sample of the kind of superstition that prevails in the East. I have spoken on this subject before, and some more details may follow now, connected with the rites of a certain oblation, also originating in superstition.

Some springs are believed to possess special miraculous powers—not their waters, but their presiding spirits. Such a spirit will do all it can for those who implicitly believe in and do honour to its power; it can cure the sick, restore lost people to their homes, arrange a good match for those who wish to marry, give childless parents their desire; it can soften angry parents, reconcile husband and wife and friends, restore lost property (such as gold, slaves, cattle, and so forth) to its owners, make poor people as rich as Crœsus; indeed there is no feat with which such a spirit is not credited.

The favourite spring in the island of Zanzibar is called Tschemschem; it is situated some miles out of the town. A visitor to this miraculous spot would gain the impression that its spirit must be easily contented, to judge from the poor quality of the gifts presented. Poor people spend only a small bit of cloth, two inches wide, left dangling about in the wind, or an eggshell. The spirit is also rather partial to all kinds of sweets (Halve), to perfumes, and incense; but to make quite sure of success, the tribute must be paid in blood.

Tschemschem is visited by many afflicted people, who have vowed to bring some such offering. There is, however, always a cautious proviso attached to these vows — the wish must be granted within a certain stipulated time, otherwise the spirit goes without his offering. If the spirit is not punctual to

time, the promise is cancelled, and there is an end of
it.   In the reverse case the promise is faithfully
kept, often by the relations of those who have died
before their vow was fulfilled.

When quite a child I was frequently taken to one
of these sacred springs, and we always had a very
pleasant time there.   But after I ceased to be called
" Kibibi," or little mistress, and had become " Bibi,"
or a real mistress, and when I was old enough to
observe and to think for myself, I only assisted
at one more oblation, which was, however, very
grand.

My sister Chadudj, now dead, had been seriously
ill for a long time, and her anxious attendants made
the vow that she should go to Tschemschem herself
to present an offering if she recovered life and health;
and when this came about she went to carry out the
promise made on her behalf.

Four weeks before the day appointed invitations
were issued to several of her favourite sisters, and
preparations on a large scale commenced at the same
time.   Ten invitations to balls in Europe, all received
at once, would not cause such anxiety and expense as
this single one to our impending pilgrimage.   It was
not a case of simply providing dresses for one's self or
daughters, but a whole regiment of slaves of both
sexes had to be equipped with dresses and jewellery
suitable to the wealth of their mistress, not to speak
of a great number of donkeys that the occasion would
require.   Artists and workmen were over head and
ears in work; and jewellers, who never keep any
stock, but make everything to order, had conse-

quently most to do, besides superintending the
polishing up of the gold and silver ornamented
harnesses and the weapons of the slaves. A pilgrimage of this sort is always something of a pageantry—
all the riding gear must look beautifully new and
resplendent ; no expense is spared, and many an
article of jewellery is paid tenfold its value on
account of the great demand.

As early as half-past five on the appointed day, I
rode to my sister's house to join her there; the crowd
was so great that I despaired ever getting there at
all. At last the signal was given to start, and we
had a long and brisk ride in the pleasant morning
breeze to the spring.

The spot, at other times so lonely and deserted,
had been changed for this day into the most wonderful fairy palace. For days the grand preparations
had been going on. The long grass was cut, carpets
spread under the big trees, mirrors nailed to their
trunks, and every possible comfort provided; a sumptuous meal had been prepared the day before.

Breakfast was taken soon after our arrival in the
shade of the magnificent trees. The picture of this
scene deeply impressed itself upon my memory; the
gorgeously-attired people, with their costly jewels,
gracefully reclining in front of the merrily bubbling
spring, and surrounded by the romantic rich vegetation of a tropical wood; truly it was a picture that no
painter's fancy even could devise — indeed, like the
enthralling descriptions of "The Arabian Nights."

Two hours later we prepared to make the offering,
the object of our excursion. The spirit of the spring

was to rejoice this day in the blood of a beautiful, choice bull, and in smaller tributes, such as sweetmeats and immense numbers of fresh eggs, dashed to pieces on the water's edge. Two flags were likewise dedicated—a red one, our insignia, and a white one—as a peace-offering.

Our camping place was only a short distance from the spring, and the whole company rose to assist at the ceremony. One of my sister's chamber-women advanced close to the water's edge to make a little speech. She spoke of the severe illness of her mistress, and how the vow had been made in the last extremity. She thanked the kind spirit for its assistance in restoring her mistress to health, who had now come in person to present the promised thank-offering.

The bull was brought forward and killed; the blood was carefully collected and sprinkled over the spring from all sides. Musk and ambergris were thrown upon burning charcoal in silver incense pans. The ceremony concluded with some prayers, which were said standing.

Besides the blood of the immolated animal the invisible spirit received the heart, liver, and a few other parts, which were strewed all round, cut up in small pieces. The remainder ought to have been distributed amongst the poor, for neither the person making the offering, nor any of her relations, are by custom allowed to partake of it. As the spring Tschemschem is, however, too far removed from town, and as there were no poor people to be found in its immediate neighbourhood, an understanding with the spirit had been come to when the vow was made, that, to overcome this difficulty, the immolated beast was to be eaten on the spot, and thus it formed part of our afternoon's repast.

When the company all sat round again to rest, one or the other of our party might be seen to disappear quietly for a while, but no notice was taken thereof, for we knew that the secret visit had been paid to the miraculous spring, and to the discreet and powerful spirit were confided many griefs and afflictions, physical and mental troubles, or, may be, the burden of an unrequited love; but for all of them its intercession was craved.

The hours up to four o'clock passed away in feasting, walking about, playing, resting, and praying. The horses and donkeys were then brought back to be saddled. It generally took above an hour before we were quite ready to start, as one of the bad habits of negroes consists in forgetting the most necessary things at the last moment.

On our return we stayed at Mnasimodja, or at Ngambo, for prayers, and after dusk we all re-entered the town to accompany my sister home. The magnificence and splendour of this feast formed the main topic of our conversation for many weeks after.

CHAPTER XXIV.

PEOPLE in the East grow up without paying any particular attention to their body or their health ; rarely, and then only in cases of severe sickness, nature is aided a little, but the remedies used for this purpose are, as a rule, more than useless.

The detestable practice of cupping plays a great part, and only the very smallest children are spared this torment. Letting blood is considered the universal remedy for all kinds of ailings—it is made use of alike in attacks of cholera and small-pox, or in any other case of suffering. It is also employed as a preventive remedy, for people in perfectly good health have themselves cupped once a year at least, as was the custom in Europe formerly.

In the upper ranks bleeding takes the place of cupping, but no particular precaution is ever observed in this practice. I once had a great fright in one of the dark passages at Bet il Mtoni, seeing one of my sisters being carried past quite motionless, and looking as if she were dead. My screams alarmed the whole house, and I would not be calm till they told me that she was not dead, as I had feared, but that she had only fainted after having been bled too profusely. She recovered very slowly from the critical state into which the careless treatment had thrown her.

I am not competent to judge whether such profuse issues are, from time to time, beneficial to the health in a hot climate; I fancy, however, that the manner in which they are practised must be extremely dangerous.

The kneading of limbs and joints produces a very pleasant effect. I have spoken of this as being done regularly every morning and evening, and of the great proficiency our slaves had acquired in it. In cases of ordinary indisposition, especially indigestion, it is much practised.

Emetics, prepared of the most nauseous herbs, are frequently taken. It is sometimes next to impossible to swallow these concoctions, the mere smell of which is sufficient to produce the desired effect.

In cases of severe illness the aid of God is alone invoked, and to this end sentences from the Kurân are considered the best cure. These passages are written by a person, generally admitted as devout, on a white plate, with a solution of saffron. This writing is dissolved with water (generally with rosewater), and the whole mixture must be swallowed by the invalid, like a dose of medicine, thrice a day, morning, noon, and night; but to do any good, not the smallest particle of this sacred liquid must be spilt. I myself had to take this remedy once for some time during a violent attack of fever.

In exceptional cases, and if the sick person was a special favourite of our father, a real medical man, or a sorcerer, was admitted to the bedside. My sister Chole once suffered severely from pains in the ear, which would not get better, in spite of all the quackeries employed. At last it was thought advisable to call in a Persian doctor (hakim), very famous at the time. I was quite a child then, and was permitted to stay in the room while he was consulted. Chole was wrapped up so completely in a schele that nothing of her whole body was visible but the ear. My father stood on the right, and my brother Chalid on the left of the couch on which she was seated, and my other brothers formed a circle round her, all of them fully armed. The doctor was conducted into the sick room by a number of eunuchs, while others were placed as guards at different parts of the house, to give the female residents the signal to retire on the approach of the Persian. The hakim, of course, was not allowed to speak to the sick, but his inquiries had to be addressed to my father or to my brothers, who also replied.

When I was down with typhoid fever, at a later period, and had been raving for some days, my aunt Asche, my father's sister, resolved at last to call in a European doctor, as none of our Arab or Suahely remedies would answer. My father's death having made me personally independent, the ceremonial just described was no longer needed. The doctor, who was well acquainted with Arab customs, insisted upon being allowed to feel my pulse, which demand was granted by my aunt after long consideration. A number of eunuchs had, however, been put in requisition, and I was completely covered by my schele, although quite unconscious of what was going on around me, and was only told afterwards by my aunt. But when the doctor required to see my tongue, Djohar, the chief of the eunuchs, aghast with horror, flatly refused this unheard-of demand, so that the doctor withdrew quite furious, without having pre-scribed anything.

Such panacea are, of course, only made use of in countries where the deepest ignorance prevails of the human frame, as well as of its functions, and the ailments to which it is subjected. The Arab is per-fectly ignorant of all these, and quite unable to dis-tinguish one case of sickness from another. He divides all inner complaints into two classes—pains in the stomach and pains in the head. No matter which be the internal organs affected, the disease goes always by the same name; and every complaint that affects the head, up to softening of the brain and sunstroke, is called headache. But as to the origin of all these, the Arab remains in utter darkness, and when all the home cures have been tried and have failed, a eunuch is perhaps sent to one of the consular doctors to ask for some medicament. A medical man who can, however, not see the sick person, and who obtains only the vaguest information about the disease itself, labours rather under a disadvantage. Consequently, the sufferer often gets a wrong medicine, or an innocu-ous one at the best.

No one knows what is meant by observing a certain diet. A person attacked with cholera, typhus, or small-pox is allowed to eat whatever he chooses, or what he can get. Nature is supposed to be proof against anything, and with the belief in predestination, the Muslim does not even guard against the danger of contagion ; people taken with small-pox, for instance, are never isolated. Needless to say, that with such rampant ignorance precautionary measures can never be effected, and that all attempts to confine cholera epidemics, or to set a strict watch over the great caravans of pilgrims, have so far failed.

I wish to say a few words more about some kinds of diseases. Small-pox, unfortunately, rules permanently in Zanzibar, and kills off many thousands. The person attacked is rubbed all over with an ointment of Djiso (curcumac), and placed in the sun ; in some cases the skin is saturated with cocoanut-milk, which is preferable to Djiso. The only other means to ease the invalid consists in removing him from his bed to a soft mat, or by placing him upon a large plantain leaf. Internal remedies are not given, and, above all, care is taken that no water comes near him.

Cases of consumption, especially of a rapid nature, are frequent, but they are taken no notice of, nor is any treatment of the disease known. Yet, of all, it is the most feared ; it is thought to be contagious, and not unjustly so, as many European physicians assert. Any one suffering from consumption is almost an outcast; nobody likes to occupy the seat just left by such an one, or touch his hand, much less drink out of the same cup with a consumptive person. One of my stepmothers, a young and very beautiful woman, was very ill with consumption, but to the last she was able to leave her bed and visit her friends. Though still quite a child, I could plainly perceive how unwelcome she was to all. I felt very sorry for her, and used secretly to go and be of some use to her when she could leave her couch no more : she had only one little boy, and no daughter to tend her.

Many of my dear relations have succumbed to this malignant disease, and the majority of them at an early age. The property left by consumptive people is treated with the greatest precaution ; their dresses and bedding are carefully washed in the sea, gold and silver objects even are put through a process of firing to guard against contagion.

Hooping cough is as frequent with us as it is in this country. The children are given large quantities of "dew-water" to drink, which is collected in the morning from the giant leaves of the plantain. A remedy, founded on superstitious belief, is likewise used. A number of round pieces, of the size of a shilling, are cut from the dried skin of a kind of pumpkin, called hawashi, and these pieces are suspended round the child's neck.

Sores and boils are very common and very painful. They are covered up with the skin of onion and with dough.

The simple home remedies are all tried in turns, but medical aid and treatment—never, in the absence of which it can hardly be a matter of surprise that people trust in the miraculous instead, and address themselves for help to fortune-tellers. These Basarin, as they are called, are consequently in great request, and do a thriving business. We generally consulted, in cases of sickness, an old, one-eyed woman from Hadramot, who was a "Schihrie." Her magic implements consisted in a dirty bag, containing a variety of things, such as small shells, sea-pebbles, bleached bones, quantities of broken bits of glass and china, rusty old nails, bent copper and silver coins, and so forth. When she was wanted to answer a question, she prayed first for aid from above for a revelation of the truth, after which, she opened her bag, mixed its contents well, and then emptied them out. Her answer was always regulated by the position of the articles she had thrown out of her bag, and then she stated whether the sick person would get better or not, &c. Chance appeared to favour this Basara a great deal more than any of the other fortune-tellers; frequently her predictions proved true, and she made a good thing out of it, for in these cases she was rewarded by large presents, quite out of proportion with the small preliminary fee.

External hurts are of course cured more easily than inner diseases. To stop bleeding tinder is generally used; though broken bones are cases of a more dangerous nature. I broke a forearm once, falling downstairs; my aunt and my brother Bargasch at once bandaged the broken limb, but unfortunately they did not understand setting the bone properly, so I have a somewhat crooked arm in consequence to this day.

I have not yet touched upon a very important subject —the devil! It is well known that in the East nearly everybody believes in the devil, and that he prefers taking up his residence with human beings. I do not remember a single child with us, that had not been possessed of the devil once, at least. A new-born

child, that is more restless and more inclined to cry
than is usual, must surely be possessed, and the
exorcising of the evil spirit is at once set on foot.
Little onions and bits of garlic are strung like pearls
and suspended from arms and neck. The remedy is a
very simple one, and not quite so foolish as it looks,
for if the poor devil has any olfactory nerves, he could
hardly withstand such an attack upon them.

Grown-up people are also frequently possessed—
men but rarely, but many women, and of the Abyssinian women, nearly one-half. Convulsive attacks,
want of appetite, and general apathy, the desire to
remain shut up in dark rooms, and such propensities,
are taken as sure signs. A person, thought to be
possessed, is treated with a tremendous amount of
respect, or rather—fear!

A special examination takes place to find out whether
a person be really possessed. For this ceremony a
party is invited, of which all the guests must be
acknowledged habitations of the evil one. These
pitiable victims form a kind of secret society, in which
they keep their movements quite dark.

The newly attacked woman sits down in a dark room,
wrapped so completely in her schele, that she cannot
be touched by the slightest ray of light. She is then,
in the true sense of the word, smoked out, a vase containing strong incense being held close to her nostrils.
The company round her begin to sing a strange song,
wagging their heads all the time to and fro. Some
Abyssinian concoction, composed of corn and dates,
which tastes rather pleasant, is a beverage necessary
for the occasion. I have been told that all these com-

bined influences put the victim into a state of second
sight; she first talks incoherently, until at last she
raves with foam at the mouth. Then is the time that
the spirit has taken possession of her. The company
present enter into conversation with this spirit, and
request to be informed what it wants; for it must be
understood that the sick are not plagued by evil spirits
alone—there are also good spirits, that may have
taken a special fancy to a person, wishing to protect
her in life. Sometimes it occurs that two spirits, a
good and a bad one, contest for the same person, and
during this exorcism they are sure to manifest themselves. It is said that frightful scenes sometimes
ensue on such occasions, which none but the very
bravest can face out.

Frequently an expert woman will drive out an evil
spirit; with a good one a kind of agreement is made,
allowing it to pay visits to its victim at times, when it
would be well received, on condition that it predicts
what may befall the possessed one, as well as her
relations.

Possessed people are in the habit of drinking the
blood of immolated animals, such as fowls and goats;
they devour eggs and meat raw. Of course the poor
people who have undergone such an examination
suffer from its effects for many a day afterwards.

In these cases I was also able to observe how fast a
bad example is followed by others. In spite of the
superstitious views of all Mahometans, the Oman
people are far from believing in all the nonsense I
have just described. When they come to Africa, they
look upon everything at first as only fit for negroes,

and would wish to return home at once. After a short stay, however, they are more susceptible and credulous than all the rest put together.

But enough of this melancholy subject !

In conclusion, I should like to ask if it would not be more humane to import female physicians into Zanzibar instead of those horribly demoralizing spirituous liquors? Must corruption always precede civilization? There is a great opening here for Christian charity, that would bear fruit hundredfold, without any great obstacles in the way. For my part I am perfectly willing, in case a society undertake to send out a qualified person, to instruct the same in Arabic and Suahely ; this is the least service I can do my dear native home. But it must be a female physician ; she will be able to do more good in the East than ten medical men combined. A kind woman with pleasing manners would be received with open arms by all Eastern ladies. She would not only find herself well rewarded, but soon acknowledge herself that she is doing a good and charitable deed.

CHAPTER XXV.

THIS chapter treats of one of the most conflicting subjects of the day. I am perfectly aware that I shall not make any friends by the opinions I hold, but nevertheless consider it my duty to state them frankly. I have met everywhere with a great deal of ignorance in regard to this question, and even those people who are more intimately acquainted with it frequently overlook the fact that it is not called into existence solely and purely by the humane efforts on the part of Europeans, but that political interests are often a secret incentive.

I was still a child at the expiration of the term after which, as convened between my father and Great Britain, the slaves of all British subjects in Zanzibar, the Hindoos and Banyans, were to be set free. These were hard times for the owners, who complained bitterly; many of the upper classes sent their wives and daughters to entreat our intercession, which, of course, was utterly outside our power. Some of them had a hundred or more slaves on their estates; all these received their liberty on one day, which caused the ruin of their owners. The latter could procure no men to work their plantations, and consequently they could get no revenues from them ; besides which, our beautiful island had the questionable good fortune of suddenly finding itself saddled with a few thousand idlers, vagabonds, and thieves. These great children thus set free enjoyed their liberty as a release from their bondage, and its inflicted duties, but what was their physical condition in life on waking from their short dream of happiness ? They found themselves for the first time in their lives thrown upon their own resources, homeless, and utterly without means of maintenance. The apostles of the anti-slavery unions, after fighting hysterically for the liberty and rights of citizenship for the slave classes, disappeared on having gained their point, making no more provision for their *proteges* than if they had been lilies of the field, except in so far—and probably to complete the grim farce—that their ladies at home sent woollen socks for the lilies on the burning soil of Africa. Everybody who has lived in the United States, Brazil, or any country where there are negroes, will corroborate the fact that, apart from many good qualities, the black race cannot be induced to work, but only forced.

As I said, only British subjects were henceforth forbidden to keep slaves. The English could not interfere with the laws and customs of our country, and slavery exists to this day in Zanzibar as well as in all Mahometan States of the East. One must, however, be careful not to judge slavery in the East by the same standard that is applied to slavery in the United States or in the Brazils. The slave of a Muslim is in quite a different and far superior position.

The worst features of this institution are the slave trade and the transport of these poor people from the interior of the continent to the coast. Great numbers perish of fatigue and of hunger and thirst, but all this is shared also by their leader. It is absurd to suppose that the slave traders cause these great hardships and privations on purpose; their own advantage requires to bring out the people in the best possible condition, as they have often invested their whole fortune in such an enterprize.

Once arrived, the slaves are for the most part well cared for. They have of course to work for their masters without wages, but they have no care themselves, and their welfare is always studiously looked after. Is every non-Christian of necessity a creature without a heart?

The negro, above all, is fond of his ease—works only when he is compelled to, and then requires the strictest control even for the little work he is required to do in our parts. Neither are they an easy family to rear and keep, for there are a great many thieves, drunkards, deserters, and incendiaries among them. What is to be done with these? To overlook their sins would be to encourage them in their practice. Imprisonment they would not resent, but on the contrary, court it, and revel in their cool retreat, eating, drinking, and dreaming their time away.

Under these circumstances there is only one expedient—corporal punishment. A great outcry is raised about this in Europe, especially by those who are more richly possessed of well-sounding theories than of practical knowledge and insight.

Cruelty and despotism is justly condemned everywhere, may its victim be a poor negro or a civilized
person languishing in a Siberian mine. But all
things must be fairly considered, nor is every institution alike justifiable or applicable. With Eastern
nations slavery is a very ancient institution. I
doubt if it could ever be completely abolished, and
in any case it is folly to attempt sweeping away old
customs in a bluster of enthusiasm. Every good
thing must take its time, and be confronted with good
examples. There are a good many Europeans in the
East who keep slaves themselves, and who buy them
if they find it in their interest to do so. Such things
are, of course, not reported home, or they are excused
on the plea that they have been done "in the interests of science." Science must serve as a pretence
to many an evil. The morality, however, remains
the same, whether the Arab puts his slaves to field
or domestic work, or whether they be employed as
carriers and porters by Europeans, the latter being
much harder and more trying work. Nor are these
European slave-keepers always humane enough to
set the slaves they have bought free when they require
them no longer, as the Arabs often do; they simply
resell them. The Mahometan population of Zanzibar
were greatly incensed on one occasion against an
Englishman who, before returning to Europe, secretly
sold his woman-slave to an Arab official.

With one or two more such cases of inconsistency
on the part of Europeans that I could quote it is not
surprising if Arabs look on their civilized visitors
with an eye of suspicion, and wish back those happy

times when they had nothing to fear from their sub-
verting ideas. They have taken it into their heads that
the object of suppressing slavery was solely to work
the slow ruin of their nation, and ultimately of their God.

If people really think that slavery can be abolished
by degrees, and that other important changes can be
effected beyond that, then the greatest caution will
be necessary, and slow advancement step by step.
The negroes must first be trained to think and to
work, and their masters must be taught in an intuitive
manner, and in a form admitting of no doubt as to
its disinterested motives, that by employing good
agricultural implements and machinery they could
easily do without those hundreds of slaves which are
now required to cultivate their lands. The Arab must
be brought to understand that there is no intention
to ruin him, and that he is to be treated and weighed
in the same balance as the negro.

In my opinion it would have been more judicious
to adopt the slow and sure course, than ostentatiously
to build a church on the slave market, for which there
was no need, as two existed already, one Catholic and
the other Protestant, and both with very meagre con-
gregations. That this must have been offensive to
Eastern people will easily be understood by those
who know a little about things there. The Arab, like
all Eastern races, is conservative by nature, and
adheres with great tenacity to his traditions. He
must not be hurried into innovations which appear
to him impossible and incomprehensible. His objec-
tions are peremptorily put down to Mahometan fana-
ticism and religious intolerance. But the following

may show that this intolerance is by no means so great as it is described. When I revisited Zanzibar after a nineteen years' absence all came to meet me with the greatest friendliness—the people even left the mosques to welcome me and to wish me all blessings; and if my countrymen had really been the religious fanatics they are reported to be, I, as a renegade, would have deserved and roused their indignation much more than a born Christian. It is therefore not intolerance which governs them, but a sense of self-preservation, increased and intensified by the fact that their most vital interests and rights are encroached upon by reckless, high-handed innovators, and often by utterly worthless, inefficient representatives of civilization and Christianity.

The negro, however, is at present still very indifferent to religious matters, and certainly such is the case in Zanzibar with the greater part of the black race. Many become Christians merely from selfish motives. An English missionary who has worked for many years at Membase (Mombas, a little island to the north of Zanzibar) complained to me once that the number of his converts had always risen and fallen with the duration of the supplies he received from England. Hence ·I regret that, before familiarizing the negro with higher doctrines, his religious sense must first be awakened and nursed with an untiring care! For this reason many of those brave men may have failed after risking their strength, their health, and their lives even in the attempt to deepen the shallow level of the negro soul, and then to lift his race into culture and Christianity.

The objection might be raised against me that I am not a fair judge on the slave question; that, having grown up with Eastern views, I am unable now to release myself from them or weigh the matter calmly. In vindication of which I here produce as momentous evidence the views of some ultra-Europeans on this subject.

The African traveller, P. Reichard, wrote in 1881 from Gonda :

"In the night of the 12th of October, I was aroused by the shrieks of a woman who asked for admittance. I sent Askart to discover the reason of this noise, and was told she wanted to get into my place, having quarrelled with her husband, and smashed some object of value, that she might, by the custom of the country, become our slave. Three similar cases happened to a native Arab within a short time, who, however, obtained compensation, and it is by no means an uncommon occurrence for a free man, dissatisfied with his position, again to become a slave in this way. This is a clear and distinct proof of the exaggeration and one-sidedness of many of the reports on slavery, which depict their condition in dark, and I might say, non-existing, colours. . . .

"The position of a slave once settled down, is by no means worse, at least as good, and frequently much better, than in his own country. The tribes south of the Tanganika, for instance, are governed by very cruel sultans, and slaves coming from that place to this would on no account go back again.

"The slave of the Arab is not at all overburdened

with work, and criminals alone are condemned to corporal punishment; greater severity than that which exists would necessitate many more overseers, and an enormous additional expense. Moreover, the slaves of Arabs are generally set free after having served faithfully ten to fifteen years.

"Slaves owned by natives are considered as members of the family, and enjoy their own free will. They are not punished even when they show their masters open defiance—as, for instance, going down to the sea-shore and hiring themselves out as pagasi (porters)."

An Englishman, Mr. Joseph Thompson, says in his book, "Expedition to the Lakes of Central Africa":

"All classes of society show a cheerfulness and happiness, which would appear uncommon everywhere, but this is an ideal land, where four shillings and sixpence suffice all day to live in plenty. Half-starved or ill-treated slaves are nowhere to be seen; for as soon as any cases of barbarous treatment come to the knowledge of the sultan (of Zanzibar) the sufferers are at once set free, and protected against the cruelty of their masters. It would seem, indeed, as if this class here is in a particularly comfortable position, and enjoys ten times more liberty than thousands of our clerks and shop girls."

Another Englishman, who had lived long in the East, and who knew the state of things there well, once expressed himself to me in a shorter and more drastic term; he simply called the anti-slavery movement, with its countless meetings, " bosh."

In conclusion, I should like to call attention to one more fact. Gordon, who at one time was one of the greatest adversaries to slavery and the slave trade, began his second short government of the Soudan by abolishing his former laws. He may not have been convinced of the necessity of slavery in Africa, but he may have been sensible of the necessity not to suppress at one stroke an institution so deeply rooted, but to gradually mitigate its effects before abolishing it completely.

CHAPTER XXVI.

SINCE my father's death I had lived with my mother and Chole at Bet il Tani, happy in their friendship and love, for about three years, when suddenly a fearful cholera epidemic spread over the town and the whole island, and snatched away many people in our house.   It was during the hottest season, and finding it impossible to get any rest in bed, I had one night got a soft mat spread out on the floor to lie down upon, but was not a little shocked, upon waking in the morning, to find my dearly beloved mother writhing with pain at my feet.   To my anxious questions she replied that she had been there half the night already, and that feeling herself attacked by cholera, she wished to die near me at least, if it was so decreed. I was well-nigh distracted at seeing my dear mother suffer from the malignant disease without being able to help her.   For two days longer she withstood its attacks, then she was taken from me for ever.

My grief was boundless, and without heeding the warnings of my friends, who were afraid I might catch the disease, I clung frantically to the dear body. My only desire was to leave this world together with my mother, but God willed that I should be spared, and to His will I at last found strength to resign myself.

I was now barely fifteen years old, an orphan, a ship without a rudder tossing in the sea. My mother's prudence and good sense had always guided me, and now I was all of a sudden to take upon myself the duties of a grown-up person, and the responsibilities, not only of myself, but also of the welfare of my servants. When I came to a clear understanding of my position, God helped me to do my duty and to manage my affairs without the assistance of others. Nevertheless, trials did come, and I succumbed to them, for, without knowing myself how it had been brought about, I found myself drawn suddenly into a conspiracy against my noble brother Madjid!

It was just as if my father's death had been the signal for general discord amongst us, instead of uniting us more, as it ought to have done. It certainly may be difficult to maintain perfect concord and unanimity amongst thirty-six brothers and sisters, and thus we divided into groups of threes and fours, according as affection drew us together. Our position was quite incomprehensible to strangers, and even our friends became, quite against their wills, involved in our feuds. A loyal friend of my brother's, or a true friend of my sister's, must needs become my most bitter enemy—unless these belonged to my special circle—whatever their personal feelings toward myself might be. Such utter disunion could of course only end in disaster. Still, with hot passion we pursued each other blindly, and hated without a cause.

We soon ceased to have any personal intercourse with our belongings, but instead kept numerous spies, who took care to widen the gulf by informing us secretly of every word said, and every project made by our adversaries. These worthy persons always made their appearance at night to receive their reward, which varied according to the gravity of the news they had to report. Gold coins had never slipped so fast through our fingers before; frequently we did not even count them, but took a handful of gold from our kis (pocket) in acknowledgment of some daring and successful deed. Sometimes we were roused at night by a muffled person demanding to be admitted by the gate-keeper—and such nightly visits not only lightened our purses considerably, but often kept us from going to sleep again if the messenger had communicated some particularly perturbing news. Indeed, we seemed to be, one and all of us, labouring under some sudden attack of madness, and no pains were spared when we could annoy or thwart an antagonist. If one seemed inclined to buy a fine horse, a house, or an estate, his opponents promptly out-bid him four and six times beyond the value, to the great satisfaction of the owners. If one sister appeared with a new article of jewellery, the jeweller was sure to receive orders from all sides for one just like it, or a still more beautiful one. The people soon found this out, and merchants and workmen rapidly learnt how to turn our discord to their advantage.

Madjid and Chole had been on very good terms up to this time, at which I was delighted, for I was very fond of both; after my mother's death they had

treated me like a child of their own. But the good
relations between them began gradually to get cooler
on account of my brother Bargasch, and this ended
finally in a complete rupture. I was always strongly
attached to Chole, but in truth I am bound to state
that the fault was hers and not Madjid's. I cannot
here give an account of all the circumstances which
preceded this rupture, only that we were all, as it
were, completely blinded and maddened.

It was a period of great conflict for me. I lived in
one house with Chole; we took our meals together and
were hardly apart all day. Without any reason, she
commenced to avoid Madjid, and ended by wishing him
every possible evil. At first, I hoped to be able to
remain neutral, and I even ventured to take my
brother's part, whose only guilt was his being sultan
instead of Bargasch. But passion knows no justice,
and Chole continued to nurse her grudge.

I was thus placed for some months between two
fires—I wished to act for the best and could do
nothing—I hesitated to choose between the two persons equally dear to me; and when I could not longer
put off my decision, I sided with Chole, whom, though
in the wrong, I cherished most, and who by degrees
ruled me completely. Is there anything we can deny
those we fondly love. What avails our faint inner voice
—justice—when love cries aloud? For their sake we
abandon our views, our principles, our most sacred
convictions—as a tree loses its withered leaves in
autumn, without its sound trunk being able to help it.

Madjid, a thoroughly noble-minded man, possessed
the love of all his people. He was, however, of weak

health, unable to act always for himself, and for this
reason he had to leave a good deal to his ministers.
One of these, Slêmân bin Ali, unfortunately had the
knack of making himself indispensable to his master.
He was a crafty, selfish man, who gradually contrived
to get all the power into his hands, and to reduce the
other ministers to mere ciphers; he even carried his
presumption so far as to act the master whenever a
favourable opportunity presented itself.   And yet with
the dignity he arrogated, he was far from having
attained those years which every Arab holds in respect
and deference, or from possessing sufficient discretion
to disguise his dandyism and libertinism.   In his
unbounded ambition, he sued for the hand of one of
my stepmothers, a Circassian named Fatme, who was
old enough to be his mother; she was foolish enough
to accept him, but lived to regret this bitterly.
Slêmân's only object had of course been to get her
large fortune into his hands.

This evil spirit gained a great influence over Madjid,
and in secret he managed to incite all brothers and
sisters one against the other in order to increase his
own power.   He succeeded too well in his plots everywhere; quarrel upon quarrel took place in our family,
many notables were insulted and neglected, and things
grew gradually so bad that the people began to mur-
mur and complain aloud.

Fortunately, there was one brave and honest man
at least among the ministers, who did all he could to
weaken the effects of Slêmân's actions, and to redress
them.   This man was Mhamed bin Abd Allah il
Shaksi, a very rich and also a very generous and

noble-minded man, who would never have committed a mean or selfish deed himself. As a matter of course, he was by no means on good terms with his colleague.

My brother Bargasch next endeavoured to turn the discord between the brothers and sisters, and the discontent of part of the people, to his profit. Madjid had only one daughter and no son, Bargasch was therefore the next successor to the throne, and had generally been regarded as the heir-presumptive since my father's death. That two elder brothers, Turki and Mhammed, were still living in Omân, was not taken into account at all, for Omân was such a long way off!

In the East, the heirs-presumptive to a throne are always in a hurry to possess themselves of it—they endeavour to forget the fact that others may have a better title, and speedily overcome all scruples about justice and honour.

This was the case with Bargasch. He had failed in usurping the power at my father's death, but had never abandoned his plans. He began more seriously to think of carrying them into effect after having removed with his sister Meje from Bet il Mtoni to the town. They resided in a house opposite to the one in which Chole and myself lived, and which had once been used as a residence for the cavaliers of the Princess Schevade of Persia.

Now began a time of great excitement to all of us. I, as a sister, cannot well recount all that occurred, although there are certain acts which almost defy silence. But even the harshness with which he continues to treat me, cannot induce me to lift the veil, for

I still remember our Arab saying, that " all the sea is not deep enough to wash away blood-relationship."

Hardly had the brother and sister taken up their residence near us, when a great friendship sprang up between Bargasch and Chole, and the former soon began spending his days with us. Meje took this as a neglect shown to herself, and complaining about it to others, there came a soreness between the two sisters that prevented them looking at each other when they met. Things assumed a more and more uncomfortable aspect, till finally peace disappeared entirely from our houses. I rejoiced at not being concerned in this new quarrel, but being made the confidant of both angry sisters, I was soon drawn into it against my will.

Chole did not act rightly with regard to Meje— indeed she was not quite herself all this time. Bargasch was her idol, to whom she sacrificed everybody without hesitation, and I, to whom she was all in all, followed her lead in everything. Secretly, I felt a sincere pity for poor Meje, for, in spite of her pride, I could not help admiring her justice and common sense. She alone foresaw that no good would come of this party conspiracy against Madjid, and she never tired of warning us.

The friendship which my two nieces, Schembûa and Farschu, had for me was soon extended to Bargasch also. They lived just opposite our house, theirs being only separated by a narrow lane from that of Bargasch. Our three houses formed thus a dangerous centre for the conspiracy.

It became now Bargasch's main object to gain over
16

a number of notables and chiefs. The Arabs are
divided into numberless larger and smaller tribes,
each of which has a chief, who is implicitly obeyed.
It is of moment, therefore, to each prince to be on
good terms, either openly or in secret, with one or
more such chiefs, to make sure of their aid in
case of need. They are, of course, always promised
some prospective post of importance or some other
advantageous remuneration. No tribe will ever desert
its chief, for their attachment is proof against
every temptation. Those who can write never omit
to sign the name of their tribe; we, for instance,
belong to the "Lebu Saïdi," a small but brave tribe,
and I have always to append this in signing my name
in full.

Bargasch gained over several of these chiefs, and
by degrees they formed quite a small court round him,
which caused a good deal of stir in the island; and
by and by it transpired that the majority of his sup-
porters were people of bad repute, men known to be
turbulent and reckless, from whom he ought to have
kept aloof altogether, but who were about his person
night and day. And no wonder either—for what
upright, honest man could have joined his conspiracy.

As the number of these bad and doubtful characters
who gathered round him increased, and as soon as we
clearly realized the true bent of his plans, all those
withdrew from him who had more the interests of our
family at heart than his wild projects. Their places
were, however, soon filled again by a class of men
that seem ever ready to grow out of the ground with
the noble and self-imposed task of fighting the cause

of the oppressed—whilst at the same time dealing a blow at a long-cherished personal grievance. Dozens of these malcontents considered themselves already his future ministers or the happy possessors of other high appointments, or of fortunes that could in no otherwise have fallen to their lot, except by a baneful violation of the laws of merit. Characters of this sort arrived from all parts to join the conspirators, apparently with the desire to serve Bargasch, in reality to serve themselves. The most desperate were not only received, but hailed with joy!

After having gathered together a sufficiently large number of such partizans, the details of the projected rising were more minutely considered. The plan conceived was to seize Madjid unawares and to proclaim Bargasch Sultan. Preparations for open fight had to be made, meetings were held upon meetings, always presided over by Bargasch himself, to gain over one or the other chief. They always took place at night, sometimes towards morning, when the moon had gone down. A state of feverish excitement and deep mistrust towards everybody had taken hold of us all; we were always in fear of being observed or espied, and frequently did domestic duties ourselves, only to keep our servants out of earshot of our dark designs, and visiting was long since at an end.

Bargasch became more excited every day. Hitherto he had regularly attended, like the other princes, all the audiences presided over by Madjid; now, however, he began to neglect them, and to appear only once a week, until he finally remained away altogether. This with us is considered a sign of great discontent, and a subject keeping ostentatiously aloof lays himself open to punishment. There could be no longer any doubt now about his hostile projects, which many would not give credit to previously. His quick temper made him behave very imprudently, for he roused the suspicion of his adversaries, and in consequence the attempt at a sudden surprisal had to be abandoned.

In secret Madjid endeavoured once more to show me the error of my ways before it was too late. As he could not come to Bet il Tani himself under the circumstances, and as I had not been to his house for a long time, he sent one of my most favourite step-mothers to beg me in his name not to take part in the intrigues of his enemies, or to allow myself to be seduced by them; that I could never expect any thanks in that quarter, but would be sure to repent my adherence to the bad cause. I was also told that in that case I must take upon myself all the consequences of my actions, as he would be unable to make any exception on my behalf or to protect me if a bombardment of the house in our neighbourhood was to take place afterwards.

My noble brother's warning arrived too late. I had already plighted my word to Chole and to Bargasch, and considered it my sacred duty to keep and fulfil my promise. My stepmother left me in deep sorrow, weeping bitterly; she had meant well, and had at a later date the sad satisfaction of recalling to my memory the justice of Madjid's prediction. To escape the risk of being distrusted or called a mother of two faces* for any supposed double dealing, I thought it best

* A byword given in our country to false women.

to avoid all further intercourse with Madjid, and to devote myself entirely to the cause of the conspiracy.

It would have been easy for Madjid at this time to have had his badly-advised brother and his adherents arrested, now that there were so much stronger grounds for suspicion, and to imprison them all in some fortress until they had repented them of their ways. But it was not in his nature to be severe, and he could not be brought to take such a measure; he still hoped to see his brother turn back, seeing that no other reason for enmity existed between them, and fearing that a premature punishment might sever them for ever. Above all, he was desirous to spare us four women, mixed up in this affair, at all hazards.

Thus for a long time Madjid shut his eyes; but when whole crowds of men, muffled in their "Barnus" besieged the doors of Bargasch's house, the Government at last decided to have our houses watched. By this measure however little was gained, for the watchers were Bluches, soldiers enlisted in Beluchistan, who were greatly attached to our dynasty and would rather have run any risk themselves than compromise any of its members. This the wily plotters knew perfectly, and made their arrangements accordingly. We women undertook to carry out the more dangerous missions ourselves, without regard to existing custom. No one ventured to molest us, while others were followed and searched. At times one or the other imprudent person was arrested, but this did no great harm to our proceedings. We were all like so many busy ants, all working hard for the success of our enterprise. Our spies informed us that the

Government had at last decided to put an end to our
doings by either imprisoning all suspicious persons
or evicting them from the island. When this news
reached us our preparations were not yet completed,
so we redoubled our efforts. Quantities of hard cakes
were got ready and brought at night to Marseilles,
which was to be our head-quarters.

Although I was the youngest female member of the
conspiracy, they made me on account of my ability in
writing, the secretary, and as such had to do all the
correspondence with the chiefs. I was indeed old
enough already to have many pangs of remorse, and
the thought preyed heavily on my mind that the
ammunition and guns I was ordering were intended
to cause the death of many innocent people. But
what could I do now? Was I to break my word and
forsake my dear sister at the very moment when
danger became imminent? It was, indeed, not
sympathy with the cause that urged me on, but sheer
idolatry for Chole.

Bargasch, the son of an Abyssinian woman, is a man
of great talent, and he was much superior to us in
intelligence and foresight. Proud and imperious in
manner, he understood the art of impressing the
masses ; but the fact that of all our large family only
four female members, and one single brother, Abdil
Aziz, who was scarcely twelve years old at the time,
and moreover Chole's fosterchild, sided with him,
proves unmistakably how little he was generally liked.
Since he had caused our father to be buried in secret,
and without the customary ceremonies, he fell into
universal odium—so that when he began to organize

his conspiracy the true estimation in which he was held by his family came to the surface. I remember encountering upon one of my rare walks one night two of my sisters; they accompanied me to within five hundred paces of my house and then hurriedly retreated from fear of approaching the neighbourhood of his dwelling.

We worked on unremittingly in spite of the searching watch set over us, and even the meetings were continued under real difficulties. Already the day was fixed for the open rebellion, when suddenly Bargasch's house was surrounded by several hundred soldiers. The time had been chosen when he was sure to be indoors, with strict orders to cut off all communication until its occupants surrendered voluntarily. This change in the aspect of affairs was naturally a great blow, but we kept up our energies nevertheless.

Of course we expected the same fate to overtake us, and then indeed our cause would have been lost altogether. We afterwards learned that the ministers and the other members of the council had voted for the blockade of all the dangerous houses, but Madjid would not give his consent to this in his desire to spare us women.

A few minutes after the appearance of the soldiers we six conspirators stood at our windows, two in each house, to take council over the narrow street as to what should be done next. We were almost on the point of breaking down for good, but Bargasch would not listen to anything like submission.

But a very distressing fact now rose to our minds. Hardly any of the houses in Zanzibar have pumps, so that people collect their water from public wells. Bargasch's establishment had been provided, for precaution's sake, with a good supply some days before, but in the hot weather this water could not be used for drinking; at the best it would only do for washing and cooking purposes. Provisions were plenty, and the besieged had a sufficient stock to hold out for weeks; but water, the one thing most needed in the tropics, was wanting. Under such circumstances it would have been impossible to resist for more than two days at the utmost.

While the men were quite helpless, the inventive genius of a woman found a way out of this dilemma and saved them from sudden defeat. She proposed to make a canvas hose and to convey water through it to Bargasch's house. The canvas was obtained, a few dozen hands got the hose ready within half an hour, and at dusk the captives could be refreshed with a deliciously cool drink. We had, of course, to use great caution to escape our watch's observation; fortunately, guards were placed only at the one door leading to the seashore—and they perhaps willingly shut an eye.

Hitherto our partizanship, I mean the women's, had been of great use; but now it devolved solely upon us to carry out the doubtful sequel. It was only through us that Bargasch from his windows was able to remain in communication with his party. Several of the chiefs had been shut up with him, and were placed in a very unpleasant position. As they could not move about the house freely while my sister Meje stayed in it, they had to confine themselves to the assembly-room on the ground floor. The most influential and energetic chief of the Hurt tribe was however at liberty and able to go on enlisting soldiers.

Our whole plan had to be changed. It was decided to collect all our followers at Marseilles, the fine estate of my two nieces, and to fortify the place. It was not a bad idea, for Marseilles was already quite a little fortress and could easily shelter several hundred men. All the arms and the ammunition were carried there, the soldiers levied were quartered in its neighbourhood, whence they would exercise their instigations to rebellion over the entire island. As we strained every nerve the plan succeeded within a short time. Common funds for our operations we had none; we therefore drew upon our private purses, from which every one of us also furnished a number of well-armed slaves.

When everything had been secretly transported to Marseilles, we took council to wield our final stroke. This was nothing less than setting Bargasch free, to enable him, by restoring the head to the conspiracy, to conduct matters personally from Marseilles. We well knew that the undertaking was one fraught with danger, but fear was far from us: we were resolved to dare all risks.

Hitherto we had not attempted to pay a visit to our captive brothers and sister, for we had no wish to call any special attention to ourselves, which would have endangered our enterprise, and we were, moreover, afraid of being refused admittance by the guards, a humiliation we were not eager to experience. But nothing venture nothing win; all hesitation was now

set aside, and the evening was fixed upon to carry out
the abduction, as the only resource now left.

After dark one night Chole and myself left our
house, followed by a large and picked retinue, to be
joined by our nieces with theirs, who, as prearranged,
had left their home at the same time, and together we
proceeded to Bargasch's house. Upon arriving at the
door our advanced guard was stopped, but the soldiers
had no idea who was to follow; we could only succeed
by undaunted courage. "Chole," I said to my sister,
"we will go ourselves to the commanding officer and
tell him who we are—surely they will respect us!"

This proposal was in violation of all custom, but the
situation was too critical to allow of scruples; our
undertaking was altogether out of the common, so we
might as well try and forget troublesome points of
etiquette!

Chole and myself went up to the officers and in
impressive language made a thrilling appeal to their
manly feelings, which extraordinary and quite un-
precedented proceedings had the effect of making their
eyes stare wildly and their tongues speechless; but
when at last the meaning of our words began to filter
through to their brains they poured forth such humble
excuses and prayers for pardon, that, conscious as I
was of our guilty purpose, I almost betrayed my
shame. However, pluck once more came to our
rescue, and with countenances on which guileless
innocence of design was depicted we proceeded on our
dangerous way.

We reached our destination, and were allowed to
pay the prisoners a short visit, and having thus

effected so easy an entrance, we dared hope that our egress in company with our brother would be attended with equal success.

We found Bargasch and Mejc in a great state of excitement. They had witnessed the scene with the guard from above, and had begun to fear that we should be obliged to turn back after all, and leave them to their fate. But now Bargasch raised another difficulty; he steadfastly declined to disguise himself in a woman's dress. For aught we knew our visit had already been reported and instructions been applied for. In his own dress he would never have been permitted to quit the house; strict orders had been given to shoot down at once every suspicious person. We felt convinced that no one had dreamt of our undertaking such an audacious deed, for if so, other measures would most decidedly have been taken beforehand. We were literally standing on a volcano, that might open and swallow us up at any moment.

Armed to his teeth, Bargasch at last consented to be wrapped in a schele, which only left his eyes free and Abd il Aziz was disguised in the same way. We chose the tallest women of our retinue to walk by the side of Bargasch, to render his height less conspicuous; and before starting we each said a silent prayer, which for all we knew might be our last.

To escape suspicion we moved on in the usual deliberate gait, while our hearts were throbbing and well-nigh bursting with suppressed anxiety. Moreover, we chatted as we went, though we must have made superhuman efforts to conceal the trembling of our voices. But now we reached the outposts, when—oh!

rapture—the guard made way respectfully, and let us pass unmolested with our treasures. I need scarcely attempt a description of our relief after the horrible suspense we had endured, the breathless hovering between life and death when we approached the lion's jaws! That memorable night passed as all earthly things do—but its memory is ineffaceable.

We had written to inform several chiefs of our purpose, and they were to wait for us at a certain place outside the town with some of their followers. It was arranged that, unless we were there to keep our appointment at a given time, they were to consider our plan as aborted, and in that case they were to disperse and wait for further news. The meeting place was a long way off, hidden among trees.

We went through the inhabited part of the town at our ordinary pace, but once on the outskirts we took to our heels so as to be in time. We rushed over the fields like a hunted band, with our delicate feet in their gold and embroidered slippers, scrambled over hedges and ditches, on—on. Then our servants, who were ahead, cried out to us that we were making straight for a stubble field; but what cared we, so long as our obstacles were not human beings; but there was no fear of detection, having put our lamps out on leaving the town. Soon, however, we had to slacken our pace, for we were getting near the appointed place, and we women had of course to observe some amount of reserve. Then slight coughs were given as signals, and a voice was heard to ask under its breath: "Is it you, Highness?" and an answer being given in the affirmative, a general,

" Praised be the Lord," burst forth. We had reached our goal in safety.

Bargasch, who had been terribly agitated on the road, but had hardly uttered a word all the time, threw off his disguise, bid us a hurried farewell, and taking his little brother Abd il Aziz by the hand, at once disappeared in the darkness, as he had to reach Marseilles this very night.

For a time we stood perfectly exhausted and speechless, looking after the retreating figures ; but it had grown very late now, and we had to return home, which we did in silence, and not without some trepidation. We separated as we approached the town, and avoiding the principal streets, reached our homes, having first divided ourselves into small detachments.

But now in the quiet solitude of our chambers, the trials of the last few hours began to tell on us. It was, perhaps, not so much to the mental strain we felt ready to succumb ; but certainly the violent and altogether unusual exertions were too great for our pampered bodies to pass over in silence. We all lay down and groaned and wept for the remainder of that night. Some of us fainted from sheer exhaustion. Sleep that would have put our shattered nerves right came not ; so we could do nothing but live over again the horror of the last few hours, and repeating over and over again for our own consolation that our wildest hopes had been realized, and that our nearest and dearest were in perfect safety. Of course, the slightest sounds our ear detected, or those imagined by our fevered brain, during that endless night, our guilty consciences magnified into the tramp of horses and the clank of arms. Our distorted vision positively saw the approach of the enemy who had come to inflict the punishment for our deeds; and when those phantom shapes had vanished at last, our poor heads were once more distracted by fresh sounds proceeding from a new quarter.

We peeped from our windows and saw the guards passing quietly up and down outside the house in which Bargasch had been confined up till a few hours before. At dawn our servants summoned us to prayers as usual. Generally Chole and I said our prayers in separate rooms; to-day, however, not knowing what might be in store for us at any moment, we met in the same room for this purpose. Our fervent desire was that Bargasch might be safe at Marseilles by this time, about five o'clock in the morning.

But soon enough bad news came in. Already at seven o'clock, we heard that our enemies had received full information of all that had passed during the night. A Bluchi soldier had recognized Bargasch in spite of his disguise, but out of respect to our departed father, in whose service he had been for many years, he deferred giving the alarm, thinking that it was Bargasch's intention to fly the country after getting free, and seeing no reason for betraying us.

The market people, on reaching the town, reported having seen many Arabs hurry on to Marseilles, and a suspicion at once arose that this might be in connection with the conspiracy, though nothing certain was known. The Bluchi now considered it his duty to reveal what he knew of the case, and with that purpose apprised the Government. Upon examination, he announced in explanation of his delayed report, that he would rather have sacrificed his life than have compromised the women. I never heard what became of the generous fellow afterwards, whom our deed had thrown into such conflict with his conscience.

Nothing was now left for the Government to do but to put an end at once to open rebellion. Several thousand soldiers were despatched to Marseilles. We conspirators had counted upon success by means of a sudden surprise or by skirmishes; but the open field had not been contemplated. The bombardment of Marseilles soon reduced that beautiful palace to ruins, and after an obstinate resistance and the loss of several hundred innocent lives, the rebels fell into the hands of the superior force.

The reader will naturally ask, what was the lot of us women for the active part we had taken in the rebellion, and what kind of punishment was adjudged to us? None. We should certainly not have come off so well had the decision rested with any one but noble and generous Madjid—for indeed we had deserved a heavy penalty.

The news of the fight and its result had not reached us when we learned one morning that Bargasch, whom we still believed at Marseilles, had been totally defeated, and had returned a fugitive to his house. Meje was our informant. As for Bargasch, he remained concealed, and would not even come to the window. But still he scorned the idea of surrender, and declared his intention of holding out to the bitter end.

Beside himself and little Abd il Aziz, who had shown the greatest bravery notwithstanding his youth, a number of notables and many servants had arrived in groups, who completely filled the lower part of the house. With their assistance Bargasch yet hoped to carry out his plans, though he had failed with a far greater force. We also, in spite of the heavy loss we had sustained in property, in soldiers, and in slaves, and though we had sacrificed the friendship of our other brothers and sisters and relations, we had not yet come to our senses. In our blindness and obstinacy we would not believe in such a miserable failure.

The news of Bargasch's return spread all over the town the same night. It was generally believed that he had come back to surrender to his brother, and Madjid himself desired to make his submission easy for him. Instead of soldiers, he sent his nephew, Sûd bin Hilâl, this time with a message to the effect that he would readily grant his pardon for all that had occurred, if Bargasch would promise to give up all rebellious plans for the future. Sûd, a very gentle and kindhearted man, should deliver this message quite alone, in proof of his peaceful intentions.

At first Bargasch would not even allow his nephew, who was considerably older than himself, to enter his house, and requested him to deliver his message from the street; but Sûd positively declined to do this. After being kept a long time waiting, the gate was just opened sufficiently to allow him to pass in alone; after which he had to climb up the barricaded stairs. Preparations had everywhere been made to shoot down any one attempting to enter by force. The staircase could be closed at its upper landing by a massive trap-door, a contrivance which was only to be found in this house, and which dated from the times of our step-mother Schesade, and this door was covered with heavy boxes besides. In this rather humiliating manner Madjid's ambassador made his entrance; and the result of his mission was equally painful, for he had to leave without having succeeded, Bargasch refusing in the most decided way to yield and to surrender.

Madjid had now no alternative left but force. In conferring with the British Consul, the latter con-vinced him at last of the necessity of putting a stop to these dangerous tumults, and offered his assistance to that end. An English gunboat happened to be in port, and owing to her small draft of water she was considered more suitable to anchor opposite Bargasch's house, than our own larger men-of-war. The crew disembarked to blockade the house, and if this step still took no effect it was resolved to bombard the palace, and to shoot every soul in it.

I had one morning left my room, which looked out upon a narrow street, and from which there was no view of the sea, on my way to Chole to wish her good morning. I found her in great agitation, walking up and down her room, wringing her hands. "Oh, Salme, dearest, where have you been all this time?" she exclaimed, plaintively; and, showing me the English ship and the disembarked marines, she told me in broken sentences all that was happening.

On reminding her that it would never have come to this if she and Bargasch had only yielded in time, I was again answered with the old reproach, that I

17

showed too little ardour in their cause. But, in the name of heaven, I asked, what could I do more? Had I not compromised myself as much as they? Had I not staked my property without hesitation? Had I spared myself personally, whenever I could be of service to our party? All this appeared to be entirely forgotten now, when in the face of my cooled sense and justice, I could not longer lend any countenance to this irrational enterprise. But I think I could have borne the taunt from any one better than from her I loved with all my being.

The marines now began to fire upon Bargasch's house, at first with their muskets only. The balls entered the windows, and one passed close to Bargasch, and struck the wall behind him. When matters had become thus serious, he fled with Meje, Abd il Aziz, and the other occupants of the room, to the back of the house, to escape the bullets which were now sent flying about right and left.

When the first shot was fired, Chole broke into convulsive crying, abusing Madjid, the Government, and the English all at one time, for the cruel measures they were adopting. The whole household, too, broke out in panic as the firing increased, for our house being immediately behind Bargasch's palace, we were likewise exposed to great danger. Some rushed about wildly, taking a tender farewell from everybody, and asking forgiveness where they thought it was needed, whilst those who were more calm packed up their jewels ready to carry away in their flight; others again stood helplessly about, moaning and weeping, unable to collect their thoughts or come to a decision.

Many prayed where they stood—in the passages, on the stairs, in the courtyard, or on the roof, which had been boarded in by palisades. Their example was soon followed by others, and instead of the general agitation we were soothed by the consciousness that not men's but the Lord's will is done, and that our fate is in His hands always. By and by we, one and all, were bent low with our foreheads on the ground in token of humble submission.

All these hundreds of people, who, after getting over their first terrors, put their faith in the Lord, might have fled easily. There was nothing to prevent us seeking a refuge at Bet il Sahel, but not one thought of doing this.

Unable to face such imminent danger any longer, Chole at last persuaded our obstinate brother to give in and tender his submission. Contrary to all rules of etiquette, she ran herself to the British Consul to announce this, and to demand a cessation of hostilities. It may be asked, why she did not go to Madjid to settle with him direct? This question was put by a good many people in Zanzibar. They could not understand that Chole's and Bargasch's hatred of Madjid should be so great as to prevent them meeting on any consideration whatever. It must have been that they were too much ashamed of themselves; that they would rather humble themselves (for it was a great humiliation in the eyes of every true Arab) in asking the assistance and the mediation of a foreign Power. At that time the English did not possess the supremacy they have at present in East Africa; they had as little to do with the inner affairs of Zanzibar

as the Turks or the Germans. It is only since 1875
—thanks to their slave policy—that their power has
greatly increased, and that circumstances are tending
to the gradual decline and ruin of our people.

Chole did not find the English Consul at home;
but as the people from Bargasch's house called out
to the marines: "Aman, Aman" (Peace), they
stopped firing, and an end was put to further ruin.
If the gunboat had been in operation instead of the
marines, there would be in all probability another sovereign seated on the throne of Zanzibar to-day, and I
should never have come to Europe. But one thing is
quite certain, that we none of us would have got off
so well if in the place of noble Madjid any other
person had determined our fate.

To prevent the recurrence of such a rebellion, it
was decided to banish Bargasch to British India. This
was done upon the advice of the British Consul; the
English, perhaps, wished to get him, as the pre-
sumptive successor to Madjid, into their power to
train him for future plans of their own. We met
Bargasch and Meje once more that evening to bid our
departing brothers good-bye, for Abd il Aziz had
declared of his free will to share his brother's exile.
They were ordered to embark the next morning, and
were conveyed to Bombay in a British man-of-war.
Bargasch stayed there for about two years, and then
quietly returned to Zanzibar, succeeding, in 1870,
after Madjid's decease, to the throne he had so eagerly
coveted.

Thus ended our enterprise, which had been commenced with such sanguine hopes. It had cost us

dear enough, especially our nieces, whose great wealth, however, soon recovered the heavy losses. Many of our best slaves had fallen, and as many more wounded and invalided, reminding us continually of the mischief we had been the means of causing, though this was the smallest punishment we could expect to reap from the evil seed we had sown. But one great grief was still in store for us—the affection and regard of our brothers and sisters, of all our relations, that we had so wantonly forfeited, were lost to us for ever, and the sting in our remorse lay in that we felt their coldness to us to be in every way justified and the only attitude they could possibly assume.

Madjid alone did not change from the large-hearted, magnanimous brother he had always been. He was repeatedly advised not to let us go without punishment, it being notorious that without our active co-operation Bargasch must have surrendered long before the sacrifice of life had been resorted to as the last means of restoring order. He replied that all this was quite true, but that nevertheless it went against his principles to publicly humiliate any woman—a generosity which we were as far from deserving as he was from meriting the public opinion that his action was a sign of weakness on his part.

I cannot say that our life henceforth was a bed of roses in the town. Remaining friends we had very few indeed; whilst our foes thought fit to watch our every action. Even the crafty Banyans so far conformed to the general odium in which we were held, by keeping aloof from us, but only during the day, for at dusk their scruples seemed to have vanished, and they would creep in stealthily and press on us those wares which they had not been able to dispose of before. So, considering the scanty attractions the city could offer me for the present, I decided to withdraw for a time to one of my estates.

CHAPTER XXVII.

KISIMBANI AND BUBUBU.

A FEW days later I was hastening at sunrise, mounted on my little white donkey, to my plantation, Kisimbani. I intended to stay and take rest here for some time, until things had become a little more quiet and peaceable at home. Chole, Meje, and my two nieces soon followed my example, and retired likewise into the country.

Since my mother's death I had been but rarely, and then only for a day or two at a time, to my three plantations; and after all that had passed I now enjoyed the quiet and repose of country life all the more. My mother had always shown a preference for Kisimbani, and many things there reminded me of her, so I revisited all the spots where she had liked to walk and to rest. I was now going to take into my own hands the pleasures as well as the great drawbacks that rise in the path of unmarried Arabian ladies, our laws of seclusion precluding every possibility of applying for male assistance. Etiquette even forbids us to speak to those of our officials who are free men. Orders and accounts can only be given by,

and settled through, the medium of slaves. Very
few great ladies can write themselves, and fewer still
of single ladies have ever received a written account
of any sort from their overseers, such as European
landowners expect from their bailiffs once in the year.
A mistress is generally satisfied if they provide the
necessities of the household, and send in cash as
many thousand dollars after the sale of the crops
as they can. These sums are realized by the sale of
cloves and cocoanuts; but it is thought mean to
sell potatoes, yams, or any other vegetables raised
on the estates; and the overseer is allowed to dispose on his own account of all the surplus. These
people, who are mostly natives of Omân, soon acquire
sufficient wealth with which they can return to their
country and live and die in peace.

While I lived in town my overseer, Hassan, used to
come once a week or fortnight from Kisimbani to
hand in his report through my slaves and to ask for
orders; but now that I purposed staying at Kisimbani
for a time, honest Hassan was very much in my way.
The poor fellow himself was made very uncomfortable at having to escape to all sorts of places lest he
might even unintentionally happen to meet us. I
therefore transferred him to another estate which he
also managed, and replaced him by an Abyssinian
slave, called Murdjän (Coral), a superior man for his
station, who could also read and write. He was full
of energy, and well able to manage a few hundred
country slaves. The Abyssinians are very smart
people as a rule, and we purchased them in preference
to negroes.

I was now able to move and ride about as much as I liked, without fear of confronting poor Hassan bin Alys at every turn of the road. I spent many happy hours daily in looking after my domestic animals, and visiting the old people in their huts, with dainties from my table for their toothless gums. The little slave children—who are considered as a sort of property by their masters—were sent to me every day to be washed at the well with Rassel (the leaves of a tree which, dried and powdered, make a lather like soap), and then fed. They remained in some part of the courtyard for the remainder of the day under the care of a trustworthy female slave, until their parents returned in the afternoon from the fields to take them home. They were much better off this way than tied all day to their mothers' backs, exposed to the heat and glare of the sun.

This free and untrammelled country life was exquisite enjoyment to me, and I rejoiced at having thus escaped all the troubles of the town. The wives and daughters of the notables on the adjoining estate called upon me, so I soon had my house full of guests for weeks and months together.

Many strangers also came in to refresh and rest themselves after a long march, in the room set apart for men. This is a custom always practised with us, and the number of these guests was very considerable, as Kisimbani stood near two much frequented cross roads.

Two sisters and one nephew had estates adjoining mine. The last was Fessal, the orphan son of Hilâl, of whom I have already spoken as a very kind, but

greatly misjudged man. I was the first to know him
really well; he attached himself to me with quite a
childlike confidence, and came over to see me nearly
every day.

I was also in constant communication with the
town. Two sets of messengers started on alternate
mornings and returned with the news in the evening.
I was heartily glad to receive now only visits of a
harmless nature, after the tangled net I had been
drawn into in the capital.

The great excitement which had followed the
miserable failure of the conspiracy had at last given
way to a feeling of greater quiet, but the dissent
between the brothers and sisters continued unabated.
I was, therefore, in no hurry to return or even to pay
a short visit, though I could have easily ridden there
in two hours; but, instead, my friends came frequently
to see me.

My happiness would have been complete had I not
missed one thing—the sea—which until now I had
had before me all my life. My three plantations
were in the interior of the island, but as I had decided
to live in the country, and did not know at that time
what it was to have an unfulfilled wish, I made up
my mind to purchase a plantation at the seaside. To
my regret this was not an easy matter, as all estates
possessing this advantage were owned by people
who cared more for the situation than for their rental.
The "Dellal" (broker) who had, through my slaves,
received instructions to make inquiries, declared that
he would not rest until he had found such an estate,
but still he failed.

He had just arrived with this dismal news when a lady friend called, who mentioned to me that a cousin of hers had a small country seat close to the sea, and that residing, permanently in town, he had no use for it, and might possibly be induced to sell or at least let it to me.

People in Europe are generally under the impression that the whole country is the private property of the Sultan and of his family, and that the subjects are quite defenceless in protecting their property against them; indeed, that we have merely to take what we covet, without asking the owner's consent. But jurisdiction is not quite as primitive as all that with the Arabs, and private property there can no more be touched than anywhere else. The difficulties I had to contend with, notwithstanding the liberal offer I was prepared to make is, I think, a very good proof of my statement. I much regretted to learn during my last visit at Zanzibar, that a deteriorating change has recently taken place in this respect, for it appears that the property of the British Consul was a present made to him by the Sultan, who had deprived the former owner of it without awarding any compensation.

On the following morning we rode over to the estate, which was called Bububu, to have a look at it. The house was shut up, and it took some time before we could gain admittance. The grounds looked as if they had been allowed to take care of themselves of late; but the house was spacious and well-built. Outside, in a courtyard, were the kitchens and servants' lodgings. A little river, reminding me greatly of my

much-loved Mtoni, ran right through the court, and
this was worth a great deal in itself in a hot clime
like ours. The view from the upper story was perfectly charming, large and small palm trees rose on
either hand, and the front was built so close to the
shore, that its walls at times were washed by the
waves.

I decided at once to buy or to rent Bububu, and
sent my friend to her cousin next morning. She
informed that he could not make up his mind to
dispose of it, but that it would give him great pleasure
to offer it me for as long as I cared to reside in it.
This, however, I politely declined, and succeeded at
last in obtaining a lease at a certain annual rental.

About a week after signing the contract—for even
that formality is gone through in Zanzibar—I removed
to Bububu, where I once more delighted in the sight
of the sea that I had known from my earliest youth.
The only thing that saddened me was the parting
from my nephew Fessal; he took our separation
much to heart, as he had no companion beyond his
old stepmother.

I took all my domestic animals with me; they
seemed not a little surprised at finding themselves
suddenly in a new place, but evidently as satisfied
with the change as myself. For hours together I
would walk about here on the shore, watching the
many ships and fishing boats that glided past on their
way to the city.

I was now much nearer to the latter, and could reach
it both by sea and by land. Almost every day my
three brothers, Abd il Wehab, Handân, and Djemschid,

came out to see me, either on horseback or by boat. Many pleasant days and hours we spent together in this place, and in their company the time passed away very agreeably.

I saw much more society here than at Kisimbani. Not a single day passed without one or two, and frequently as many as ten, ladies coming to stay with me for some days. I always look back with pleasure and regret on this beautiful, unclouded period of my youth.

My stay at Bububu was not, however, to be of long duration. I was sweeping the sea one day with my glass, to see if any of my brothers were coming. A single boat soon came in sight, in which Abd il Wehab was alone this time, his looks betraying to me at once that he was the bearer of unwelcome news.

"What news do you bring, Abd il Wehab, my brother?" I asked, when he entered.

"I have been sent with a request to you to-day, sister Salme, which is far from pleasing to me," he replied. "Only guess from whom." At my pressing questions, he continued:

"You are aware that a new British Consul has lately arrived?"

"What do I care for him? Has he sent you, perhaps?"

"No!"

"Well, then, speak out and tell me all, without tormenting me any longer!"

"But won't you be angry with me, Salme?"

"No. no; but now out with it quick," I exclaimed.

"Well, I am commissioned by—Madjid, who entreats you, if you still have any love for him, to give up Bububu. The new British Consul sent yesterday to him to inquire if he could have Bububu as his country seat."

Madjid's request was a great blow to me. Any one else I should have refused point-blank, but could I again thwart Madjid, against whose government and life I had so wickedly conspired? I had so far made no attempt at meeting him, although I felt convinced that he had condoned the past and wiped it from his memory. Now that he, the injured and offended one, took the first step himself (this was his meaning, for otherwise he might easily have told the consul that Bububu was not his to dispose of), I thought I might repay a small portion of the debt I owed him, by granting his request; and I spoke to Abd il Wehab to this effect.

Madjid had sent me word that if I consented he would get Abd il Wehab to procure a proper town residence for me, as he was aware that I did not wish to return to Bet il Mtoni. But I had not yet made up my mind where to go, and I asked for time to consider his proposal.

I was, perhaps, for the first time in my life, really grieved at anything so material. But I had been so happy at Bububu, and could have had no desire for anything better. When Abd il Wehab left me after dinner, it was with the earnest request not to return to Kisimbani. Then I took a tearful leave of all my favourite spots.

I struggled long before making up my mind to

return once more into the turmoils of the capital, for it seemed as if I could not shake off certain gloomy presentiments.

Next morning I wrote to Abd il Wehab that I should be ready to leave Bububu in a week's time, and would then place it at Madjid's disposal, and as I had decided to return to Kisimbani I made all necessary arrangements for this purpose. But in the afternoon my three dear brothers appeared, crying out simultaneously: "Salme, we will hear no more of Kisimbani! If you care for us in the least, you must return to live in town!" And Djemschid jestingly continued: "If you are going to hide yourself on your plantation, we shall come at night and set it on fire!" At the same time they begged me in their mothers' names (who were Circassian women all three) to come back to town. For the last time we all spent the day together at pleasant Bububu, and then they left me and rejoiced at having prevailed on me to live in the town again.

CHAPTER XXVIII

MY LAST RESIDENCE IN ZANZIBAR.

I HAPPENED to be, a few days afterwards, one moonlight night, on the roof of my new town residence, procured for me by Abd il Wehab, talking to an old acquaintance, when Selim suddenly appeared to announce Chole.

"Oh, Salme, I never thought you were so bad as all that!" These were the first words she exclaimed on entering.

"Good evening, Chole; and what ill have I done to you?" I asked, quite taken by surprise, leading her to the seat of honour, the "Tekje."

"You really pretend you have done nothing to me? Is it nothing that you have given up Bububu to oblige Madjid and the godless Kafer?" (Englishman).

"But, my dear sister," I replied, a little hurt, "surely if I don't mind—and, besides, I explained the matter to you fully in my letter the other day."

"I suppose you wished to insinuate yourself again into the good graces of the damned?" (by whom she meant Madjid).

"No, you are altogether mistaken; it is no favour I want of any one, and that you know well enough yourself."

"Yes, I know that; but why did you grant his request?" she persisted, getting more and more excited. "And I understand it is he who induced you to live here instead of at Bet il Tani."

"No, it was not he who asked me to do so, but Abd il Wehab, Hamdân, and Djemschid wished me to live here," I said.

"Well, I see now that you have turned against us," she replied, rising and refusing the refreshments offered to her by the servant. "You may now choose between myself and Bargasch on the one side, and the slave of the Englishman on the other! Goodbye!" And without listening to another word she turned and went.

I have never seen Chole since that day, though I lived for some years longer in the same town with her, and it was only after my departure that she relented. I often asked myself in what way I could have offended her, but could think of no intentional offence on my part; my only object in giving up Bububu had been to relieve my own conscience of some of its load. And now this absurd reproach that I had been moved by motives of ultimate gain! But on the evening when Chole had vented her displeasure on me I remembered she was very much excited, and might have said more than she meant.

Up to this time I had seen neither Madjid nor Chadudj; and in order to avoid giving fresh grounds for Chole's suspicions, I resolved to keep out of their way altogether. But it was to be otherwise, for hardly had I been a fortnight in my new place when Madjid himself came, followed by a great retinue.

18

"Good morning, Salme," he cried; "you see I am
the first to come, though I am so much your senior,
to thank you for getting me out of that dilemma with
the Englishman."

"Oh, my brother, that was nothing, really nothing
worth speaking of," I stammered, for no one was
taken more by surprise by this visit than myself.
Nor did Madjid, in his kind and generous way, allude
to aught that had occurred, but tried to put me at
my ease at once by talking of all sorts of other
things.

"You will, I hope, come and see Chadudj one of
these days?"

"Yes, surely I will come," was the reply I naturally
gave.

"And our aunt Asche, who loves you so dearly,
now lives with us, and she will be so rejoiced to see
you again."

Madjid stayed about an hour, and we parted perfectly reconciled. The news of his visit spread all
over the town the same day, and it was of course also
reported to Chole.

Now that Madjid had been the first to come to me,
which I could never have looked for, the only course
left open to me, even if I had remained unforgiving in
my heart, was to return his call and also inquire for
Chadudj and my aunt Asche. I could not then fore-
see how dear this simple act of courtesy was to cost
me afterwards. This step is still considered the
greatest crime on my part. Such excess of jealousy
may appear incomprehensible, yet at the time it was
unfortunately but too well in keeping with the rest of

our family affairs, as I found out by and by. Indeed it had to be neck or nothing. Friendliness with both factions of our family was a thing utterly out of the question.

The two parties existed as before, and the intrigues continued unabated, only more secretly.

It is the nature of Eastern people to be very candid. They are unable to dissimulate in the masterly manner that answers so well here. An Oriental rarely conceals his aversion to a person who has affronted him by look, word, or deed; he at once betrays his feelings as a child would. Dissimulation, if such a thing could be practised with any degree of success by our quick-tempered Southerners, would be simply put down to cowardice. They reason thus : " Why should I show myself otherwise than I am ? Are not all my thoughts and feelings known to the Lord ? Why then should I try to dissemble in the face of men or be afraid of them ? "

The engagement and subsequent marriage of two of my sisters with two cousins happily caused a little diversion in our life; indeed, the continual quarrels and dissensions in our family were suspended for some months. As is frequently the case, these sisters married to two brothers, had drawn a very different lot. The unhappy one had children and the happy one had to go without, however much she might long for them. Our circle was further increased by a good many of our Omàn relations, who had come to our country on account of the precarious position of our brothers there, and for a time at least I could once more taste the pleasures of family life.

Above all, I shall never forget one of my friends. I may not mention her name or be more explicit here as to our relations or separation. All I can take on myself to state is that this true friend helped me to the last when I was about to leave my home under great perils. Being fully acquainted with all my domestic concerns, she could not fail to perceive what was going on; still she remained, until I was compelled to remove her by gentle force till half an hour before I left. "Highness," she said, in taking leave, may the Lord of the universe protect you! I am aware that I shall have to give up my life within twelve hours; but for your sake that is not too much!" Her parting words still ring in my ears, and I may well exclaim: A friend in need is a friend indeed!

If people wish to know what is really understood by perfect devotion and self-sacrificing friendship, they must go to the East. I do not mean to say that such friendship is not elsewhere to be met with; but certain it is that where an Arab once loves, his life is for evermore consecrated to the object of his heart.

Though the distinction of classes is nowhere more observable than in the East, it is not taken into account at all in a case of real friendship. A prince will be on the same friendly terms with the son of a poor stable-man, whom he is fond of, as with any of his more distinguished friends, and without making the least distinction between them; and a princess will treat the wives and daughters of a simple overseer as affectionately as the most exalted lady. My sister Meje, for instance, formed an intimate friendship with the daughter of an overseer. She invited her to her palace, and her attachment to the poor, shy, but highly-gifted girl remained a very close one until they were separated by death.

It is no rare occurrence either, that a lady of high rank makes a friend of one of her female slaves, not a negress of course, but some Abyssinian or Circassian; which ends in her being bought by her benefactress for five or six times her value, if purchase in her case be possible; her freedom being secured by a legal act for all times.

In case of imprisonment a friend will always spend several hours every day with the prisoner, and a banished person is everywhere accompanied by his friends. In misfortune and poverty the friends assist the luckless person with their fortune, nor is it ever required to appeal to the public for contributions on such occasions. All this is, as it were, instilled into us from early youth, and is thenceforward regarded as a matter of course.

●

CHAPTER XXIX

GREAT CHANGES.

WHILE all this bitterness prevailed in our family I was made happy by the affection of a young German, who lived at Zanzibar as the representative of a Hamburg mercantile firm. A good many untrue reports have been published with regard to these, to me, important events, and I feel it incumbent on me to briefly mention them here. During the reign of my brother Madjid the Europeans enjoyed a very respected position; they were often and gladly received as guests at his house and on his estates, and were always treated with marked attention on such occasions. My step-sister Chole and myself were on most friendly terms with all foreigners in Zanzibar, which led to various courtesies, such as the custom of the country admitted. The European ladies of Zanzibar for the most part called only upon Chole and myself.

Soon after my removal from Bububu I made the acquaintance of my future husband. My house was next to his; the flat roof of his house was a little lower than my own. He held his dinner parties in a room opposite to where I could watch them; for he knew that this display of a European festivity must be very interesting to me. Our friendship, from which in time sprang love, was soon known in the town, and my brother Madjid also was well aware of it, but he never showed any displeasure, much less made me suffer imprisonment on this account, as the gossips had it.

I was, of course, desirous of leaving my home secretly, where our union was out of the question. The first attempt failed, but a more favourable opportunity soon presented itself. Through the mediation of my friend Mrs. D., the wife of Dr. D., the British Vice-consul at the time, I was one night taken on board by Mr. P., Commander of the British man-of-war, *Highflyer;* and everything having been in waiting and preparation for me, we started at once and steered to the north. We reached Aden all safe, where I was received by a Spanish couple, whom I had known at Zanzibar; and there I was going to wait till my affianced husband could join me; for he was as yet detained at Zanzibar in winding up his affairs.

In the meantime I had been instructed in the Christian religion, and was baptized in the English Church at Aden with the name of Emily, and married immediately after according to the English rite. After our marriage we left for Hamburg, *via* Marseilles, where I was received in the kindest manner by the parents and relations of my husband.

I accustomed myself soon to my strange surroundings, and endeavoured to learn all that was necessary for me. My dear never-to-be-forgotten husband helped me on in all these stages, with the deepest interest. Especially fond he was of observing the first impressions that European life and the customs of the civilized world made on me. I have retained a most faithful memory of them, and may speak of some on a future occasion.

Our quiet, happy, and contented life was only to last a short while. Little more than three years after our removal to Hamburg, my dear husband had the misfortune of falling while jumping from a tram-car, and was run over. He expired three days later after great sufferings, leaving me quite alone in the world with three children, of which the youngest was only three months old. For a time I thought of returning to my native home, but fate decreed that two months after this unspeakable grief my dear brother Madjid was also to die, he who had always been so kind to me. He did nothing to harm my *fiancé* after my departure, but allowed him to settle his affairs at Zanzibar without hindrance, nor did he ever after manifest the slightest resentment at my secret flight. Like a true Moslem he believed in fate and predestination, and was convinced that it was this that took me to Germany. He gave me a touching proof of his brotherly love shortly before he died by despatching a steamer with a full cargo of all kinds of things to Hamburg for presents. The generous donor suddenly departed this life while the ship was yet on its way. I have never seen or received any of the goods intended for me, nor had I received any intelligence at the time of Madjid's generous intention. I only learned afterwards that his kind purpose was intercepted, and that the appearance of the ship at Hamburg at the time was reported to be for the purpose of repairs. Nine years later I heard from a friend, who had been on board the vessel at Gibraltar, and who had then seen the captain, that the cargo was intended for me. In spite of every effort to keep their arrival in port dark, the dusky crew had by some means found out my dwelling in Hamburg. The poor fellows were wild with joy at having succeeded, and showed their attachment in the most touching manner.

Two years more I lived in Hamburg, but never free from misfortunes. I lost a considerable part of my property through the fault of others, and learnt now that the management of my affairs must be undertaken by myself. The deepest aversion to the place where I had formerly been so happy now completely overpowered me—in addition to which my life among the people of that city was not made as pleasant as I could have wished or expected.

I removed to Dresden, where I met with the kindest advances from all sides. From that place I went to London, of which I am going to speak in the next chapter. Wishing to lead a quiet life for a time, I lived for some years in pretty Rudalstadt, and there also I made many dear friends, foremost among whom I must mention with gratitude their Royal Highnesses. I soon recovered my shattered health so far that I could think of removing to Berlin, for the better advancement of my children's education. There, also, my social life was of the happiest. I shall remain deeply grateful all my life for the interest evinced for me by the most exalted persons there.

CHAPTER XXX.

I HAD always kept up a correspondence with my native country, and had never given up hoping to see it again, but the obduracy of my brother had rendered any reconciliation hitherto impossible. His implacability was not, however, on account of my desertion of the faith—it was what he chose to consider a personal affront to him—viz., my renewed friendship with his old adversary Madjid! But I continued to yearn for all my dear ones at home, and secretly I never relinquished the hope of being once more reconciled to them.

All at once a report was spread through the press —in the spring of 1875—a report that stirred my whole being, to the effect that my brother Bargasch, the sovereign of Zanzibar since Madjid's death, was about to visit London.

I took no steps at first to verify this news, nor did I betray the uneasiness it caused me. I had experienced too many disappointments in my life to allow of sanguine hopes, and it required all the power of persuasion on the part of my friends to decide me to go to London myself. The Secretary of State, Herr von Bülow, held out hopes to me of the diplomatic

aid of the ambassador, Count Münster, which I regret
to say, however, proved of little assistance to me.

The short time previous to my departure I employed
in learning English, so as to render myself a little
less helpless. For nearly eight weeks I was busily
poring from morn till night over my books, learning
English words and reciting dialogues. The thought
of having to leave my three children behind damped
my ardour not a little all the time.

After an exhausting, wearying journey, I arrived at
last in the giant city, where rooms at a hotel had
been prepared for me by some friends of mine, the
only persons I knew in all London, and those but
slightly. I had only seen them once, when they paid
us, or rather my dear husband, a short call on their
wedding tour, yet they were ever after kindness and
devotion itself to me.

My brother's arrival was only expected a week
later, and in the intervening time I made myself
acquainted with all that was new and quite strange
to me. Count Münster, on whom I had called at the
earliest opportunity, kindly promised to assist me
to the best of his ability.

Some few days after my arrival, while sitting in the
drawing-room of my hotel, buried in sad thoughts, the
card of Dr. P., M.P., the brother of a dear friend of
mine, was handed to me. I was a perfect stranger to
him and to his wife, since deceased, but in both I subsequently found two of the most kind-hearted persons,
ever ready to pluck the thorns from under my feet.
They had come to offer me their services, and to
make at the same time the welcome proposal of carry-

ing me off to their own home. I dined with them the
same day, and removed on the following to their
house, and as things had thus acquired a more pleasant aspect, I took fresh courage, hoping that the end
of my mission would take a favourable turn.

My friends in Germany strongly advised me before
starting to proceed as cautiously as possible, and in
the first instance to try and procure the aid of the
British Government in my behalf. I at last gave way
to their earnest entreaties, though I had at first been
resolved—after having often before realized to my cost
how inexpedient it was of me, a stranger, to negotiate
matters in Europe—to trust to God and myself alone.
Pictures rose up in my mind of vague, empty shufflings,
of diplomatic periphrases, of slight coughs given to
gain a little time before speaking; these and many
more such signs I was soon to be brought face to face
with. I was to learn that my fate lay in the hands of
those who study and practise, and finally excel in the
art of prevarication.

It was not long after my removal to the residence
of my kind friends, that the visit of Sir Bartle Frere,
afterwards Governor-General of South Africa—a
gentleman whom I had hitherto only known by name
—was announced to me. If ever I received a proof
of the truth of certain presentiments, it was on this
day, on which the hopes most dear to me and the
future of my children were buried for ever. A most
unpleasant feeling took possession of me the very
moment I beheld the great diplomate, who governed
my native country as he chose, and who held my
brother Bargasch altogether in his power.

After an exchange of civilities, Sir Bartle began to make inquiries about my affairs, and appeared particularly anxious to learn the reason of my visit to London. I told him—although he seemed fully informed on these points already—all about my wishes. There was not much to tell after all, as I had only the one thought of being reconciled to my relations.

My surprise may be more easily guessed than described, when Sir Bartle, after I had done, put the plain question to me : " What did I consider of greater value to me—a reconciliation with my relations, or the securing of my children's future prospects ? " Even now I am unable to say what I felt on hearing these words; I had been prepared for anything but for this question. I trust I shall not be accused of inconsistency or of want of courage, if I wavered and hesitated for a moment. What were my own personal hopes and wishes when the welfare of my children was at stake ?

After recovering somewhat from the surprise and embarrassment into which this unexpected diplomatic move had thrown me, I requested an explanation as to the meaning of this question. Sir Bartle then declared, and in a very decided manner too, that the British Government was by no means disposed to mediate between myself and my brother; and that, as its guest, it would be highly unbecoming to cause him any annoyance.

It is to this day a matter of grave doubt which annoyance he would have considered the greater had he been at all consulted in either matter; signing the slave treaty, and therewith giving a formal countenance to the English protectorate, or holding out a reconciling hand to his sister.

On the other hand—and this was Sir Bartle's positive proposal—if I would promise not to approach my brother during his London stay, either personally or in writing, the British Government would undertake to secure the future of my children.

I was as sad and disappointed as a person can be, who, pining for a refreshing drink from a cool spring after a long and dreary march, finds the longed-for well closed up by some magic power. I had to choose between two alternatives : to act either for myself, and without any help from the British Government— and this with the certain knowledge, that almost unsurmountable obstacles would be raised in my way, which I was too weak to overcome—or to accept the proffered aid of the Government in the interest of my children. Mindful of the promise I had given to my motherly friend, Baroness D., at Dresden, not to go alone and unprotected to my brother—though I never doubted that he would respect English law everywhere; and in England especially, if I were to confront him suddenly—I finally accepted the proposal of the British Government.

A proposal, however, so vague, that a friend of mine could not refrain from inquiring of Sir Bartle what inducement had actuated the Government to take so sudden an interest in my affairs ; whereupon the astute diplomate adduced three reasons : (1) We do the Sultan a favour therewith ; (2) We keep the princess quiet for a time, and (3) we deprive the chancellor, Prince Bismarck, of all pretext of ever taking up the matter himself. All these reasons seemed on the surface perfectly plausible and reassuring.

In order to avoid even the appearance of a premeditated meeting with my brother, either in such public buildings to which everybody has access, or in the park and in the streets, I studied the programme of my brother's daily excursions in the papers; I even requested my kind hostess not to take me with her in her drives; but to this she would not agree, saying that my health would suffer, and proposed that we should take quite opposite routes, and thus we went West when the Sultan had gone East, and *vice versâ*. Such a precaution was indispensable as far as I was concerned, for I could not have trusted myself to remain mistress of my feelings if a meeting had taken place. On the other hand, there was but little danger of a recognition on his part—my own dear mother would not have known me again in my present attire—much less any one of my brothers, who had hardly ever had an opportunity of seeing me without a mask.

I should have preferred to leave London at once, where I had seen all my hopes destroyed, and to return home. But even this I was not allowed to do. I had to stay many weeks longer far away from my children, full of anxiety and care. Sir Bartle Frere had so willed it. Before taking my departure I was requested to send in a detailed memorial. Not only was I wholly inexperienced and unversed in this branch of business, but my sorrows had reduced my mental energies almost to those of an automaton.

I, therefore, with what remaining hope I had of
eventual success, accepted the offer of my kind friends
to draw up the memorial for me, and after a protracted stay of seven weeks I was at last able to leave
England and to return to my children; but with what a
heavy heart I quitted its shores may be easily imagined!

Zanzibar was already considered at that time a
future British colony, so my memorial was first to be
submitted to the Indian Government. Several months
had passed in nursing my hopes, when they were
suddenly broken in upon one morning by the receipt
of a letter from London, enclosing the copy of a
document, forwarded to me by the British Government through Count Münster, declining to enter upon
any of the terms of my petition that Sir Bartle had
so warmly urged upon me. As a reason for this
refusal was adduced: that, as I had married a
German, and was residing in Germany, my case came
within German jurisdiction. This flimsy prevarication was the more contemptible, as I had asked no
alms of either of the two Governments, but, in the
name of justice, the moral support of both. Sir
Bartle Frere had himself incited the memorial—the
same diplomate who had shortly before annihilated
the object of my mission to London with the bribe of
securing the future of my children! I had been
given to understand that the memorial was intended
to be a formal compliance on my part with the compact the English Government had entered into with
me, and that the former would now carry out theirs
as I had carried out mine. But oh! how dearly I
was to pay for my credulity!

My husband had been a German, and I, therefore, would be regarded as a German subject also. Oh! now I perceive! I could lay, of course, no claims to English chivalry or generosity. And yet why, I ask myself, had the truth of my nationality never been realized till my concordance had been extorted ; why did I receive strict injunctions to conform to the compact as though it had been entered into with an English woman. I can only explain it thus : that until my brother had signed the treaty, and so long as he was within reach of any hints I might feel inclined to give him, and be *able* to give him,· from my better knowledge of European tactics, I was bound over on my honour, as any ordinary English citizen, "to keep the peace," and thereby acknowledging my power, as the Sultan's sister, of possibly " disturbing it." But no sooner had my brother regained his shores and I mine, than the last card was played, and I suddenly became once more a pure German subject. All this I concluded slowly and painfully, and learnt subsequently that I had interpreted the whole course of events rightly, that I was, in a word, the victim of the "Humane Policy" adopted by Zanzibar. Let me, however, here distinctly impress my readers with the fact that though I may trace the source of all my miseries to the wily machinations of the Government of England, I feel in my heart not only gratitude, but the deepest affectionate remembrance of kindness and sympathy received at the hands of English society.

19

CHAPTER XXXI.

RE-VISITING MY HOME AFTER NINETEEN YEARS.

WHEN I wrote the preceding chapter some years ago, I did certainly not dream of the possibility of ever seeing the most ardent wish realized that filled my thoughts and my very being. The eventful years that had elapsed since I had last seen my dear home, had been fraught with many storms and hardships. I had meanwhile passed through the most wonderful changes of life—I had outlived the most cruel trials. Thanks to my good constitution, I was able to brave all the rugged duties that devolve upon the dwellers of the North, but only for the first few years. As they went on I was made aware of my decreasing powers of resistance.

About two years ago, I said one evening to my two daughters : "Children, I cannot help thinking—and have been pursued by the thought for some time—that this would be a favourable moment for returning to Zanzibar." I then explained my views more fully. One of them reminded me of the evil star that had frustrated so many of our dearest hopes, and then drew a sad picture of the renewed anguish and disappointment this enterprise might have in store for us. The other one, however, replied eagerly : "No, mamma, nothing must be left untried. You might reproach yourself afterwards with the thought that you had missed the right moment." And she thought as I did.

I took the necessary steps confidently, and was met in high official quarters with a kind encouragement, but the matter did not progress for a long time After several disappointments, and when I had already given up all hope of ever satisfying my longing for home, I one day received a summons from the foreign office to hold myself in readiness to depart for Zanzibar shortly. The surprise caused by this news was so overwhelming as almost to deprive me for a time of all power of realizing my good fortune. Next to God I felt most thankful to the Government, and to our beloved emperor, for whom I as well as my children will always preserve the deepest gratitude.

I need not dwell on the preliminaries of our departure—they were those usually accompanying a long voyage. And as for the political features of the expedition, they were sufficiently explained by the daily papers at the time.

On the 12th of July, 1885, I was to be at Port Said. On the 1st of that month I left Berlin with my children, and went *via* Breslau and Vienna to Trieste, where we arrived on the 3rd. My children were charmed with all the beauty they saw. As for myself, I could not well help being more keen on the issue than on the incidents of our journey. The peace and quiet I had not known for weeks I found again on board the Lloyd steamer *Venus* after we had put out to sea, and here I tasted the first sweet enjoyments that offered on all sides. The weather was so beautiful that we could remain on deck nearly all day long.

On the 5th we touched at Corfu, visited the most beautiful spots in the island by a few hours drive, and rejoined our steamer in the afternoon, highly pleased with what we had seen. Past barren Ithaca on the south point of Greece, and lofty Candia, our vessel brought us, on the 8th, to Alexandria. A hushed and almost holy feeling of home overcame me as I entered this city with palm-trees and minarets, a feeling that can only be experienced but not described, and which only those understand who have, under similar circumstances, been long absent from their home. Of the real South I had seen nothing for nineteen years, and my winters had been passed in Germany by the fireside. Busily as I had always been engaged with the duties of house-keeping, my thoughts had ever wandered far away. To me the greatest pleasure and recreation had been to sit down quietly and alone with a book all about the South. Now that I was actually face to face again with Eastern life in the bustling port of Alexandria, I stood as one in a dream—afraid of waking to the fact that I had only been steeped into it by the perusal of some well-told, life-like description.

We were requested at the custom-house to show our passports, but I had decided to give my name only in case of absolute necessity, and I therefore asked my travelling companion if I might use one of her own cards, and, curiously enough, this was considered quite satisfactory, and we passed on. After this we had positively to fight our way, with the help of constables, through the clamouring crowd offering their various services; and finally, having reached a cab, we got in and asked to be driven to the hotel. But even here one of our persecutors managed to fasten himself on again, warning us, with much agitation, against proceeding any further without his assistance as interpreter, when, to his utter astonishment, I told him in Arabic that we were perfectly able to take care of ourselves.

The two days we spent in our expensive and dirty hotel passed quickly enough. I was most delighted with a visit to the Arab quarter, where I remained for hours watching the ever-varying scenes of its animated life. After being eyed rather suspiciously at first I began to talk to them in Arabic to their intense astonishment. "Mother *" they cried on all sides, "where didst thou learn to speak our language so beautifully? Surely thou must have been to Bagdad; how long didst thou live there?"

Mhammed, our Arab cabdriver, soon took such a fancy to us, that he beseeched me to take him with me as my servant. He assured me he would serve us faithfully all his life, and never touch a single bottle of our wine. He was quite downcast when he came next morning to drive us to the port, and I scarcely knew how to console the poor fellow.

Our short stay at Alexandria had been a most

* "Mother" is a friendly term of address.

happy one. After a passage of eighteen hours we
arrived at Port Said, where we went on board the
Adler, one of the tugs of the East African squadron.
Port Said is only a small harbour town, but everything is to be obtained there, and the shops contain
everything one can possibly wish for.

Here the desert begins, through which runs the
"canal" that connects the Mediterranean and the
Red Sea. The channel is so narrow that two ships
cannot pass each other; crossing stations have
been established at various points, and their names
put up, as "Gare Limite Sud," or "Gare Limite
Nord." Ships have to wait here sometimes for
hours, until a vessel coming the other way has passed
the station. At Port Said or at Suez a channel-
pilot is taken on board every steamer, who understands the meaning of the ball-signals, indicating
by their number and position whether you may go on,
or how many ships are expected to pass by. No ship
is allowed to go through the channel under full
steam, to prevent the undulation damaging the
sandy banks; at night all traffic is stopped. Notwithstanding these several hindrances, the passage
is quite an interesting one—especially when some of
the ships race through the large salt lake to reach
the canal first.

Near Suez the channel widens, and we entered the
Red Sea at last under "full steam." The heat,
which had been great before, became almost unbearable when we entered this branch of the sea
enclosed by high rocky walls. We could not keep a dry
thread on us night or day. I felt more at ease in

this, to me, familiar heat, than I had felt all the long years I had been away; but my children were quite prostrated with it. The port holes could not be opened, as the sea was running very high; and the air became so oppressive below that we preferred sleeping on deck at night on chairs instead of retiring to our cabins.

Seven days it took us to get to Aden, and in that port we had to remain five days before the *Adler* received orders at last to proceed on the voyage; and then who more rejoiced than myself? I was to see my home again at last in eight days more.

We had not suffered from a rough sea as far as Aden, but hardly had we got clear of that rocky port, when that fearful south-west monsoon began to blow. We were now in those dangerous regions, where H.M.S. *Augusta* had gone down some weeks before. One morning at eight we were just having breakfast on deck with the officers, when the first tremendous sea came over and speedily dispersed all the company. And now began three awful days and nights! We were in the midst of an appalling hurricane. The foam of the waves broke over the funnels, which, after the storm was over, stood there perfectly white with the brine. I must despair of giving an adequate description of our dangerous situation; and our bodily sufferings and discomforts, too, were very great. The pitching and rolling the first day made us, of course, very ill, but our miseries even increased. Our cabins were swamped, so that we could not get into them. Indeed, in the face of our great danger, we did not think of undressing for three nights running. We all had to sit in the gentlemen's saloon under umbrellas, for although the ports and skylights were tightly screwed down, and the latter covered with tarpaulins—the state of our atmosphere may be better imagined than described—the water oozed through the decks. Toilet was dispensed with, for we had no dry changes to replace the sopping garments we were wearing.

After three days, at last the storm abated a little, but though the sea still came over at times, we could' at least stay on deck, on a raised seat, under an awning.

My anxiety had naturally been very great at first, but I soon became quite calm and composed, remembering that we are at all times in God's hands, and filled with gratitude that I had my three children with me.

The island of Pemba came in sight on the 2nd of August. The distance thence to Zanzibar is only thirty miles, which can easily be travelled over in three hours. As it grew dark we made for the north-cape of Zanzibar, it being dangerous to enter the port at night on account of the many sandbanks.

It was a curious coincidence that I was to see my native home again in the same month in which I had left it nineteen years before, and exactly on the same day and at the same hour I had lost my husband fifteen years ago. I need scarcely speak of my heart's anguish on that day. Earlier than usual I retired to my berth, but never closed an eye all night. My whole soul shaped itself into a prayer, and God, in His mercy, heard it, and gave me comfort once more.

Our ship drifted slowly during the night towards

the lighthouse, and when I came on deck early in the morning the palm-trees of my native home greeted me from afar. At sight of them I again broke down. I went back to my cabin and prayed. The conflict of my feelings was only an echo of the many conflicts my life had known. What indeed are we poor human beings but frail skiffs tossed on the ocean of life. I had left my native home an Arab and a true Mahometan; I returned an undeserving Christian, and half a German.

But at this moment it was given me to live all my youth over again. Everything stood vividly before me, and the merry pictures of the past rose one by one, and filled me with exultant joy. Even my happy, light-hearted children seemed silent and thoughtful in this hour. They clung to me all that day, and through their glistening eyes I could read the sympathy that their full hearts could not speak. Though my life has been robbed of some of its dearest possessions, God, in His mercy, has made me rich in giving me my loving children.

On nearing the town we learned, to our regret, that the German squadron had not yet arrived. As the *Adler* was to be of its number, there was nothing for us to do but to steam back to the east coast of the island, and wait about. In this manner we passed eleven days. On the 11th of August at last the man on the bridge called out, "Ship in sight!" which, however, did not raise great hopes in us, as we thought it might be a passenger steamer. But very soon we saw the vessel make straight for us, so we got up steam, and hoisted our flag. The vessel turned out

to be the tender *Ehrenfels*, which had been in search
of us all the morning, to bring us the commodore's
order to come into port, the squadron having already
arrived there four days ago. We made for the port
at once, but could not run in that night.

Next morning at six o'clock we were all astir. Far
off in the distance we saw the forest of masts in port;
steaming close in shore we passed many fine palm-
groves and small negro villages. Come to an anchor
at last, we found four German men-of-war present,
H.M. ships *Stosch*, *Gneisenau*, *Elisabeth*, and *Prince
Adalbert*, two English men-of-war, five steamers of the
Sultan, and several sailing ships.

Commodore Paschen thought it advisable to treat
me at first as " secret cargo," a name which caused
much merriment to all the officers of the squadron.
However, on the arrival of Admiral Knorr in H.M.S.
Bismarck, matters were soon smoothed for me. I
was free to go on shore when I liked. Apart from the
feelings that moved me at seeing my home again, it
struck me as very strange that I should be able to
walk about those streets in broad day, accompanied by
gentlemen, where I had formerly only been permitted
to pass at night, veiled. It may be thought that,
after nineteen years of European life, I might have
got over this, but Zanzibar brought it back to me
with far greater force than Egypt, where I had been
twice since, and did not realize my emancipation
nearly so much.

I fancied I could see the most undisguised surprise
in the faces of all the people who crowded round us
when I visited the town for the first time. They

pressed round me on all sides, calling out to me in Arabic and Suahely, "How do you do, my mistress?" Large numbers collected in the narrow streets before the shops we had gone into, but made room respectfully when we emerged again. Our escort increased day by day, and the welcome on the part of the inhabitants grew daily more cordial and more affectionate. All this, of course, did not a little annoy the Sultan and his counsellor, the British Consul-General; the former even thought fit to have a number of the persons whipped, who had followed us. He, as well as the Consul-General, made a complaint to the commander of the squadron about this friendly demonstration in my favour. When I heard of this I thought it best to tell the people not to accompany me any more, but they replied that no fear of punishment should prevent them from showing their joy at seeing me again.

Frequently slaves came up to me cautiously, to bring me their master's compliments. I was begged not to have any doubt of their attachment and fidelity; they placed their houses at my disposal, and expressed their earnest desire to pay me visits on board. These slaves also brought me letters secretly, which, in the absence of pockets, they had concealed in their tiny caps. In passing the houses I often saw a troop of ladies retire behind a door when they saw me in the distance, and on my approach they would either address me or merely call down a blessing—such as: "God be with you and keep you in good health." My brothers and sisters, my relations and old friends, asked me frequently to come and see them, but I always declined their kindly invitations, not from any lurking resentment of former days, far from it, for my heart yearned for my own flesh and blood; but circumstances compelled me to act as I did.

Whenever we passed the palace in boats, or walked under the windows of the harem, we could see the wives of the Sultan waving their hands to us in a friendly manner. As I was accompanied on these excursions by several naval officers, I had to request these gentlemen, in the interest of the women, not to salute in return, not wishing to be the ruin of these imprudent fair ones. I avoided doing so myself, for I had been told that their lord and master was in the habit of concealing himself in some place from which he could easily watch and find out all that passed on the sea and in the streets unknown to them, and then follow up his discoveries with cruel punishments. This is not conjecture, but a fact well known; even to the Europeans in Zanzibar that happened scarcely a year ago. The Sultan from his hidden post had seen a Portuguese, gliding past on the water, bow to his favourite, a beautiful Circassian, and also saw her return the greeting; a custom she was by no means alone, or the first in observing, for thirty years ago, when I was quite a child, the English and French naval officers, who visited our island, and the foreign residents, always bowed to us, and we as invariably returned their courteous salutation; our gentlemen had never objected to it, and no one saw any harm in it. Bargasch, however, was of a different opinion; he whipped his Circassian for the crime she had committed, with his own hands, and in so cruel a manner that she expired some days afterwards in consequence. He is said to have entreated, vainly however, her pardon on her death-bed, and even now has prayers said over her grave.

On our excursions into the interior we often encountered people mounted on donkeys. To show us their respect they always dismounted, led their beasts past, and then only remounted. Nor could any punishment inflicted by the Sultan make the inhabitants desist in showing their attachment, and it must have vexed him to hear the crowd crying beneath his palace windows: "Kuaheri Bibi! Kuaheri Bibi!" (Farewell, Mistress!) every time we got into our boat to return on board. I was told that whenever we neared the shore somebody would beat an old biscuit-tin like a drum to summon the people together.

Of course we were well set round with spies, mostly Hindoos, but to their great disgust we only conversed in German. Even on the night preceding our departure two of my friends (who had come on board to bid me good-bye under the shelter of darkness) called my attention to the dusky figure of a man, who had often honoured our ship with his presence in the guise of a hawker, and who in truth was a very active and clever tool employed by the now influential but former lamp-cleaner and court-barber, Madoldji Pera Daudji.

This Pera Daudji, a very wily and cunning Hindoo, has become the Sultan's jack-of-all-trades. The lamp-cleaner of old now devotes his services to the sovereign of Zanzibar in the highest and lowest positions. All diplomatic negotiations pass through his hands, but the same hands wait upon the guests of the Sultan's

table. His salary, thirty dollars a month, every one
will admit to be a low one, but I was told that he
made it worth any one's while to increase it.   This
omnipotent Pera Daudji is not above bartering his
influence.   Of course, his thirty dollars, that do not
even suffice to pay for his costly dresses, are replenished
from other sources of revenue.   The court jeweller,
who refused to give a certain percentage on all orders
to the ex-lamp-cleaner, lost his custom in consequence.
Pera Daudji honoured and entrusted a more accom-
modating competitor with the execution of such
orders.

My birthday happened to fall in this time, and
now I celebrated the same for the first time in
my native country, where it is not customary so
do so.   The officers of the squadron did all they
could to make this day a real festive one to me,
and they succeeded well.   I can hardly thank them
sufficiently for all their kindness.   One very remarkable thing happened on this occasion.   In honour of
my birthday (a born Mahometan's!) a pig was killed
on board the *Adler*, and almost in sight of Islam's
most faithful worshippers.   If this had been predicted
to me nineteen years ago by the cleverest of our
fortune-tellers, I should have scorned the idea, in
spite of all superstition.

Viewed from the sea, the town of Zanzibar made
upon me quite as favourable an impression as it had
done of old.   Perhaps it looked even more pleasant
now, many new houses have been built, the lighthouse
in front of the palace, lighted by electricity, looks
really quite fine.   By the officers it was always called

the Sultan's Christmas-tree, on account of its many rows of lamps. I was much less pleased with the appearance of the inner town.

During my long residence in Europe I may perhaps have become more fastidious than Oriental practice will allow of; I thought the inner town in a sad condition of untidiness. Nearly every house in the narrow and dirty streets was a heap of ruins. Weeds grew everywhere, and even big trees flourished amidst these ruins. No one seemed to care; people in the most natural manner were picking their way over ash-heaps and waterpools. The introduction of a good Board of Works does not seem to be quite so easy, otherwise this state of affairs would have been remedied by the Sultan long since, who has had sufficient opportunity during his stay at Bombay, as well as in England and France, to become acquainted with clean streets. But he has deemed it necessary to introduce the manufacture of ice, also electric light, a so-called railway and, I know not what else in Zanzibar, not to mention French cooks and French gastronomy.

The evident decay of the heart of the town struck me painfully indeed. I had not then an idea of the condition in which I was to see my old Bet il Mtoni again, or Bet il Ras, that was only just finished when I left. I was deeply moved when we went to revisit the house in which I was born. What a sight! In place of a palace there was nothing but a fast decaying ruin; one of the staircases had altogether disappeared, the other was choked with weeds, and so tottering that it could not be ascended without peril.

More than half of the house was a rubbish heap, just left as it had tumbled down; the baths, once such a favourite place of resort, and always filled with a merry throng, had lost their roofs; ruins again indicating the place where some of them had been. There I stood, gazing with burning eyes at the neglect and desolation around with the recollection of former and happier days filling my heart with a painful mockery of all things earthly and human.

My companions little knew what anguish was mine—they laughed or chatted, or played on those heaps. Had I suspected what was awaiting me in the old house of my birth, I should have paid it a preliminary visit by myself. The figures of former residents seemed to me to be hovering around and gliding from under the dangerously-leaning roofs, the half-hanging doors and falling beams. More and more vividly did their faces and shapes grow upon me. I was moving in their midst, and could hear their own familiar voices. How long this delusion lasted I know not, but I was suddenly roused into the actual present again by the kind officers and my children coming to draw me away from the scenes that affected me so deeply.

It is commonly thought, but without reason, that the Arabs, in token of their love and respect to their dead, allow the houses formerly inhabited by them to fall into ruins. This is incorrect—it is not this sentiment, but their innate indolence that makes them look with indifference on decay. Arab houses are but seldom repaired or renovated—their lime and bricks are of a nature to be easily decomposed by the climate

—so that when a house gets rather too much out of repair, a new one is built instead, and the old one is left to crumble away. The value of building ground is merely a nominal one.

My nephew, Ali ben Sund, the son of Zuéne, had lived, up to his death, in one part of the house, which still contained a few comparatively well-preserved rooms. His attachment to the old ancestral seat of our family was so great that he could never live anywhere else, and so he died in this place two years ago.

In this wing we found two Arab soldiers, who had come from Omân but a few months previously. They had left their families at home, hoping to take back to them some of their earnings from the wealthy Zanzibar; but so far they had fared very badly, and were yearning to get back to Mesket as soon as they possibly could. Both complained of bodily afflictions, and begged me to cure them; one of them had sore eyes, and the other some internal disease.

When I inquired, somewhat surprised, why they lived in the ruins, I was told that they were not alone, but only formed part of the guard, which, incredible as it may appear, were set to watch over the ruins. This, I should think, could hardly have been a military measure, but probably one connected with the dread of the evil one. I may, however, be mistaken in this, as I have for too long a period lost sight of this kind of superstition and its adherents.

As a memento I took with me some grasses, a few leaves, and a stone I found in the niche where my dear father used to say his prayers.

20

On leaving the house a well-dressed, rather distinguished-looking Arab came up to us, introducing himself as the commanding officer of the guard. He remained some time with us, and finally escorted us to our boat. On approaching the Mtoni we observed a venerable old man standing in it, engaged in ablutions previous to saying his prayers; and when we came nearer we saw that he was stone-blind. Since my arrival at Zanzibar I had made it a point never to be the first in addressing any one, so as to get them into no trouble; but in this case, and with a blind man, I thought I might make an exception, so I went up to him, and wished him good evening in Arabic, not without some misgiving for disturbing him at his devotion, and I, a Christian too, was not calculated to draw forth a pleasant acknowledgment, especially as he could hear that we were a European party. I was not a little surprised however when he stretched forth both his hands, drew mine to his lips, and pressed them for a while to his face. I was really touched, and wished to remove the doubt of being mistaken for some other person. "But do you know who I am?" I asked. "Indeed, I do know you," he replied, "are you not my mistress Salme, whom I have often carried about as a child? Oh, we were so rejoiced when we heard you had come back. God help and protect you, you who are so dear to us all!" Such and other words like these the poor helpless blind man addressed to us on parting. The Arab officer, who had been a witness to this proof of faithful attachment, told me the old man acted as the Muedden (Muezzin) to the colony of Bet

il Mtoni, and was at the same time appointed by the
Sultan to say prayers over the tomb of Abd il Sund,
whom the latter had so bitterly persecuted all his
life.

The last remark struck me particularly, for I was
quite well aware of the heartless and yet childish
conduct of Bargasch to Ali ben Sund, and to my
elder sister Raje. Raje, a real sister of Ali's mother,
removed to Zanzibar from Mesket at a pretty advanced age some years ago, and was provided by the
Sultan with a house and an annuity. It was but
natural that his aunt Raje went to nurse him, when
Ali ben Sund, who, without any cause whatever, had
incurred the bitter hatred of Bargasch, was lying
mortally ill at Bet il Mtoni, having no wife or
children to look after him. But Bargasch disapproved
of the step she had taken—he was perfectly unable to
understand or to appreciate any service of charity, or
to show compassion. To make her feel his wrath, he
not only withdrew her annuity, but actually, without
any compensation, deprived his aged sister, who was
old enough to be his mother, of her home. He did
not appear at Ali's burial, a disregard hardly ever
shown even to an enemy. And now he has prayers
said over his grave! What unaccountable conduct!

As I am just talking about the head of our family
in Zanzibar, I am tempted to lift the veil from
another part of his life's history. I might feel a great
reluctance to make known to the world the wickedness
of people of my own blood—in spite of the many years
I have been alienated from them, and notwithstanding
the heartlessness and harshness shown to me by the

same Bargasch, in whose interest I have risked and
imperilled my life and my fortune, for we cannot, do
what we may, wipe out a certain compassion for the
flesh of our flesh—were it not that Bargasch's bowels
of mercy are closed alike against subject and relation.

It is a fact well-known in Zanzibar that Bargasch,
on coming to the throne in 1870, suddenly, and
without any cause, cast our second youngest brother
Chalife into prison. The poor fellow there languished
upwards of three years heavily chained, with irons on
his legs. An explanation hereof could only be
guessed—Bargasch probably feared that Chalife,
being next in succession, might behave to him in the
same dastardly and treacherous manner as he had
done himself to Madjid.

His conscience, however, suddenly smote him.
When one of his sisters, whom he had likewise
injured, was about to set out on a pilgrimage to
Mecca, and dreading the efficacy of a curse pronounced in the holy city of the Prophet, he went to
her to beg forgiveness. But his sister positively
refused it until he had set Chalife free again.

In spite of this, he continued to have Chalife and
his friends continually watched, and soon found out
that the latter had a very faithful and wealthy friend.
He well remembered the time when it had been a
matter of great importance to himself to be allied to
rich chiefs; nevertheless, he determined to deprive
the successor to the throne, at any cost, of such
valuable adhesion and assistance.

He sent for Chalife's friend, and thus briefly
announced: "I understand you intend to sell your

plantations; tell me the price you want for them, as I should like to buy them." "That must be a mistake," the man replied, "I never had the least intention to sell my property." "It will be to your own advantage, however, if you do sell them to me," he was answered. "Now go and consider the matter."

Some time after, the unfortunate man was again summoned before the Sultan, and received with the following words: "Tell me, now, what is the price for your plantations?" "I have never thought of selling any of them, your Highness." "It is quite indifferent to me what you think. I shall give you 50,000 dollars for them. Here is a cheque for the amount; go and make yourself paid."

The poor fellow departed perfectly heartbroken from the presence of the man who in this manner acts as the "father of his people." But even here the mortification did not stop. When about to cash his cheque, he was informed that the whole amount was payable only within twenty years, in annual instalments of 2,500 dollars, the first of which was at his command now. The poor man was completely ruined, just what the Sultan wanted.

Another occurrence makes me blush with shame, and fills me with the deepest pity. One of my sisters had been most vilely calumniated—she was said to love some one whom Bargasch objected to as brother-in-law. When he heard of this report he went to her himself, and taxed her with it. In vain she protested her innocence and utter ignorance of the whole matter—the conscientious brother carried duty so far as to personally administer fifty lashes to his own sister! In consequence of this brutal treatment the poor girl was ill in bed for more than a month, and suffered from the effects long after. I have no doubt that he will have prayers said over her grave after her death as he does over those of his wife and of Ali ben Sund.

Europeans may frequently be heard to praise the engaging manners of the sovereign of Zanzibar. From the above it may easily be judged how much of this praise is deserved. One thing, however, is certain, that from the bottom of his heart Bargasch has never hated anything so much as the mere name of Europeans.

It may be presumed that I did not expect much from him as to my private claims. The press made a gratuitous statement that I had returned to Europe in full possession of my inheritance, consisting of the proceeds from the sale of no less than twenty-eight houses. This is absolutely untrue; I have not received a penny, and my claims—admitted as just ones even by the British Consul-General, and that is saying a great deal—remain unsettled to this day. My generous brother offered to pay me the large sum of 6,000 rupees in full settlement of all my claims, which kind offer I declined with thanks, this sum being only the merest fraction of what I am entitled to. Five of my brothers, five sisters, my aunt Asche, three nephews, one niece, and a very rich stepmother of mine, have died since he has held the reins of government; and I am entitled to part of the inheritance from all these. The Sultan waived, under some futile pretext, our reconciliation urged by the German

Government; and no doubt his delight was great when their interest in my cause was finally submerged by political ones.

Everything was tried from official quarters to set the people against me. Some of our officers had asked me to select for them some articles of jewellery they wished to take home to their friends. To get these we went several times to a jeweller, who worked also for the Sultan, without our being aware of it.

The Sultan no sooner heard of our purchases from his faithful Pera Daudji, who had to report all news to him, than he sent for the jeweller, upon whom he poured out the full measure of wrath and abuse for daring to sell us his wares. But the tradesman, generally so pliant, quietly replied he could not presume to turn his master's sister out of his shop. This answer displeased the Sultan still more, so he threatened to withdraw his custom altogether. But the jeweller, with great composure, announced the fact that he had for some time contemplated taking his departure from Zanzibar, and that he would embrace this opportunity for shutting up his shop, and thereby avoid giving me offence.

In the same way an attempt to annoy me was made by prohibiting the owners of donkeys to let out their beasts to me, while some of my former slaves, who had ventured to pay me a visit, were imprisoned.

Such and other absurd measures were taken, but had just the opposite effect. The people gave their opinion of such proceedings in words like these: "Pija kana kasi ja watoto, Bibi!" (He just behaves like a little child, O Mistress!)

When I arrived at Zanzibar I was doubtful of the reception I should meet with there, but confident, too, that my brother would not delay in carrying out the expressed wishes of Germany, and I was not mistaken. He would, at all events, out of respect for Germany, *tolerate* me. But the bad treatment that my other brothers and sisters had experienced at his hands could hardly lead me to expect any friendly advances on his part; and, as for the rest of the inhabitants, it gives me the greatest pleasure to state that they gave me tokens of their kindly feelings only. Arabs, Hindoos, Banyans, and natives repeatedly entreated me to remain in Zanzibar for good, which could only strengthen my belief that there was no religious aversion felt for me. One day I met two Arabs, with whom I entered into conversation. Hearing from a third person that they were relations of mine—I had not recognized them—I told them afterwards I should not have addressed them had I been aware of this, as I knew my relations were not all inclined to be friends with me. But they both replied at once that, whatever happened, they could never forget that I was the daughter of my father. And when I touched upon the religious question, one of them said "this fate had been destined to me from the beginning of the world." "The God who has severed you and us from our home is the same God whom all men adore and revere. His mighty will has brought you back to us, and we all rejoice at it. And now you and your children will stay with us henceforth, will you not?"

Proofs of affection and love like these, and the deep and indescribable joy of beholding my native land once more, will always associate that voyage with some of the sweetest hours of my life.

But the hour for parting came at last and found me oh! so loath to say a long farewell once more to the few but very dear friends I had still. They fully shared my grief, and perhaps I could convey its expression best to my readers, and thereby put a fitting close to my book, by giving the English rendering of a letter that they jointly sent to me after I had reached Germany again. But its sweet tenderness and originality I cannot reproduce :—

You went from us without a word at parting;
This has torn my heart, and filled my soul with sorrow.
O! that I had clung to your neck when you departed hence,
You might have sat on my head, and walked on my eyes!

You live in my heart, and when you went
You poured grief into my soul such as I né'er felt before ;
My body is wasted, and my tears fall fast
One after one down my cheek like the waves of the sea.

O Lord of the universe, let us meet again ere we die!
Be it only one single day before death.
If we live, we meet again ;
When we are dead, the Immortal One remains!

O! that I were a bird to soar to thee on wings of love;
But how can the bird soar whose wings are clipped ?

In the foregoing pages I have endeavoured to draw a picture of Oriental life and its customs, especially with regard to life at Court, and the position of woman in the East. Some of the subjects contained in this book may be thought to possess less general interest, but, as part of the whole, my description would have been incomplete without them. It must be remembered that I have not been writing a novel or a tale of fiction, but the faithful recollections connected with the life of my native land in all its phases.

If I have naturally felt tempted to exalt such of our customs and institutions which, in my opinion, are deserving of commendation, I have, on the other hand, never endeavoured to excuse or disguise others which, in the eyes of more highly-cultured nations at least, may justly be ridiculed or thought objectionable; and if, in drawing comparisons between foreign and Eastern customs, I have not shrunk from speaking my mind openly and candidly, and have sometimes sent home a shaft, I may aver, in justice to myself, that I have by no means spared myself, but have readily and frankly admitted the errors into which I fell.

Even in this century of railroads and rapid communication, so much ignorance still exists among European nations of the customs and institutions of their own immediate neighbours, that one can hardly wonder how little is actually known about those of races far removed. The ablest and most conscientious writer must always, to some degree, fall short of giving a perfectly precise and faithful picture of a foreign nation; and, in the case of an Eastern nation, he will, of course, find himself heavily handicapped out of all proportion when family and domestic life generally is so jealously guarded from the gaze of the outer world.

Having been born and bred in the East, I am in a

position to set down the unvarnished reflection of my
Oriental experiences—of its high life and its low life—
to speak of many peculiarities, and lift the veil from
things that are always hidden from profane eyes.
This, I hope, will constitute the main value of my
book, and my object will have been fully gained if I
have been able to contribute my share, and, above all,
if I have succeeded in removing many misconceptions
and distortions current about the East.

My task is done—and, in conclusion, it only remains for me to say farewell to my kind readers, who
have followed me through these pages, and who, I
trust, will always bear a friendly memory for one
whose life has already gathered so rich a store of
changes and vicissitudes.

NEW FICTION.

12mo, paper covers, 50 cents each.

Thraldom.* By Julian Sturgis.

Red Spider.* By S. Baring-Gould.

A Terrible Legacy. By G. W. Appleton.

Romance of the Canoness.* By Paul Heyse.

Dick's Wandering.* By Julian Sturgis.

Tempest-Driven. By Richard Dowling.

A Zealot in Tulle. † By Mrs. Wildrick.

Lil Lorimer.* By Theodore Gift.

The Master of the Ceremonies.* By George Manville Fenn.

Miss Churchill. † By Christian Reid.

The Silence of Dean Maitland. † By Maxwell Grey.

Aliette (La Morte).* By Octave Feuillet.

Pepita Ximenez.* By Juan Valera.

Roslyn's Fortune. ‡ By Christian Reid.

Noble Blood. By Julian Hawthorne.

A Conventional Bohemian. ‡ By Edmund Pendleton.

John Maidment.* By Julian Sturgis.

Double Cunning. By George Manville Fenn.

Jacob Schuyler's Millions. By Thomas Dunn English.

Mrs. Lorimer. By Lucas Malet.

Colonel Enderby's Wife. By Lucas Malet.

The Money-Makers. † **A Social Problem.**

Adventures of Timias Terrystone. † By Oliver B. Bunce.

Vice Versa; or, A Lesson to Fathers. † By F. Anstey.

The Black Poodle and other Stories. By F. Anstey. Illustrated.

The Giant's Robe. ‡ By F. Anstey. Illustrated.

Love's Martyr. By Miss Laurence Alma Tadema.

* Also half bound, 75 cents; † also in cloth, $1.00; ‡ also in cloth, $1.25.

NEW FICTION.

(Continued.)

12mo, paper covers, 25 cents each.

Autobiography of a Slander. By EDNA LYALL.

The Bag of Diamonds. By GEORGE MANVILLE FENN.

Miss Gascoigne. By Mrs. J. H. RIDDELL.

The Great Hesper. By FRANK BARRETT.

Old House at Sandwich. By JOSEPH HATTON.

Dawn. By H. RIDER HAGGARD. Half bound, 75 cents.

The Witching Time. Tales for the Year's End. By F. MARION CRAWFORD and others.

The Broken Shaft. Tales in Mid-Ocean. By F. MARION CRAWFORD and others.

In One Town. By EDMUND DOWNEY.

Dear Life. By J. E. PANTON.

Little Tu'penny. By S. BARING-GOULD.

The Dark House. By GEORGE MANVILLE FENN.

The Crime of Christmas-Day. By the author of "My Ducats and my Daughter."

The Witch's Head. By H. RIDER HAGGARD.

The Secret of Her Life. By EDWARD JENKINS.

The House on the Marsh. By FLORENCE WARDEN.

At the World's Mercy. By FLORENCE WARDEN.

Deldee; or, the Iron Hand. By FLORENCE WARDEN.

Doris's Fortune. By FLORENCE WARDEN.

A Vagrant Wife. By FLORENCE WARDEN.

A Prince of Darkness. By FLORENCE WARDEN.

Addie's Husband.

Matt; A Tale of a Caravan. By ROBERT BUCHANAN.

The Tinted Venus. By F. ANSTEY.

A Nemesis; or, Tinted Vapors. By J. MACLAREN COBBAN.

The Maurice Mystery. By J. ESTEN COOKE.

Struck Down. By HAWLEY SMART.

NEW FICTION.

(Continued.)

12mo, paper covers, 25 cents each.

The Rabbi's Spell. By STUART C. CUMBERLAND.

The Master of the Mine. By ROBERT BUCHANAN.

For Maimie's Sake. By GRANT ALLEN.

Tales of Eccentric Life. By WILLIAM A. HAMMOND and CLARA LANZA. 12mo.

Babylon. By GRANT ALLEN.

12mo, paper covers, 30 cents each.

His Helpmate. By FRANK BARRETT.

A Dateless Bargain. By C. L. PIRKIS.

NEW EDITIONS.

Frederick the Great and his Court. By LOUISA MÜHLBACH. 12mo. Paper, 30 cents.

Henry VIII and Catherine Parr. By LOUISA MÜHLBACH. 12mo. Paper, 30 cents. 12mo. Cloth, $1.00.

Mrs. Gainsborough's Diamonds. By JULIAN HAWTHORNE. 12mo. Paper, 25 cents.

A Struggle. By BARNET PHILLIPS. 12mo. Paper, 25 cents.

Samuel Brohl and Company. By VICTOR CHERBULIEZ. 12mo. Paper, 25 cents; cloth, 60 cents.

Meta Holdenis. By VICTOR CHERBULIEZ. 12mo. Paper, 25 cents; cloth, 60 cents.

Geier-Wally. A Tale of the Tyrol. By WILHELMINE VON HILLERN. 12mo. Paper, 25 cents.

Modern Fishers of Men. By GEORGE L. RAYMOND. 12mo. Paper, 25 cents.

Dr. Heidenhoff's Process. By EDWARD BELLAMY. 12mo. Paper, 25 cents.

John-a-Dreams. By JULIAN STURGIS. 12mo. Paper, 25 cents.

An Accomplished Gentleman. By JULIAN STURGIS. 12mo. Paper, 25 cents.

An Attic Philosopher in Paris. By EMILE SOUVESTRE. 12mo. Paper, 25 cents.

NEW FICTION.

(Continued.)

NEW EDITIONS.

In Paradise. By PAUL HEYSE. 2 vols. 12mo. Half bound, $1.50.

Tales from the German. By PAUL HEYSE. 12mo. Paper, 25 cents; cloth, 60 cents.

The Felmeres. By S. B. ELLIOTT. 12mo. Paper, 50 cents; cloth, $1.50.

The New Nobility. A Story of Europe and America. By J. W. FORNEY. 12mo. Paper, 50 cents; cloth, $1.50.

The Oddest of Courtships; or, The Bloody Chasm. By J. W. DE FOREST. 12mo. Paper, 50 cents; cloth, $1.00.

Remorse. By TH. BENTZON. 12mo. Paper, 25 cents; cloth, 60 cents.

Not Wisely, but Too Well. By RHODA BROUGHTON. 8vo. Paper, 30 cents. 12mo. Cloth, $1.00.

Cometh Up as a Flower. By RHODA BROUGHTON. 8vo. Paper, 30 cents. 12mo. Cloth, $1.00.

Red as a Rose is She. By RHODA BROUGHTON. 8vo. Paper, 30 cents. 12mo. Cloth, $1.00.

Good-Bye, Sweetheart! By RHODA BROUGHTON. 8vo. Paper, 30 cents. 12mo. Cloth, $1.00.

Cherry Ripe. By HELEN B. MATHERS. 8vo. Paper, 30 cents.

Comin' thro' the Rye. By HELEN B. MATHERS. 8vo. Paper, 30 cents.

Bressant. By JULIAN HAWTHORNE. 8vo. Paper, 50 cents.

Garth. By JULIAN HAWTHORNE. 8vo. Paper, 50 cents; cloth, $1.25.

Sebastian Strome. By JULIAN HAWTHORNE. 8vo. Paper, 75 cents.

The Lost Manuscript. By GUSTAV FREYTAG. 8vo. Paper, 50 cents.

James Gordon's Wife. 8vo. Paper, 25 cents.

Arius the Libyan. An Idyl of the Primitive Church. 12mo. Cloth, $1.25.

A Game of Chance. By ANNE SHELDON COOMBS. 12mo. Cloth, $1.00.

A Politician's Daughter. By MYRA SAWYER HAMLIN. 12mo. Half bound, 75 cents.

D. APPLETON & CO., Publishers, 1, 3, & 5 Bond Street, New York.

www.ingramcontent.com/pod-product-compliance
Lightning Source LLC
Chambersburg PA
CBHW060531030726
47498CB00004B/1159